Queen of the Cookbooks

Center Point
Large Print

Also by Ashton Lee and available from
Center Point Large Print:

The Cherry Cola Book Club Novels
  The Reading Circle
  The Wedding Circle
  A Cherry Cola Christmas

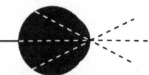

Queen of the Cookbooks

Ashton Lee

CENTER POINT LARGE PRINT
THORNDIKE, MAINE

This Center Point Large Print edition
is published in the year 2017 by arrangement with
Kensington Publishing Corp.

Copyright © 2016 by Ashton Lee.

All rights reserved.

The text of this Large Print edition is unabridged.
In other aspects, this book may vary
from the original edition.
Printed in the United States of America
on permanent paper.
Set in 16-point Times New Roman type.

ISBN: 978-1-68324-243-7

Library of Congress Cataloging-in-Publication Data

Names: Lee, Ashton, author.
Title: Queen of the cookbooks / Ashton Lee.
Description: Center Point Large Print edition. | Thorndike, Maine :
Center Point Large Print, 2017.
Identifiers: LCCN 2016044599 | ISBN 9781683242437
    (hardcover : alk. paper)
Subjects: LCSH: Librarians—Fiction. | Cooking—Competitions—
Fiction. | Large type books.
Classification: LCC PS3612.E34253 Q44 2017 | DDC 813/.6—dc23
LC record available at https://lccn.loc.gov/2016044599

For Aunt Gail Jenkins Healy Beach

Acknowledgments

This fifth installment of the Cherry Cola Book Club series was so much fun to write. My editor at Kensington, John Scognamiglio, wanted a novel full of good food talk and the chefs who provide it, and I want to thank him for the initial inspiration for *Queen of the Cookbooks*. Of course, my hardworking agents, Christina Hogrebe and Meg Ruley, did their part in negotiating the new contract, and I would be "lost in New York" without them.

But I owe special thanks this time around to Alexe van Beuren and Dixie Grimes of the B.T.C. Old-Fashioned Grocery and Dixie Belle Café in Water Valley, Mississippi (btcgrocery.com), for giving me permission to use their wonderful business in the plot. After a visit there, I just knew I had to write a scene that took place in this nationally recognized enterprise to help bring *Queen of the Cookbooks* to life.

I am also indebted to one of my biggest fans and food enthusiast, Ana Raquel Ruiz, for attending all of my signings in the Atlanta, Georgia, area and providing me with the inspiration to create a new character, Ana Estrella, who graces the pages of this novel. Ana was also willing to share one of her treasured family recipes at the back of the novel—one that is also an integral part of the plot. She, Alexe, and Dixie illustrate perfectly the T-shirt I sometimes wear at book talks and signings—CAREFUL OR YOU'LL END UP IN MY NOVEL! Who knows which of you out there will be next?

Queen of the Cookbooks

1

Out of the Rain

Would it ever stop raining in Cherico, Mississippi? First, the winter storms had come with a vengeance, never letting up, even bringing occasional fits of ice and snow. After all, this was the extreme northeast corner of the Magnolia State—might as well have been Tennessee as the crow flies. Then, March and April had rolled in with the promise of a letup, but no such thing had happened. There had been the usual clashes between the warm air of the Gulf and the Alberta clippers that had roared down like freight trains with tornadic results. Fortunately, Cherico had avoided the physical damage but not the thorough soakings. Lake Cherico, where Maura Beth McShay's new state-of-the-art library was struggling toward completion, was as high and muddy as anyone could remember in recent memory. Fishing had become somewhat of a lost cause, at least until the water table was lowered and the fish could see the lures.

So here it was May, and the rain was continuing, as if sticking its tongue out at Maura Beth's plans for her long-anticipated Grand Opening on the Fourth of July. There was so much riding on the celebration: an elaborate, hour-long fireworks display, followed by a concert, thanks to the generosity of sexy, young country music star Waddell Mack. It was he who had secured the location of the Spurs 'R' Us cowboy boot plant in the town's new industrial park, thereby reversing Cherico's recent economic spiral; even if the rainy weather was also slowing down construction of the manufacturing facility itself. Worse yet, having the library ready to open to the public was beginning to seem doubtful at this point, and Cherico's favorite young redheaded librarian was letting her nerves get the better of her.

"I have to get away from all this. I mean—we have to get away," she told her husband, Jeremy, one rainy May evening at the dinner table inside their Painter Street cottage. "No cell phones, no texting, no way for anybody to get in touch with us—we just leave the Cherico universe behind for a while. Something tells me it's vital that I do this right now."

He looked up from cutting the fried green tomato on his plate, grinning as if he'd just heard some inside joke. It was part of the playful ribbing they had developed since they had become a married couple. "Tell me the truth. You aren't hearing voices in your head, are you?"

"Very funny."

Like the good husband that he was, however, Jeremy knew when to stop kidding around and take his wife seriously. "How long have you been thinking about this, Maurie, and where exactly do you want to go? Do you have one of those Triple A itineraries mapped out?" He dipped the manageable bite of tomato into his reservoir of remoulade sauce and happily munched away at the down-home appetizer his wife had managed to perfect in recent months.

She had even given her sudden interest in cooking a name—My Post-Honeymoon Recipe Period. She had christened it with a perky smile one afternoon in her bright yellow kitchen with the potted palms that she had inherited from the previous owner—Miss Voncille Nettles—now Mrs. Locke Linwood. Where the impetus had come from, she could not say. But suddenly, all she wanted to do was try out new dishes on her husband of nine blissful months. He would be her culinary guinea pig, and so far nothing she had prepared for him had backfired on the two of them: grilled fish, pork and beef, stir-fries, casseroles, overstuffed sandwiches, sorbets, cookies, cakes and pies. Of course, the reality was—everything always tasted good where true love was involved. To a point.

"No, I don't have any definite place in mind. I just mean I absolutely need a day off," she continued, tapping her index finger on the table for emphasis. "Every time I go out to the construction site all full of energy and hope with a vision of the

13

library being completed on schedule, all I get is more bad news—or rather no news that amounts to anything from The Stump."

"The who?"

Maura Beth leaned back, making him wait just a bit for the payoff. "Oh, that's what I've decided to call that sweaty, tobacco-spitting foreman, Kyle Hoskins. Every time I ask him a question about anything, he never has an answer. 'When will that new flashing for the roof be in?' I'll ask. And he'll say, 'Not sure, ma'am. Last time I called about it, they just hemmed and hawed.' And then he'll spit. Or I'll ask him, 'What about the furniture?' And he'll mumble, 'Still can't say, ma'am. There's been some mix-up at their warehouse, they told me.' Then he'll spit again." Maura Beth narrowed her eyes, looking like a hungry feline about to ambush her prey. "He's not just always stumped, I believe he's as dumb as a stump."

"Fence post."

"What?"

Jeremy snickered, screwing up his handsome features in the process. "The official saying is 'dumb as a fence post.'"

Maura Beth frowned at first, but her features eventually morphed into a skeptical smile. "You high school English teachers. You have to nitpick the language to death, don't you? Anyway, getting back to my original thought. What would you think of just taking a day off, jumping into The

14

Warbler, and driving somewhere—not particularly caring where it is."

Jeremy beamed at the mention of his souped-up yellow Volvo, which he considered his one and only guy-toy, finished the last of his fried green tomatoes, and sat with her question for a while. "Do you want to spend the night and then get under the sheets and make a little of our rockin' good lovin'? I'm always up for a session of that big-time, you know."

"Depends on how far away from home we end up. What I really want to do is play it by ear. Be totally spontaneous. No cataloging, ordering books, reading reviews, or doing anything related to being a librarian for just one day. Because the truth is, all this waiting around for the new library to open makes me feel like I'm going to give birth, if you catch my drift."

He nodded with a brief smile, but then a hint of consternation flashed across his face. "You know, maybe I should go out to the construction site with you next time. I wonder if The Stump would be a little more forthcoming if a man asked him all the questions you've been asking. Sounds to me like he doesn't take you seriously. Do you think he might actually be one of those male chauvinist pigs who doesn't want a woman within shouting distance of his daily routine? And God forbid there should ever be a female on his sacred crew."

Maura Beth shook her head and abruptly held up her right hand like a school crossing guard trying to prevent a restless child from darting into traffic. "The last thing I want is for you to start anything up with that quick temper of yours. I didn't marry you because of your macho qualities. I mean, I know you have them, and there are times when they've come in handy, but it's the man who kisses me on the eyelids before he makes insane love to me that I'll proudly claim."

"I won't turn that compliment down."

"I'm sure. Besides, I can always go to City Hall and ask our dear Councilman Sparks for the inside story."

Jeremy's features hardened at the mention of the man's name. The time-honored phrase "fightin' words" flitted across his mind, and his fingers curved inward slightly as if he were getting ready to make a fist. "I can remember a time when Councilman Sparks made a career out of keeping you in the dark on everything. You were his everyday obsession. You know, it still definitely gets under my skin that he wanted to get rid of the library so you'd have to come and work as his secretary with those good ole boy perks for him on the side. What a sleazebag!"

"But that didn't happen, and those days of him trying to intimidate me are over. I think Waddell Mack bringing Spurs 'R' Us to town has given our fearful leader a new outlook on life with all those jobs and new people on the horizon. I really think he's finally called a truce."

"If you say he's waved the white flag, then fair enough," Jeremy said. Then he leaned in, returning to the issue as yet unresolved. "So when did you think you wanna get outta Dodge?"

"As soon as possible. Let's say—tomorrow. Renette handles Saturdays just fine—she always does. She's wise beyond her nineteen years—well, except for . . ." The pregnant pause was not lost on Jeremy, who had observed more than once what an asset the efficient, sweet-natured teenager had become to his Maurie as her chief assistant and most-reliable front desk clerk.

"Except for what?"

Maura Beth exhaled quickly and made a dismissive gesture with her hands. "Well, I haven't made a big deal out of it, but our little Renette Posey has had this mad crush on Waddell Mack since he first came to Cherico last year. You might remember that I got her a seat at that dinner our Periwinkle threw for him and his band down at The Twinkle. Renette's been gaga over him ever since. Says she's bought all his CDs and has a poster or two of him hung on her bedroom wall."

Maura Beth paused, lowered her voice, and began talking out of the side of her mouth. "If you ask me, she's become a genuine Waddell Mack, country music, long-distance groupie."

"That can happen with nineteen-year-olds. I assume it's not interfering with her work?"

Maura Beth brought her napkin up from her lap and dropped it to the side of her plate. "Well, no. I suppose her fascination with him is harmless enough. I guess I worry about her a little too much. She confides in me all the time at work, and it's mostly unsolicited. The thing is, I've discovered she doesn't have a very good relationship with her parents. They're very judgmental, hard-line churchgoers. One of those really quirky, generic-sounding denominations that I've never heard of before—Church of the Eternal Something-or-Other, if I recall. It's tucked away out in the bushes somewhere, but I can vouch for the problems she has with her parents. The Poseys came to the library once but haven't been back since. After they'd browsed around for a while, they approached me and said they'd found certain books on the shelves they didn't approve of— even thought should be removed."

"This should be good. Such as?"

"Would you believe *Harry Potter* for starters?"

"No, I wouldn't. You mean to tell me that a boy wizard fighting for justice set them off?"

Maura Beth turned slightly toward one of the potted palms Voncille Nettles Linwood had left behind in their bright yellow kitchen, as if searching for inspiration and the strength to continue. The Poseys had worked every nerve in her body. "They claimed all the *Harry Potter* books were promoting witchcraft. Of course, I'd read about that line of reasoning before—if you can call it that. Then, they ranted and raved about our books on Halloween for the same reason. Even innocent little books on making original costumes and planning children's parties kept them going. They wanted those gone, too, since they were the work of the Devil, they said. I suppose I've been lucky in that I've yet to have a challenge to anything in our collection before that little encounter with them. You'd think it would be something of a more serious, reasonable nature, though. But I told them that while I respected their right to their views, I could not in good conscience remove those books for the reasons they'd given me. I told them as nicely as I could that the overwhelming majority of our patrons simply didn't feel the same way they did."

"And what did they say to that?"

"They actually threatened to picket the library. Both the old one and the new one when it opened up."

Jeremy gave her an incredulous stare. "Ambitious, aren't they? Well, how did you handle that?"

"I was rather proud of myself, actually," she told him, with an imperious grin. "I invited them to browse the collection and find books that appealed to them and their views and check them out. 'Our books on religion and spirituality are quite diverse,' I told them. And then I finished with, 'If there's a particular book you don't like, no one will force you to check it out, I can assure you.' "

"Did they buy it?"

Maura Beth shrugged. "Who knows? I did what I could do. I directed them to the two hundreds. Then I walked away, thanking them for their input and hoping that I'd put out the fire. Although something tells me I haven't heard the last of them. What a can of worms that is—letting any of your patrons censor what's available to the public. The last time we discussed her parents, Renette said they definitely didn't approve of her new interest in country music. Told her they thought it was 'trashy,' I believe she put it, and that the only kind of music she should be listening to was hymns sung by a choir in church. Anything else was just way beyond the pale."

Jeremy had a distasteful look on his face. "So? She doesn't have to live with them. She has her own apartment, right?"

"Yes, but you've gotten to know Renette a little. She wears her heart on her sleeve. When she gets enthusiastic about something, her emotions just spill over. She probably never should have told her parents about the Waddell Mack thing. She says the last time she went over to their house for dinner, they practically gave her the third degree about the kind of music she was listening to. She told me she lied to them and said she'd thrown all her Waddell Mack stuff away, and they just bowed their heads and said, 'Ay-men. Our little girl is saved.'"

Jeremy was shaking his head vigorously now. "Wow! That sounds like a train wreck of a relationship. But as long as it doesn't affect her job performance, I guess she's still good to go with you."

"I've come to think of her as a daughter in a way—even though I'm only ten years older than she is."

He put a finger to his lips thoughtfully, knowing exactly where he wanted to go. "Hold that maternal thought, Maurie. I think it's a safe bet that you'll need it eventually."

Lately, they had seriously discussed the matter of her getting pregnant. Was it too soon, or did they want to wait a little longer to become parents? Both her parents, Cara Lynn and William Mayhew, as well as his, Paul and Susan McShay, had been pressuring them not so subtly on the subject of becoming grandparents. When could they all expect a blessed event? Would it be sooner rather than later? Oh, and please let them know the minute they knew! They had booties to knit and names to suggest and a hundred other things to consider that were always the purview of grandparents. It was high time they perfected the art of spoiling, Cara Lynn, for one, had pointed out.

"We could start playing the ovulation game seriously. I've had all that down for some time now," she had told him at one point recently. "That is . . . if you really think we're ready."

Jeremy had told her that he thought they should wait until she was good and settled in the new library—the Charles Durden Sparks, Crumpton, and Duddney Public Library, it was going to be called. But although Cherico's scheming head councilman and its three most generous female benefactors—Mamie and Marydell Crumpton, along with Nora Duddney—had donated the money to make the library's construction possible, it was Maura Beth who had had the tenacity and vision to force the issue and bring Cherico into the twenty-first century. The more she thought about it, the more she realized that Jeremy was right— she needed to put this baby by the lake to bed before she considered taking on one that would involve a lifetime commitment of a different kind of love and understanding. Everything in its time. Still, there was a part of her that was definitely warming to the idea of being pregnant, and she couldn't envision herself being the least bit upset if it happened sooner rather than later.

"All right, then, you've convinced me," Jeremy continued at the table, sounding very much like the man in charge that he was. "We'll load up The Warbler and head for the hills . . . or the swamps . . . or the Delta . . . or whatever part of Mississippi we happen to end up in tomorrow. We can pack our lunches together. And if you say you need to get your mind off dealing with The Stump, you're way golden with me. Just remember—if you think he needs a little man-to-man talking-to, you let me know, and I'll take care of it pronto."

She sat back, eyeing him with a bit of a territorial attitude and looking thoroughly pleased with herself. She had always been attracted to his intensity, even if he occasionally got too carried away and into trouble because of it. Intelligence was certainly something to admire, but a woman also needed to know that her man would stand up for her in a physical way when necessary. "I knew there was a reason I married you. A man who likes to listen to a woman is a rare treasure, you know. Matter of fact, a man who likes to listen *period* is rare. I have to say, you've done a pretty good job of it as we've been sitting here."

He cupped a hand around his right ear playfully. "Hey, it's what I do for a living—I listen to all those teenybopper students of mine all day long and try to cope with the fallout. I think I've gotten pretty good at it, if you ask me."

She didn't speak for a while as she revisited something that had been nagging at her lately. She just wasn't completely satisfied with the big day coming up. "I think we need something else. For the Grand Opening of the new library, I mean. Waddell Mack's concert and the fireworks and the tours of the building will all be well and good. But something is missing—something that will get everyone involved in an even more personal way."

Jeremy was frowning now, trying to follow her. "Don't know what on earth that could be, Maurie. I assume that you're not envisioning something like a Woodstock on Lake Cherico. That's not the kind of publicity you really want, and there probably aren't enough porta-potties available in this neck of the woods to handle that."

Her laughter was prolonged, indicating her surprise. "I halfway love the idea, and yes, the library will be renting plenty of porta-potties anyway. We certainly don't need to get down and dirty and make a mess of things on opening day. I still think we need something more to keep interest up throughout the event, though. And I'll know what it is when it comes to me."

It wasn't that Jeremy was lost. It was more that The Warbler didn't have a GPS, and neither he nor his Maurie was particularly successful at reading the roadmap at the moment. Not that they couldn't actually see the red threadlike, meandering lines that represented their whereabouts, but it was as if their brains had been dilated, and they simply couldn't focus properly.

"We never should have gotten off the Natchez Trace," Maura Beth was saying as she squinted at the map once again. She had come to the sudden realization that she hadn't ventured outside of Cherico very often over the last six or seven years, and now she was paying the price. "I think we've been a little too adventurous. We may never get back to civilization at this rate. They'll find our skeletons someday, and we'll be the subject of a future documentary on one of those travel channels. The narrator will say, 'What do you suppose they were doing way out here? No one ever comes out this far.'"

"What an imagination you have. But I thought this is what you wanted. A little adventure, I mean."

He managed a perfunctory smile and drove on along the narrow, winding, two-lane back road with the occasional pothole that they had been trying to negotiate for about twenty minutes now. The first flush of spring was nearly over, and the leaves on the overhanging trees were beginning to darken and proclaim their victory over the long, rainy winter. Except that the rain had still not been vanquished, and Jeremy had the wipers going intermittently against the annoying drizzle they had run into some time ago. Was there anything worse than playing the halfhearted windshield wiper game? Especially when the blades started squeaking against the glass and set teeth on edge like fingernails across a chalkboard.

"Best as I can tell," Maura Beth continued,

looking up from the map after thumping it for emphasis, "there should be a little town called Water Valley about five miles ahead. I've heard of it before—just never been there since moving up from Louisiana seven years ago."

"As I recall, it's a little southwest of Oxford," Jeremy said with a little more certainty in his voice. "I hope they've got a place to eat that's not fast food. I'm hungry, but I hate settling for burgers and fries and that kinda stuff. Your cooking has spoiled me, you know."

She reached over and rubbed his arm affectionately a couple of times. He had indeed been the world's greatest sport throughout her culinary successes and the occasional failure that they had chosen never to bring up again. "Thanks for bearing with me, sweetheart. I was so afraid I'd burn things up and make a martyr of you. I didn't want you to have to gulp things down out of pity."

"Eating pity meals? Now there's an idea."

"Please tell me you didn't have to do that with some of my dishes."

"Nope, there was nothing in that category that I can recall. I've ended up asking you for seconds most of the time. If I had to give you a grade, it would definitely have to be an A-plus."

She was remembering the long succession of recipes and the care she had always taken to pull them off successfully. Was she on fire or what?

"You're my favorite guinea pig," she told him.

"I guess I *have* made a pig of myself sometimes." They both exchanged amused glances. Then the rain started to fall a bit harder, coming down in fat drops that seemed to impart a sense of aggression, and Jeremy gratefully changed the wipers from squeaky intermittent to seamless continuous. "So what else is new? More rain. Is there a dark cloud following us wherever we go? Seems like we've been coming out of the rain every day for months now."

Maura Beth put the map down and snapped her fingers. "Oh, you know—there was a really nice article in the Tupelo paper I saw online not long ago about this charming little combination grocery store and café in Water Valley. Their menu sounded very sophisticated but also like Southern comfort food. I'd really like to see someone pull that off. I made a mental note that if I ever got anywhere near Water Valley, I was going to try it."

"Do you remember what street it was on?"

"Oh, it shouldn't be too hard to find," Maura Beth said. "Water Valley's just a small town, and if I remember correctly, I think it might have been on Main Street. But since you're not opposed to the concept like most men are, you could always stick your head out the window and ask for directions if we have any trouble."

Jeremy sped up a bit, even though the rain was coming down even harder now with a bit of thunder and lightning for emphasis. Obviously, the immediate goal was to get out of the storm as quickly as possible, but stomachs were growling as well. "That sounds really good to me. I'm starving to death."

Maura Beth was pleased with herself. She had wanted to get away for one day to someplace different and special, and Water Valley's B.T.C. Old-Fashioned Grocery with its Dixie Belle Café inside fit the bill perfectly. The simplicity of the charming, two-story brick building with its benches out front, big sidewalk planters with seasonal flowers, and blackboard with daily specials scrawled in colored chalk were the essence of small-town curb appeal. If a building could have spoken, it would have said in a soft drawl, "Come on in and try me, y'all!"

Inside, there was much to recommend it. Fresh produce labeled with the first names of the farmers who had supplied it filled the rustic shelves: blueberries from Joe, Hal's tomatoes, Mike's sweet potatoes, Sam's figs, and Miss Patsy's cucumbers. It was like walking into a garden tended by close friends and neighbors who were offering up their pride and joy for consumption. A lot of other items seemed to have a "local" label on them as well: jars of local honey, cartons of local eggs—even packages of local pork. After browsing through it all with smiles on their faces, Maura Beth and Jeremy were seated in the crowded, brick-walled café full of tempting aromas and chatting customers; then they began looking over the eclectic menu.

"I like the sound of this Lola Burger," Jeremy said, pointing while nodding his head crisply. "It says here it's got flat-grilled beef on a Rotella bun with some white cheddar, pickled red onions, and something called Lola Sauce. I think I'll give that a big 'yum.'"

Maura Beth had a whimsical look on her face. "Lola. Wasn't she a character in *Damn Yankees*? Wasn't she the Devil?"

"The Devil's mistress, I think. Or maybe his personal secretary or something like that. At any rate, she was plenty saucy. I believe she sang 'Whatever Lola Wants, Lola Gets.'"

She began mouthing the words, finally nodding her head enthusiastically. "Yep, I didn't know you were that up to speed on musical theater."

"Oh, didn't I tell you? I dabbled in high school," he said, waving her off. "Got a small part in the chorus of *Oklahoma!* and thought at the time I might even want to become an actor. But my voice wasn't *that* good, and my love of the English language prevailed instead."

"Well, I think I'm going to have this Jive Turkey Sandwich," Maura Beth told him. "Says it's smoked turkey on wheat-berry bread with Muenster cheese, alfalfa sprouts, avocado, and some real fancy mayo with jalapeño and some other stuff. I do love me some spicy food."

Just then the waitress arrived—a breezy young thing with short blond hair and a bright smile plastered on her face. "Hello, folks. I'm Melba, and I'll be taking care of you this afternoon. We have a few specials today and—"

Before she had a chance to say anything further, however, Jeremy took over and ploughed right ahead. "That's okay about the specials, thanks. But the deal is, we're really hungry, so we'd like to go ahead and order everything, if you don't mind." He paused and chuckled to himself. "Well, I don't mean we want to order everything on the menu. We just want to go ahead and order."

Maura Beth wagged her brows at the waitress. "English teacher."

Melba smiled and said, "Oh, I knew what you meant, sir."

With that, Jeremy rattled off their choices exactly the way he gave homework instructions to his students at Cherico High, and Melba was off to the kitchen. Then Maura Beth quickly rose from her chair.

"I'll be right back."

"Ladies' room?"

She pointed toward the front of the store with its wide display windows. "No, I saw something that interested me when we walked in. I think I'm getting that idea about something extra for the Grand Opening."

"I know that look."

"What can I say? I love it when things fall into place."

"Then I'll just sit here twiddling my thumbs and wait for you to tell me all about your brainstorm."

A few minutes later, Maura Beth returned with a book in hand and handed it over to Jeremy, who read the title out loud. *"The B.T.C. Old-Fashioned Grocery Cookbook."* He fanned through it briefly. "Looks very interesting. I'd certainly like to try some of these dishes. But you bought it before we had a chance to eat the food?"

"Oh, I can smell that the food we ordered will be good. Just look around. Happy locals munching away. And this is definitely what's missing in our Grand Opening celebration for the library—food, food, food. I mean, why should we settle for the store-bought cookies and punch we had originally talked about? I can't believe I was about to settle for something that lame. What was I thinking?"

She sat down across from him and began painting a picture, her hands framing an imaginary canvas. "Can't you just see it? Food tents. Tasting booths. We invite everyone who can cook—or thinks they can—to come and offer their specialties to the public. They can charge nominal prices—no one'll get rich. But some might benefit from the exposure. It can go on all day while the library

31

tours are taking place. People will get hungry and thirsty, of course, since it'll be the Fourth of July and hot as all get out. We can have contests for best overall recipe and best dishes in all kinds of categories—just like a county fair. We can give out ribbons or trophies or maybe even a little cash to really give them some motivation to participate. There's plenty of money in the library till for the prizes since my Cudd'n M'Dear left us that incredible endowment to do with as I please."

Jeremy sat back, admiring his wife's tenacity where the library was concerned. "Maurie, you thought of all that just now?"

"We librarians think of lots of things on the spur of the moment. It's our nature. Our brains roam around like the generalists we are."

Jeremy mumbled something under his breath and slouched a bit in his chair, his mood nearly undecipherable.

"What did you say?" Maura Beth wanted to know.

"Roaming Brains. Sounds like the title of the novel I may someday actually write, since I don't seem to be able to get anywhere with the one I started in Key West on our honeymoon. Of course, I should have known better, since it *was* our honeymoon. I . . . or rather, we had something else on our minds."

She reached over and gave his hand a reassuring squeeze. He truly had not been making much progress with his writing, and she wanted to be as supportive as possible of his aspirations. "Your muse will come. Just be patient."

Shortly after the food arrived and they began sampling the Lola Burger and Jive Turkey Sandwich they had ordered, Maura Beth took a moment to puff herself up. "See? This is beyond delicious, just as I knew it would be. And besides that, people who love to cook take an enormous amount of pride in their food. They live for it, and nothing makes them feel better than getting compliments on what they've fixed. I'm betting the citizens of Greater Cherico will stand in line to set up their tents for the big day." She took another bite of her Jive Turkey and slowly ruminated. "Yummy. This mayo is really spicy. And this trip proves that I was absolutely right to get away from the library and Cherico to get a little perspective on things. Do you see what's happened as a result?"

"You are preaching to the choir, sweetheart. I never doubt your ability to get the job done right. You have vision."

Suddenly, she put down her sandwich, sounding particularly triumphant. "A queen. We need to crown a queen. Everybody loves to think of themselves as royalty in the Deep South. I think it started with Mardi Gras in New Orleans and the Natchez Pilgrimage, both of which have oodles of kings and queens. So we'll have a top prize. We'll call her the Queen of the Cookbooks, and we'll give her a little tiara, too."

Without hesitation, Jeremy looked at her sideways. "And if the winner happens to be a man?"

Maura Beth thought for a while and then snapped her fingers. "I say we give the winner both a tiara and a trophy to do with as they please. King or Queen—it'll all be in good fun."

"There ya go. Hey, I'm not one of them, but some men love to cook, too."

"We could always give the winner a cigar, too," Maura Beth said, stifling a giggle or two.

On the way back to Cherico with a light drizzle still accompanying them, Maura Beth sat in the passenger seat scribbling on her notepad. She was clearly lost in her scheming, furrowing her brow and biting her upper lip throughout the process. "I need to get some flyers made up right away," she said at one point. "I'll get Periwinkle and Mr. Place to spread the word down at The Twinkle to all their customers, and James Hannigan will let me put flyers up on the bulletin board at The Cherico Market, and he'll make announcements over the PA system in the store like he always does with my projects. Oh, he's such a sweet, sweet man." She paused briefly for a breath and a self-satisfied grin.

"And then I'll get all the rest of the gang in the book club involved and work even more of the angles. I just know people will come from miles around for everything—Waddell Mack's concert, the fireworks, and the food tents. It'll be a regular carnival—just without the crazy rides. Except . . ."

"Except what?"

Her voice went all gloomy as she considered the calendar in her head. "I'm still a bit worried about the library completion date. The one thing we can't change is when the Fourth of July shows up on the calendar. We can't stop the sun from rising and setting. Honestly, there are times I could swear that construction company is delaying things on purpose."

"Now, why would they do that? Some of these construction contracts have incentive clauses to finish early for bonuses. It would cost them money to fool around too much like that."

Maura Beth always seemed to end up with the same old talking points when it came to her tenure at the library. "I'm sure you're right. I guess I've become somewhat cynical after dealing with City Hall and Councilman Sparks all these years. I mean, things appear to be much better between the two of us, but that doesn't mean there isn't something going on behind the scenes. I know that sounds paranoid, but I speak from my long experience."

A mile or so of slick, winding road went by in silence, as Jeremy tightened his grip on the wheel and concentrated on keeping the low traction in check. When the road finally straightened out a bit and a big patch of sunlight broke through the overhanging trees as if The Warbler had reached the promised land, he exhaled softly and said, "Well, you could still have all the festivities without the library tours. Or you could have the tours even though everything wouldn't quite be finished. I don't think your patrons would mind all that much. You know they'll love you no matter what. After all, you're the one who got Cherico buzzing again about something besides yard sales, football, hunting season, and drinking beer. Hey, who knew a librarian could become the real mover and shaker in Cherico—instead of Councilman Sparks?"

Maura Beth played at being difficult about it all. "Yes, I know all that, Jeremy. But I'd have tours of an unfinished facility only as a last resort. I want everything to be perfect for my patrons. After all these years of living with that dark, tractor warehouse of a library that we've been saddled with, I want them to be able to celebrate the state-of-the-art building they'll finally be getting. I want this to be a bright, shining moment for our little town of Cherico. No matter what else I accomplish here in the years ahead, this will be my proudest legacy."

Jeremy briefly took his right hand off the steering wheel and offered her a high five. "That's my Maurie. Brava!"

2

Out of the Woodwork

The Queen of the Cookbooks contest flyers that Maura Beth quickly produced began getting sensational results over the next few weeks and well into June. Not a day passed that someone didn't appear at her outmoded, soon-to-be-discarded library on Shadow Alley asking for more details about the competition. Perhaps they were hoping to get some tips for an inside edge from the enterprising library director herself. Maura Beth knew or recognized almost all of them, diplomatically prodding them to return and use the library even after the contest was over; but a couple of interesting new faces turned up, much to her delight, causing her to think that Queen of the Cookbooks might turn out to be as much of a game changer for Cherico as the creation of The Cherry Cola Book Club had been nearly two years earlier.

Of course, many of the club members were doing their part to advertise Maura Beth's brainstorm as the Fourth of July Grand Opening grew ever closer. Periwinkle and her waitresses at The Twinkle included a flyer and a bright smile at the end of every meal. "If you like to putter around the kitchen—not ours, but yours, I mean—be sure and check this out. You might even win you some mad money," Lalie Bevins would tell them all as she handed her customers their tabs.

Elsewhere, the retired Connie and Douglas McShay made the rounds door-to-door soliciting their neighbors out at the lake where they had also footed the bill for temporary bleachers for the Waddell Mack concert taking place next to the new library; Cherico's most famous "married pushing seventy" couple, Locke and Voncille Linwood, got their daily exercise walking up and down Painter Street handing out flyers to passersby and people working diligently out in their yards despite the midsummer heat; Jeremy got permission to tack up a few flyers on Cherico High School's bulletin boards even though he wasn't teaching summer school; Justin "Stout Fella" Brachle had nailed flyers to telephone poles on every piece of real estate he was currently peddling both inside and outside the city limits; James Hannigan had displayed them on the big message board at The Cherico Market; and downtown merchants like Audra Neely had managed to integrate flyers into their window displays. The buzz for the culinary competition was building exponentially, and people seemed to be coming out of the woodwork to announce their participation.

Was it all too good to be true?

"I'm Ana Estrella," a slim, young, dark-haired woman with smooth olive skin explained, shaking Maura Beth's hand at her office door one morning just after the library had opened. After the two women had taken their seats and Maura Beth had graciously welcomed her, Ana continued with a great deal of poise and confidence—her hands folded neatly in her lap. There was even a definite sense of being carefully rehearsed about her tone. Not robotic, but rehearsed nonetheless.

"You're probably wondering why you've never seen me around before, Mrs. McShay. I'm brand-new to Cherico. I've moved down here ahead of the construction of the Spurs 'R' Us cowboy boot plant. I'll be doing public relations for the company once it opens, but the owners wanted me to get the feel of the community well in advance. Mr. Waddell Mack in particular said he thought it would be a great move, and I decided to take his advice."

"Oh, we adore Waddell. He single-handedly saved our economy by getting the plant to locate here after everyone thought it was backing out. And we have more than a few of our citizens who swear by his country music now." Maura Beth paused, wondering if she should say more, but soon relented. "If I may say so, I don't quite understand the popularity of some of his songs—and I have listened intently to his current CD. More than once, as a matter of fact. I'm more the classical music type and so is my husband, Jeremy. But Waddell's a charmer and a true gentleman, so who am I to judge his talent? After all, I'm a librarian, and we're just about the most inclusive people you'll ever meet."

Ana nodded and quickly flashed a smile. "Yes, I certainly believe that. You came highly recommended from a couple of sources as a good place to start in getting to know Cherico. First, there was Councilman Sparks at City Hall. My, what a looker he is with that touch of gray at the temples and that smile. Maybe I shouldn't say this, but he almost reminded me of one of those game-show hosts the way he gestured all the time and put me right at ease."

"Aptly put. Did he say, 'Come on down'?"

Ana enjoyed a good laugh, and said, "Oh, I can see we're going to work well together."

Maura Beth was tempted to say something more about her favorite politician, revealing a bit of her often-tempestuous relationship with the man who ran the town with an iron fist and had never really understood what a library's mission was; in the end she opted for discretion. "I would definitely say that meeting with our esteemed head honcho would be your first order of business here in Cherico. I can't wait to hear how it all went."

"Well, our meeting was quite productive. I didn't know what to expect, but he gave me the key to the city and couldn't have been more gracious to me. You could tell that he's very excited about Spurs 'R' Us coming to Cherico."

Maura Beth could picture Councilman Sparks putting on a show for Ana. He was excellent at creating first impressions, particularly where one of his hidden agendas was concerned. At the moment, however, she was inclined to give him the benefit of the doubt. "He should be excited. We've desperately needed the jobs to get us really going again. Cherico has had a run of bad luck recently, and there's not much of a margin for error in a town as small as this one is."

"So I understand. Well, the same day I met with Councilman Sparks, I was given one of your Queen of the Cookbooks flyers when I ate dinner at The Twinkle that evening—which also came highly recommended by Mr. Mack. I believe he and the band stopped there on one of their tours last fall. I remember all his tweets quite well. He was burning up his account, and he trended quite nicely. Sometimes all this technology makes my head spin."

"They certainly did have themselves a grand feast at The Twinkle. They left fat and happy, as the saying goes, and they swore by Periwinkle's fried catfish, cole slaw, and her husband Parker's crème brûlée. I was witness to the whole thing, doing a bit of indulging myself with my own husband."

Both women laughed, and Ana said, "Well, what can I say? I love to eat, and I love to cook, too. I thought I'd even have one of those tasting booths for your library opening out at the lake on the Fourth of July. My specialty is Hispanic food, since my family is originally from Puerto Rico. We're from the San Juan area, actually."

"Oh, I've heard so many wonderful things about San Juan. My family grew up in New Orleans, so charming, historic architecture is certainly something I can appreciate. I must put San Juan on my bucket list."

Ana leaned in, her dark eyes sparkling and her tone suddenly more confidential. "You won't be disappointed if you do. Of course, I'm very proud of my Hispanic heritage, but I always say that history can only get us so far. What really counts is what we do with ourselves in the present, and that's the big reason I've come to Cherico. I want to be sure that Spurs 'R' Us is a good citizen once it's up and running, and to do that, I need to understand what makes this town click. Many people have assured me that you can give me the lowdown. So here I am—more than happy to get your take on everything and everyone."

Maura Beth was unable to contain her amusement. Once again she debated how much she should reveal. If only she could tell this newcomer everything there was to know, all that lurked beneath the surface of what appeared to be a quiet, conventional community. But now was the time to be welcoming and avoid any sort of controversy. Perhaps the best thing would be for Ana to discover certain things for herself and then take it from there.

"Well, you've come to the right person. I'll be happy to put down some names and identify the movers and shakers for you. Sort of a 'Who's Who in Cherico?'—which incidentally is also the name of our well-established genealogical society here. It meets every month right here in the library under the direction of Voncille Nettles Linwood. We used to call her Miss Voncille until she got married last year. Anyway, I can do some mini-sketches for you if you'd like."

"That would be wonderful," Ana said, waving her hand about. "I've come here from Nashville where the Spurs 'R' Us headquarters is, you know. The big city. Well, at least it's big for the Deep South. I imagine that a small town like this will be a lot easier to figure out."

This time, Maura did not restrain herself, sitting up straighter in her chair. "You'd be surprised. But I'm going to do you a huge favor by suggesting you join our Cherry Cola Book Club, which meets right here in the library. Our next meeting is in a couple of weeks at the end of June. You'll meet everyone who's anyone in Cherico. Most of our members bring potluck dishes, so you could whip up one of your Hispanic recipes to introduce yourself. I always say that most everybody can be won over and impressed with some good food. We're breaking with tradition this time out, though. Usually, we review one classic work of Southern fiction at a time, but we're doing what I call a free-for-all. Everyone will comment on their favorite, outside-the-box novel of whatever genre. We don't quite know what to expect—in fact, we've come to expect the unexpected in our little group, but it should still be fun."

"You've convinced me. Unless something comes up, I'll be there. And I think I know just what I'll fix."

Maura Beth reached across and patted her hand. "Good move." Then she picked up her pen, looking thoughtful. "Perhaps I should get busy on those mini-sketches I promised you."

Ana clasped her hands together dramatically and smiled. "Almost like one of those programs you read when you go to the theater. Are you the critic of Cherico?"

Maura Beth could not help but laugh heartily. "I have to keep a low profile on that, but you have no idea what you've just said. Cherico is nothing if not home to some of the biggest drama queens— and a few kings, I might add—in the annals of the history of the Deep South."

She began writing down all the pertinent information for Ana and then cheerfully handed over the sheet of paper. "My handwriting is perfectly awful. I think I must have been out sick the entire year they taught penmanship in grade school. So I printed everything for you. Legibly, I trust."

Ana glanced down quickly and began reading out loud. "Justin . . . how do you pronounce this last name spelled B-R-A-C-H-L-E?"

"Like broccoli."

"Ah. And it says here he's a real estate tycoon. I guess all these small towns have one."

"Trust me on this one. The man could sell air conditioners to scientists at the South Pole."

Ana continued, her tone full of amusement. "Becca Brachle—retired radio cooking show celebrity. And it also says here she turned her difficult married name into a clever and unforgettable ratings success."

"Yes, Becca is Justin's wife. For years she was the star of the local *Becca Broccoli Show*—spelled like the vegetable, you understand—and she even has a cookbook of her best dishes coming out in time for the library's Grand Opening. She'll be doing a signing inside that very morning, and we're counting on her drawing a crowd. But what's even more important, she's the mother of my godson, Mark Grantham Brachle. Markie is six months old now and so adorable I could just eat him with a spoon."

"How nice for you, and I know just what you mean. I have a few little nieces and nephews of my own whom I just love to spoil whenever I can." Ana returned to her list. "Connie McShay—retired ICU nurse. Douglas McShay—retired trial lawyer. Quite a few retirees living here, I see."

"Oh, more than a few. Many of them are out at the lake where the new library is located. In fact, Connie and Douglas donated the land next to their lodge for the library. They went above and beyond the call of their civic duty in saving us a ton of money with that gesture. They're originally from Nashville. But I guess you never met them up there, huh?"

"Afraid not. Nashville's a big city and getting bigger by the minute. But they sound like wonderful, generous people. You can't beat that." Ana ran her finger down the list and continued. "And next we have Voncille Nettles Linwood—retired schoolteacher and town genealogist of note . . . yes, you mentioned her before. And then Locke Linwood—the most gentlemanly of Southern gentlemen, you say here. He sounds absolutely charming."

"That he is. His recent marriage to Voncille is his second. His first wife, Pamela, died of breast cancer a few years ago. They were both regulars at the 'Who's Who in Cherico?' meetings."

"How sad. But I'm happy to hear he's remarried."

"Yes, Locke and Voncille are an inspiration to everyone looking for love in all the right places."

After a respectful pause, Ana resumed.

46

"Periwinkle Place, owner of The Twinkle, Twinkle Café, the town's premier restaurant. But I don't believe I met her while I was eating there." Ana looked up with a curious expression on her face. "Periwinkle. Is that her nickname?"

"Nope, that's her real given name. Well, part of it anyway. She's actually Periwinkle Violet. Her mother was fond of flowers. Hey, what can I say? This is the Deep South, you know."

"So it is. Now, let's see here . . . Mr. Parker Place—The Twinkle's accomplished pastry chef. I didn't see him, either, but the slice of caramel pie I had was downright sinful. My figure isn't going to thank me for indulging, I'm afraid. I did have a very nice waitress, though. She had an unusual name, too."

"That was probably Lalie Bevins. She's been with Periwinkle since The Twinkle opened, and her son, Barry, delivers all the takeout orders in their van. They've done quite well with that, and I've called them up many a time when I was just too tired to cook."

Then Maura Beth looked thoughtful for a moment, figuring out how to phrase things. "Believe me, Peri and Mr. Place were working hard behind the scenes. The Twinkle is their baby. They were married just a few months ago in a very sweet, simple ceremony in the Cherico African Methodist Episcopal Church. They had it there out of respect to his dear sweet mother, who died unexpectedly last year, unfortunately. That threw everyone in Cherico for a loop."

Ana looked properly sympathetic, took a deep breath, and continued reading. "Mamie Crumpton— the town's wealthiest spinster. Best to steer clear." Ana cocked her head. "A warning?"

"Just between the two of us, she's . . . well, let's just say that she's anything but shy and retiring," Maura Beth explained, lowering her voice. "Very opinionated. But she and her sister, Marydell, who works for me at the front desk, does a great job, and is nothing like Mamie, did contribute a substantial amount of their trust fund to enable us to build the new library. I'm indebted to them for that."

"Ah, then all's well that ends well."

"In this case, yes."

Ana scanned the rest of the list quickly. "Well, perhaps I ought to look over the last part of this at my leisure." Then she rose from her chair and extended her hand. "And if I have any questions, I can call you?"

"Of course. And do think seriously about coming to our next Cherry Cola Book Club meeting. Don't even worry about bringing a novel to talk about at this late date. If you want, all you have to do is listen and eat some good food your first time out. It's right here at six-thirty on Wednesday the last week in June, and it's the last one we'll be having in this old tin shack of a building. It goes without saying that we can't wait to move into our new home out at the lake where we can finally do things up right in a real meeting room instead of forever hauling folding chairs out of the closets and into the lobby. Of course, all our meetings have substance, but there's nothing wrong with adding a little style."

After Ana had left, Maura Beth couldn't help but trot out her last-minute worries about the new library's completion. The computer terminals had still not arrived, and neither had the furniture. To be sure, the shelving was in place, but there was an enormous opening day collection half in and out of boxes to be processed. The new staff hires—a third front desk clerk, Helen Porter, technical processing librarian, Agnes Braud, and the library's first-ever children's librarian, Miriam Goodcastle—had not yet been introduced to the public but were working diligently behind the scenes moving what was salvageable from the old collection into the new building.

Would it all come together in time?

The next newcomer to approach Maura Beth could not have been more different from Ana Estrella, both in style and physical appearance. Where Ana had been polished, diminutive, and relaxed, Mrs. Bit Sessions practically roared into Maura Beth's office after Renette Posey's quick introduction in the doorframe. Without having to be told to take a seat, this bosomy matron with snow-white hair piled high atop her head in imitation of Dairy Queen soft-serve vanilla ice cream plopped herself down across from Maura Beth and cut right to the chase.

"What I want to know is this—I'm from over in Corinth. Am I allowed to participate in this Queen of the Cookbooks thingamajig? Or is it just limited to you people here in Cherico? Or as you people like to call it—Greater Cherico. Honestly, what nonsense I've always thought that was. You don't have more than five thousand people here, and I hear by the grapevine that a couple of your businesses are moving to Corinth. Now I'd like to know just what's so great about that? Who wants to publicize that a town is dying on the vine?"

Maura Beth's brain was spinning. Where to start with this maelstrom of a woman? So she took a deep breath and plastered a smile on her face. "The . . . uh, contest is open to everyone who's interested. There are no mileage and distance limits, if you will. I guess theoretically you could enter if you lived in Chicago or in New York City, that is, if you found out about it in time. Wouldn't that be a hoot if we had entrants from places like Detroit and Kansas City?"

Bit drew back, her blue eyes widening farther and the hint of a smile creeping into her face. "So you're the clever, humorous type, I see. Well, I'm glad you don't take yourself so seriously. Because

50

I certainly do. I intend to win that Queen of the Cookbooks grand prize of five thousand dollars, or my name is not Elladee Martha Simpson Sessions." She paused with an expectant look on her face, waiting for a reaction. As Maura Beth offered none, however, she moved on.

"I know my name's a mouthful, but when I was just a little bit of a thing, everyone started calling me Bit. I was small for what seemed like forever, but as you can see, I've made up for that now. Yes, I eat way too much and it shows on my hips and everywhere else, but it's because I'm the best darned cook in the Western Hemisphere, and I'll prove it by winning this contest. If my fourth and last husband, Talbot, were still around, he'd walk up to you and swear by me and demand that you give me that prize without even tasting a forkful. My Tally Boy—that was my nickname for him and maybe you can guess why—was a retired Army Ranger, you see, and he took no nonsense off of anyone. But, boy, did he ever have an appetite. You should have seen our grocery bills back in the day. Believe me, his army pension came in handy whenever I went shopping for us."

Maura Beth was trying her best to warm to the woman and finally seized upon something resembling a compliment. "Your . . . uh, Tally Boy sounds like a fascinating man, and I admire your spunk. I've always been pretty spunky myself. So tell me, what exactly is your specialty?"

"Down-home is what I expect people would call it. It's nothin' fancy. But it's all so good you can't possibly pull away from the table. My spicy lasagna is to die for, and so is my squash casserole. It's a little on the sweet side, but it's not a dessert, you understand. Have you ever had butterbean soup with ham? Now that's on the savory side, of course. And then there's my sweet corn kernel cornbread. Doesn't that all sound just scrumptious?"

Maura Beth nodded with a pleasant smile on her face, struggling to keep up with the culinary onslaught. She was, in fact, salivating just a bit.

"Believe me, you don't know what you're missin'. That's what anybody who's ever tasted my food has said. I tell you, the others won't have a chance. There'll be a line a mile long for my tasting booth. But I've been thinkin' that maybe I'll just concentrate on one of my dishes—like my ham and butterbean soup. I could enter it in the appetizer category."

Thinking on her feet, Maura Beth continued to smile and said, "Enthusiasm like yours is just what we need. It's sure to make for a heated competition. Ha! There's a little cooking humor for you."

Surprisingly, Bit's demeanor went all dark and sullen, her eyes narrowing to slits. "Now, about that . . . I know we've just met, but may I speak to you frankly about something?"

"Of course."

"Is there any way you could tell me if a particular person has signed up for the contest? Maybe she's even entered already. Do you happen to keep track of that sorta thing?"

Maura Beth was frowning now, unable to see where the woman was going but sensing that Bit had "hidden agenda" written all over her. She had run across more than a few patrons like that, and they had turned out to be the bane of her existence. "I . . . uh, suppose she could have. Everyone who enters has to register here at the front desk. Why do you ask?"

Suddenly, Bit launched into a diatribe complete with sweeping hand gestures and constant eye rolling. No televangelist could have done it with more conviction and panache. "It's that nauseating, whining Gwen Beetles. She's always been my rival at everything. She and I grew up together over in Corinth, and I just know she's gonna want to hog the spotlight and beat me out of winning that top prize. Why, she just thinks she invented the kitchen and every utensil in it. To hear her tell it, she was born with a spatula in her mouth. Heh. I'd like to shove one up her . . . well, you get the picture. She's such a know-it-all, especially when it comes to secret ingredients. You would think God himself gave them to her, like Moses delivering the Commandments. She presses the church metaphors ad nauseam. Her sauces are a revelation, she's always saying. Her icings are angelic and heavenly, she insists. One time, I'd just about had enough, so I told her she ought to have all her recipes published in a cookbook and call it *The Hubris Collection.* For all I know, she may already have done that. So, I'd appreciate it if you could let me know the moment she enters the competition, if you don't mind. Forewarned is forearmed, you know."

Once again, Maura Beth was speechless, struggling desperately to formulate a sensible reply. Such was always the objective of the public servant. "Well, I don't think anyone by that name has signed up yet, but you are certainly welcome to come in and check the sign-up sheet at the front desk whenever you want," she managed finally. "I'm afraid I don't have the time to monitor it for you with all I have to do around here. I mean, I have the new library opening soon on the Fourth of July, and we've already begun moving the collection out there. I'm sure you can appreciate all the work we have ahead of us. It's been overwhelming."

Bit shot to her feet, slightly off balance, almost as if something had stung her ample rear end. "I suppose I can. So, now, where did you say these sign-up sheets are again that your flyer talked about?"

Maura Beth rose more slowly and pointed helpfully to her office door. "Right through there at the front desk. Renette Posey, the young lady who showed you in, will take care of you. And welcome aboard."

With a quick nod and a mumbled, "Thanks," the anything-but-a-wallflower Bit Sessions was off and running.

A few seconds later, Maura Beth realized she had not invited the woman to join The Cherry Cola Book Club as she had done with Ana Estrella. She started to call out after her. Then some sort of alarm went off in her brain and kept on clanging away. Maybe later, if ever. Bit had "first-class disruption" written all over her, and there was no lack of members already in the club capable of providing that and more. No need to add more fuel to the fire.

At least Maura Beth was somewhat prepared when Gwen Beetles showed up at the library about thirty minutes after Bit Sessions had left. What was the adjective Bit had used to describe her nemesis? Oh, yes—*whining!* And that turned out to be quite the understatement. In addition to the whining, anyone would have found the droning on and on somewhat difficult to bear. It was as if the woman were in a trance of some kind—her eyes half-lidded while she fingered her stringy gray hair absentmindedly.

". . . and so I followed her over here all the way from Corinth, you see," Gwen was saying in

Maura Beth's office. "I tailed her in my car just like in one of those detective movies, and I was quite clever about it, if you ask me. She's not about to pull the wool over my eyes, even though she'd been hinting around. Well, actually, I overheard her at a party talking about entering the contest, and she didn't know I was listening. She's always up to something, you know—she's in on the town gossip without fail. That and cooking are the only reasons she's living."

Maura Beth steeled herself with a smile, as she always did when she encountered difficult patrons. In such instances her objective was always to conceal what she was really thinking. "Well, we certainly want people to register who have a knack for making good food, don't we? I think we can concentrate on that and let everything else go."

Gwen's face dropped considerably. "Well, maybe you could. Too much has happened between me and Bit for me to forget, though. But no matter. I intend to win that money because everyone in Corinth thinks I'm the best Southern cook around as God is my witness. Except Bit, of course, who's always thought the whole world revolved around her, you know."

Then she leaned in, widening her eyes and showing some intensity for the first time since she had shuffled into Maura Beth's office almost as if she were sleepwalking. "You heard it here first.

Bit will do anything to win this contest, and I do mean anything. She will cheat if she has to, and believe me, I know what I'm talking about. You can ask anyone in Corinth who knows her—they even say she cheats on her income taxes. She has more money than she knows what to do with. Why, she buried four husbands, and it's my considered opinion there might even have been some foul play afoot here and there. She's an evil one, if you ask me."

Maura Beth didn't really want to dignify all the heinous charges coming her way but felt she had to say something. Silence might be interpreted as agreement. "I don't think we need to start accusing people of dastardly deeds, Mrs. Beetles. Besides, I don't see how anyone could cheat and get away with it. The people who taste the food will determine the winners. They'll fill out their ballots and drop them in a bowl. And I'll make sure that bowl is under the strict supervision of my assistants, Helen Porter and Marydell Crumpton. This won't be anything like a county fair where you have a handful of judges who could be bribed or where nepotism could even enter the picture. Whoever gets the most votes in the appetizer, entrée, and dessert categories will win those prizes. And then Overall Best Dish will win the Queen of the Cookbooks top prize. I believe everything will be aboveboard."

But Gwen was shaking her head emphatically.

"Doesn't matter how tight a ship you think you're running. She'll find herself a way around the rules. She'll pay people if she has to, and I really think you should have someone keep an eye on her the whole time. I'd volunteer to do it myself, but I'll have my hands full at my own booth with my heavenly dishes. Just you wait and see if I don't win out."

Maura Beth listened to the woman ramble on in that monotone of hers while concocting an interior monologue of her own to keep her wits about her. What had she wrought with this contest? Suddenly, they were crawling out of the woodwork with their rivalries and jealousies and outright spite. Would there be more of them coming down the pike like Bit Sessions and Gwen Beetles? Had she inadvertently opened Pandora's Box of Recipes?

In any case, this was not what she had envisioned. Women in starched white aprons wearing colorful oven mitts and sunny smiles, and men in tall chef's hats handling long wooden spoons had been her hopeful, charming fantasy. But so far, all of the disagreements and unpleasant behaviors that had broken out spontaneously during meetings of The Cherry Cola Book Club heretofore were beginning to pale in comparison to the worrisome possibilities looming ahead during the Queen of the Cookbooks competition.

• • •

The parade continued. Another entrant who wandered in later that afternoon fared better when it came to a more normal, even-handed personality in Maura Beth's estimation. Perhaps the two women from Corinth had unduly influenced her judgment, and she needed to make an attitude adjustment. In any case everything about this third woman was restrained and elegant down to her tasteful, navy blue business suit, flawless bouffant hairdo, and ramrod-straight posture. The ensemble gave her an ageless appearance—she might have been thirty-five, or she might have been fifty, or possibly even older than that.

"I'm Aleitha Larken," the woman said in an even, cultured tone, shaking hands before seating herself in Maura Beth's office. "I live in the North Crossroads Community, which is about halfway between Corinth and here. I know it's way out in the country, but the family home is there, and I wouldn't think of moving. We have quite a tract with pecan orchards and beaucoup herds of cattle. As we're so fond of saying among ourselves—we deal in nuts and beef in no particular order."

Maura Beth laughed brightly. "I like that. And I'm glad we have another out-of-towner coming to us on the Fourth. We're flattered so many of you have chosen to participate in our contest. We'd hoped to attract more than just our fellow Chericoans, and it looks like we're doing just that."

59

Aleitha adopted a more confidential demeanor. "Actually, I'm doing this on a dare. My husband, Phillip, says I've always underestimated my cooking, but I've always thought that was something he had to say because he was married to me. 'Go see if I'm not telling you the truth,' he told me the other day. 'Sign up for that Queen of the Cookbooks competition over in Cherico. I bet you'll win it.'" She paused to shake her head thoughtfully.

"Well, I don't know about that, but here I am giving it the old college try. I'm offering only one dish, which everyone in my family swears by. It started out as Chicken Divan Parisienne—and don't ask me where that came from—but my kids couldn't handle something so fancy and complicated. My eldest, Julia Rachel, was in middle school and had just won her sixth-grade spelling bee when I first trotted out the recipe. She was up on all the words in the English language, just a little wizard." Aleitha drew back smartly with a chuckle.

"Then, one day at the dinner table, Julia Rachel pointed out to all of us quite obviously that *divan* was just a fancy word for a sofa. 'Why don't we start calling it Chicken on the Sofa instead of that other thing?' And, of course, everyone at the table laughed and that just stuck. I know, it's probably the corniest thing you've ever heard. But not a week passed by when the kids didn't ask for it, all

60

giggly and conspiratorial about it. So serving Chicken on the Sofa has become a cherished Larken family tradition, and I've decided to share it with the world for the first time. Well, maybe not the whole world. Maybe just everyone who lives within a fifty-mile radius of Greater Cherico. Isn't that what you folks down this way like to call it?"

Maura Beth's grin was wide and genuine. She was feeling as comfortable with Aleitha Larken as she had felt awkward with both Bit Sessions and Gwen Beetles. There was nothing to fear here. "I'm afraid Chericoans have a somewhat inflated opinion of themselves. The truth is, we're just a little town by a big lake, and it's our own fault that we've let ourselves be overlooked as time has marched on. But some of us are bound and determined to correct that."

"Fair enough. Anyway, my tent will be the one with the GET YOUR CHICKEN ON THE SOFA sign over it. I think it's kinda cute and should attract some attention, don't you?"

"I'd be curious about it, I know that. And who knows how many couch potatoes it'll win over?"

Aleitha laughed warmly. "Very nice touch. And they say librarians don't have a sense of humor."

"Well, I don't know about the rest of 'em out there, but I try."

The last entrant that particular day pressed the envelope in a way that Bit Sessions and Gwen

Beetles would likely never have considered—and that was saying something. For all intents and purposes, Marzetta Frieze was a miniature adult, although she was definitely not a little person. She was normally proportioned but just happened to be a few inches short of five feet. But that was not what truly distinguished her from the pack. Rather, it was her run-on sentences, along with her downright loopy exuberance that had Maura Beth in awe, unable to get a word in edgewise.

". . . and I really think I can win the Best Appetizer category and as a matter of fact," Marzetta was saying after introducing herself, "I've actually brought a couple of my cheese balls for you to taste and I'm sure you will agree they're the best cheese balls you've ever tasted because it was my mother's recipe and all of her friends who came to her parties begged her over the years to give it out, but she wouldn't because she said that once you give out a recipe, people will change it on you and then if they do something really terrible to it, then you get the blame, but anyway I have a couple of cheese balls in my purse for you to taste and I just know you're gonna love them as much as everyone else does and—"

Maura Beth could not restrain herself and finally broke in. "Did you say you have cheese balls in your purse?"

Marzetta looked and sounded as if she'd just

heard the most ridiculous question in the world put to her. "Why, yes, I wanted to be sure no bugs landed on them on the way over here and my purse is the perfect place to make sure that doesn't happen, and just wait until you taste them because I made them fresh this morning, although I think they're at their absolute best when they're warm, but maybe if you have a microwave here in the library I can go run them in for a few seconds and bring them back—" Marzetta came to a sudden halt. "I see what's bothering you, I should have known, but let me assure you that I didn't make that mistake twice."

"What mistake was that?"

Marzetta's tiny body shook with laughter. She almost seemed like a windup toy that was out of control or getting ready to run off the tracks. "Keeping the cheese balls away from my lipstick and my compact, of course, because a couple of times I didn't wrap them in anything, not even napkins, and I don't know what I was thinking, but there was this time I got powder on them when my compact opened up and some of it spilled out, though I don't know how. Another time, there was a penny stuck to one of them. A brand-new, shiny penny. Can you imagine? People thinking I rolled my cheese balls in pennies? But, of course, I learned my lesson, so naturally from then on I carried them around in a ziplock bag and that's what I've got them in right now to let you taste, so you needn't worry about a thing, Miz McShay, everything is really quite sanitary, I can assure you."

Maura Beth was speechless at first; then she realized that the real reason she couldn't think of anything to say was because she wasn't sure if the woman had really come to the end of her long, rambling monologue. Finally, she managed a half-hearted, "Is that it?"

"Is what it?"

"No, I meant, did you have anything more to say about your cheese balls? That's an amusing little story you just told."

"I can't think of anything, except that I'd love for you to taste one and all I have to do is get the ziplock bag out of my purse and it'll only take me a second to do that and then you'll see why everyone always raves about my cheese balls and why I think I'll win the Best Appetizer category for sure, and I sure could use the extra money because ever since my husband divorced me, he's always behind on the alimony payments, that good-for-nothing, lazy slob. Do you know that he used to store his money behind the heating vent in the bedroom? Imagine what would have happened to it if the house had caught on fire. He'd have been broke and—"

Fearing even more of the woman's life story to come, Maura Beth once again broke in. "By all means, let me have a nibble, please."

Marzetta retrieved the bag and handed over one

of the perfectly round, orange-colored savories, then leaned back with ever-widening eyes in anticipation.

Seeing no sign of powder, lipstick, or coin of the realm on the surface, Maura Beth summoned her most adventurous spirit and took a bite, consuming half of the cheese ball in the process. She chewed somewhat tentatively at first; but then, as the extraordinary flavors burst in her mouth, she picked up speed. The other half soon disappeared and Maura Beth held nothing back.

"That really is quite delicious, Marzetta. I've never tasted anything like it. You may very well win. Although I hope you realize that I can't vote, and I'm not supposed to influence the outcome in any way."

"I figured as much, but can you guess what my secret ingredient is in my cheese balls? Now, some people have guessed right, but most people don't, so let's see if you can."

Maura Beth waited once again to see if more words were forthcoming and then she went to work on trying to identify the aftertaste in her mouth. "Is it . . . by any chance . . . ham?"

Marzetta puffed out her cheeks, looking like she might explode at any moment. Then she let the air out of her face and went straight into the widest smile she could manage. "Bingo. You're a winner. I don't think the word's meant to be used this way, but everyone says my cheese balls have a hammy flavor. And some of 'em say I'm downright hammy myself."

"That's cute, but these really are the best cheese balls I've ever tasted. But once again, I have to keep my opinions to myself."

Marzetta's energy level seemed to shift into yet a higher gear. "I know that and I think my cheese balls speak for themselves, but now, if you don't mind, I wondered if you'd give me your opinion of the sign I'm having made up for my food tent, and what I mean by that is, do you think it's too corny and I should go in another direction because here's what I was thinking of doing, and it's that I wanted to make a play on the letter *z* in my last name and spell out my sign like this—capital M-R-S and then F-R-I-E-Z-E-apostrophe-S and then C-H-E-E-Z-E and then finally B-A-L-L-Z. What do you think, Miz McShay?"

Maura Beth was conjuring up a mental picture and took a few seconds to consider the scheme while sweeping aside any lingering confusion. "Well, why not? It's all in fun, so maybe that'll get a few more people to your tent. I say go ahead."

Marzetta wrinkled her little bunny nose and then winked. "Yeah, that's what I'm gonna do, but you mark my words, I'm gonna win on the Fourth and nothing or no one's gonna stop me."

"You're overreacting," Jeremy told Maura Beth in bed that evening. At the moment he was a bit miffed that his wife's worries over the contest and the completion of the library were interfering with their ordinarily energetic lovemaking. So far, nibbling her earlobe tenderly and his trademark kisses on her eyelids were having no discernible effect, and those little romantic canapés had rarely failed to work their special brand of magic before.

"No, I'm not. You should have heard those two women from Corinth scratching and clawing at each other today, and they weren't even in the same room at the same time." Maura Beth propped herself up on her pillows and folded her arms, looking anything but ready for a little romance.

"Now, listen," he began, inching closer to her and determined to defrost her for the occasion. "You've handled a lot worse in the book club than those two quarreling biddies. Why, I'd put Mamie and Marydell Crumpton up against those women from Corinth—what did you say their names were again?"

"Bit Sessions and, uh, Gwen Beetles."

Jeremy practically guffawed. "What names! Do you think they actually might be aliases or in the Witness Protection Program?"

"I doubt it. This is the Deep South, after all. You can't make this stuff up, you know. Of course, there was another woman who came in—Aleitha Larken—and she restored my faith in humanity. She was perfectly delightful, and I know I shouldn't be saying this, but I sort of hope she wins. And then there was still another woman who went by the unlikely name of Marzetta. She was this tiny little thing who talked a mile-a-minute about her cheese balls and even brought me one to taste. Actually, she lifted it out of her purse."

Jeremy put a finger to his temple. "Aha, the old purse maneuver. Sounds like an extremely novel way to serve things. How was it?"

"It was very good, and she insists she's going to win Best Appetizer. I'm telling you, sweetheart, I was a bit overwhelmed today. Of course, it was all for a good cause." A hint of a smile crept into Maura Beth's face, and Jeremy decided to be audacious and run with it.

"I think the best remedy for your troubles, Miss Scarlett, is a little first-class romp in the hay." He could tell that Maura Beth was pretending to be offended by turning up her nose halfheartedly. His naughty ploy was definitely working, and he was within sight of port.

"Why, Mis-tuh Jeremy McShay," she said with a smile, working a drawl for the fun of it, "I hope you don't talk that way to your English classes, suh. You'd never hear the end of it at all those very proper PTA meetings."

Then he made his move, planting a juicy kiss on her lips and waiting for her to come up for air.

"Okay, you've convinced me," she told him, sounding a little breathless. "I'll put the new library and all the rest of it on the back burner just for a little while. Have your way with me."

"You better know I will," he said, wagging his brows wickedly. "You need to soar, Maurie."

She was whispering now. "I'm ready. Take me to the heights."

They were good at this sort of racy banter, keeping their love for each other an inventive exercise that never grew stale and usually contained a surprise or two worth repeating. They were never left unsatisfied and always ended up unwinding in each other's arms after their pulses had finally wound down, the way it should always be for people who are very much in love.

Maura Beth would long remember every detail of the dream she had that night. Because it would recur. She was somewhere ethereal, surrounded by a cloud-like mist that obscured everything else from view. She was wandering about, searching for something but had no idea what it was. No one else was around. Not Jeremy. Not her parents, nor his. Not a single member of The Cherry Cola Book Club. Thankfully, not Councilman Sparks with his City Hall lackeys.

She recalled a feeling of panic when this oppressive veil failed to lift no matter how far she walked. She began to pick up her pace, as if to outrun the fog. She wanted to call out for help, but no name seemed appropriate for that purpose.

Then, just when she was about to scream, gripped by that insistent feeling people get when they realize they are in the midst of a nightmare and need to wake up to escape it, a small clearing appeared ahead of her in the gray mist. The moment she walked into it somewhat tentatively, shafts of bright sunshine streamed down upon her uplifted face. Then she suddenly realized her hands were outstretched as if preparing to welcome someone or something into her open arms.

At that point she woke up, no longer afraid. She sat up in bed and blinked a few times, as if trying to establish what was real and what was not in the darkness of the room. This dream, she decided, was going to stay with her, tucked away in her memory bank for future use. She would tell no one about it for the time being, since she was certain they would dismiss it as just an ordinary dream—one among many that people had from time to time that was probably inconsequential. But Maura Beth definitely felt otherwise.

Funny how instinct could rear its convincing head when it needed to, overcoming logic and the other tenets of waking life.

3

Free-for-All

It was a magnificent sight to behold. There it stood, a sparkling, imposing façade covered in Tennessee sandstone with great panes of glass and a vaulted ceiling dotted with skylights to let the sunshine in below. No more repurposed dark, windowless, corrugated iron tractor warehouse for the deserving patrons of Cherico: The Charles Durden Sparks, Crumpton, and Duddney Public Library was nearly complete only a few days away from its Grand Opening on the Fourth of July. Maura Beth and Jeremy took it all in from the parking lot in front, which had just been freshly paved with asphalt and caused their nostrils to twitch at the overpowering smell of creosote baking in the merciless sun.

"I can't believe we're almost open for business now that the computers are in—and none too soon," Maura Beth said, fanning her face in the heat and leaning against Jeremy for support. "Yep, we are ready for business except for some of the landscaping and the furniture."

"I think your patrons will forgive the lack of greenery. A few missing bushes never kept people away. Besides, you can always blame

71

everything on the heat. No one'll dare dispute it."

"Probably so." She checked her watch and gave an impatient sigh. "He's late, of course. Everyone must always be kept waiting for His Highness. Sometimes I think he does it on purpose."

"So our good City Hall councilman wouldn't even give you a little hint about the furniture?"

Maura Beth shrugged and managed to sound complacent, even though she was anything but. "He just loves teasing me, you know. I'm halfway convinced he has all of it in storage somewhere around here just because he can. If you look in the dictionary under 'control freak,' there's a picture of our Councilman Durden Sparks smiling like the charming devil he is."

They both chuckled, and Jeremy said, "I want to see the lake from the deck around back again. While it was under construction, I really couldn't believe the view. Water has such a calming effect on most people. I know it does me. I can look out over a body of water and somehow feel like I'm home. Probably the Lemming effect. They say we all want to return to the water anyway. It just occurred to me that I ought to bring my English classes out here to see what a state-of-the-art public library looks like. Our school library is pretty much the pits, and it just doesn't get the job done with its limited hours."

"Well, I'm still convinced some patrons will come out just to read their books on the deck. That is, if we can ever get something for them to sit on. Of course, they could stand at the railing for a while, but we ordered up four cast-iron tables and sixteen cast-iron chairs so they could relax out there to their hearts' content. But where are our outdoor tables, and where's the rest of it? Where are our browsing couches and comfortable chairs for the periodicals area? Where are our chairs for the study carrels and the computer terminals? Oh, it's driving me crazy, and our supplier just keeps giving me the runaround. Frankly, I think they've lost track of the shipment. Wouldn't you know it?"

Jeremy put his arm around her shoulder and gave her a gentle squeeze and then a peck on the cheek for additional reassurance. He had become an expert at relieving her stress the moment it reared its ugly head. "Don't let it get to you, Maurie. Even if the furniture doesn't arrive in time, your patrons will still be blown away by the light and space and the professionalism of your new staff. You've done well, and even if everything is not perfect, I'm sure the Grand Opening will be a huge success. We'll still have the fireworks and Waddell Mack's concert and your Queen of the Cookbooks contest with all the food booths. I'll bet you anything that your patrons will be so excited they may not even want to sit down."

It was then that Councilman Sparks drove up and made a show of maneuvering his SUV into one of the nearby, freshly painted parking spaces, waving at them as if he didn't have a care in the world or was watching them sail into the sunset on a yacht. Patented grand entrances and exits were an affectation of his, and he had won many an election by honing them to perfection.

"Sorry I'm running late," he said, stepping out in his crisp gray suit, silver tie, and sporty dark glasses and approaching them with the usual cheesy, reelection smile plastered on his handsome face. "Shall we go inside out of this heat? I think I'm about to melt."

When Maura Beth punched in the code for the sliding glass doors in front, she felt an overwhelming sense of ownership. Not that the library belonged to her, but it had definitely come through her, just as children do, according to the philosophy of Kahlil Gibran. She had found her niche in the universe of possibilities and brought this twenty-first-century building into being, and that was a commendable act of creation. Perhaps it would never get any better than this, so she was savoring the moment, which was captured for posterity on her smartphone.

"Whew! The AC is certainly working to beat the band. Glad we didn't spare any expense there," Councilman Sparks said as they entered, wiping the sweat from his brow with the handkerchief from his pocket while gazing at the vaulted ceiling above them with a look of amazement on his face.

Even he had to be impressed with what they had accomplished together.

"Now that would be the opening day problem to end all problems," Maura Beth answered. "That would have really done us in. We may not have the furniture we ordered, but at least our patrons won't be roasting in this July heat. So about the furniture—"

Councilman Sparks cut her off. "Yes, yes. I know you've been waiting for some last-minute good news, and I can't say I blame you. I didn't want to get your hopes up until I had everything pinned down precisely. The bottom line is I just got off the phone with the carrier again, and after much investigation on their part, it seems our shipment was mistakenly sent to the library in Jericho, Missouri. How that could have happened, I have no idea."

Maura Beth was livid and clenched her teeth. "Oh, no, please. Not that again. We've had that happen before with shipments of books and even some of our movie posters for our Cherry Cola Book Club meetings. This has to be the worst déjà vu ever. What on earth is wrong with people? Don't they know the difference between MS and MO? Children in middle school know simple things like that, don't they? I'm beginning to believe there's a conspiracy against us."

Councilman Sparks sounded sympathetic but kept the self-serving grin on his face all the same.

"I don't think we need to be paranoid about this. But the shipment is definitely on its way here now. We just have to keep our fingers crossed that it'll be here in time for the Grand Opening."

"You mean there's still a chance it won't?"

"I was told it might be under the wire. But the library's really not about the furniture, is it?"

Maura Beth was in no mood to be diplomatic and set her jaw defiantly. "No, of course not. We expect the patrons to lie on the floor or stand around until their feet ache. Well, that's just great, isn't it? I'm just about ready to sue them for breach of contract. Can we actually do that?"

"No, I don't think we need to go that far," Councilman Sparks told her. "But I understand your frustration. Once you're up and running, I think the public will forget about any temporary inconvenience they experienced on opening day. Don't underestimate the 'wow' factor."

Jeremy spoke up for the first time. "But it sounds like you really don't expect the furniture to get here. Am I reading you right?"

"I authorized them to put a rush on the shipment back to us, and they've agreed to do that at their expense. I read them the riot act over the phone, believe me. I want our Grand Opening to be as much of a success as both of you do. After all, my name is on the building."

Somewhat placated, Maura Beth sat with her thoughts for a while. "Maybe I can come up with an emergency backup plan just in case," she said finally.

Councilman Sparks looked somewhat wary. He had been burned before by Maura Beth's clever schemes—and deservedly so in every instance. "Are you at liberty to divulge exactly what you have in mind, Miz McShay?"

"Not sure yet. We've already sold off the comfortable chairs and the big table we had in our old meeting room, and we still have a few of our creaky folding chairs that we've been using for our book club meetings. But even those wouldn't be nearly enough for our needs. So my thought here is that I ought to get my Cherry Cola Book Club members involved. That's always seemed to work in the past when we've had a problem of any kind."

Jeremy nodded and pointed to his wife in exaggerated fashion. "Believe me, when she says something like that, you just have to wait it out. She'll come up with something."

"Sounds good to me."

Maura Beth finally allowed herself to exhale even though the issue still wasn't definitely resolved. "Meanwhile, Councilman Sparks, would you like the grand tour of what we've done for the citizens of Greater Cherico? And by 'we,' I mean both you and me."

"Okay, then. I've got a few minutes. I've been out a few times during construction, but there were some things I couldn't make head nor tail of. As you know, I've never been much of a library user. So put on your tour guide hat and show me the way. I almost feel like I'm in a cathedral."

"Good description. It's a cathedral of knowledge. I also like to think of it as the repository of our culture."

"You librarians with your vocabulary!"

They began with a peek into the children's room, which featured thick, brown papier-mâché trees growing out of the gold carpet all the way up to the ceiling. At the back of the room was an expansive stage with steps leading up to it, and a big backdrop featuring colorfully painted animals, clowns, and famous comic book heroes in the middle of it all. At the extreme left were down-to-the-last-detail drawings of The Cat in the Hat and Horton; at the extreme right, illustrations of Junie B. Jones and the Oompa-Loompas. There were also huge framed posters on the walls of noted children's authors such as Beverly Cleary, Roald Dahl, Maurice Sendak, Beatrix Potter, Eric Carle, Dr. Seuss, Shel Silverstein, and Mo Willems. For all intents and purposes, it was an indoor children's literary playground that would ultimately give them access to the world as they grew into adulthood.

"Our new children's librarian, Miriam Goodcastle, will be doing her morning story hours there onstage. We've devoted a generous portion of the

Children's Department's budget to costumes and props so that Miriam can portray any number of characters for the little ones and their mothers. I've tried to do the best I could over the years with story hours here and there, but that's not really my training. I just had to wear too many hats—doing the ordering, processing, and paying the bills. Miriam is very creative and full of ideas to get the children into reading, and that's one of the primary missions of any library. Those children grow up to be our much-needed taxpayers, and I'm sure you can understand that."

"Yes, I do," Councilman Sparks said, though his tone lacked conviction. He seemed more animated, however, when they moved along and the bank of gleaming computer terminals came into view in the middle of the library's sunlit central corridor. "So this is where they can surf the Internet, right? These computers are the bells and whistles everyone is yakking about?"

"Yes, and they were just installed yesterday. I was on pins and needles waiting for them to arrive. These terminals are what you wouldn't let me have all those years, remember? I must have gone before you at least five or six times to beg for them, but I was always denied. 'Everyone has one of these at home,' you always said. But, you know, that's just not true. Some people simply can't afford them. It's another high-demand service any library should always provide in the millennium."

He cleared his throat noisily while fiddling nervously with the knot on his tie, a sure sign he was uncomfortable. "That may be, but I've heard that some of these kids can get into lots of trouble watching all kinds of porn on those things. If I had a son or daughter, I know I'd be keeping an eye out for that; and if kids here in Cherico start coming out here just to do that, I know their parents won't like it at all. More to the point, I'm the one who will have to deal with all the complaints, if I know my constituents. And I think I do by now."

"I'm quite sure you do, but, no, you won't have to deal with any of that. I'll be the one to field those complaints, and I feel more than competent to handle them. Besides, we have filters that will effectively block those questionable sites, Durden. And we won't let people have unlimited time on the terminals. They can't just come in here and stay on them all day. We'll be fair to everyone, of course, but it'll all be supervised, I can assure you."

Councilman Sparks turned away slightly and mumbled an unintelligible sentence or two under his breath.

"Did you have a little something to add?" Maura Beth asked him. "I didn't quite catch that."

"I was thinking . . . uh, doesn't that amount to censorship? Can you get away with that?"

Maura Beth thought carefully before speaking.

She knew quite well that he delighted in setting traps for her. Time for another application of her Librarianship 101 to put out this latest little fire he wanted to start. "Many libraries want to avoid getting into trouble by allowing certain patrons to hog their computers visiting those pornographic sites you mention. So you can't have it both ways, Councilman. You either allow the cyber free-for-all and suffer the consequences, or you assign some limits to it according to reasonable community standards. That's very different from allowing any patron to barge in and decide which books need to be pulled off the shelves because they disapprove of them. That's the slippery slope of all time, I can assure you. We never want to go there."

He was nodding now, however reluctantly. "Okay, I get your point. Let's move on. I trust you know what you're doing here."

"Things would have been a lot easier for me if you'd felt that way from my first day on the job several years ago."

"Maybe so. At any rate, I see the deck and the lake ahead. I have to admit—that's a spectacular view out there. Why don't we go out and take it in? Maybe we'll even catch a breeze."

"We will sample the deck soon enough. But not before we make the rounds and I show you the teen room and our technical services room where we process all the books, both of which you fought against so hard when we were drawing up the plans," she told him. "If you've never truly understood how a library works before, you will by the time we get through with this tour."

Jeremy winked and gave Councilman Sparks a friendly nudge. "There's no use fighting it, Councilman. You're here on her territory. But don't worry—it's a good place to be."

A few minutes later, it was the glitzy teen room, however, that really had Councilman Sparks shaking his head with his mouth wide open. "This looks more like one of those rock and roll-era diners from the fifties with all these booths. Can these kids order food in here?"

"It's just the design theme we chose. We thought the kids would 'really dig it,' to borrow a phrase from the fifties. For the record, though, there is never any food or drink allowed in the library," Maura Beth said, watching his facial expression with an amused satisfaction. "That's always been a hard and fast rule, and if you'd ever come to the library enough, you'd know that. Of course, the exception we make is if a club is holding a meeting in one of the rooms. Like 'Who's Who in Cherico?' or The Cherry Cola Book Club, for instance."

"Yeah, I knew you'd find a way to bring your pet project in somehow. You're nothing if not predictable about that, Maura Beth." He continued to survey the setup. "And there's that big-screen

TV over there hanging on the wall that you said was absolutely necessary to get these teenagers into reading. But if you don't mind, I'd really like for you to explain to me again how that works. I really don't get the connection at all."

"One more time, then. Listen closely. The goal is to get the teens into the library and make it the cool place to hang out after school with their friends. That's the biggest hurdle to overcome. But once they start coming in with their laptops and tablets and smartphones and maybe checking out the DVDs, they might move on to books and actually like them. That's the strategy, at least."

"If you say so. Still seems like a real expensive strategy to me." He pointed to the framed movie posters on the wall. "You have all these films for the kids to check out? I thought video rental stores had gone out of style. There certainly aren't any left in Cherico last time I looked."

"You're correct about that. They are definitely passé. But I can assure you that libraries are not, and we can incorporate any technology we need to as part of our mission."

He began rattling off the titles. "*Indiana Jones, E.T., Close Encounters, Star Wars*—" He came to a dead halt. "What, may I ask, is *Downtown Abbey*? Pardon my English, but that sounds like the adventures of a streetwalker to me."

Maura Beth tried as hard as she could to hold back but was unable to suppress a giggle or two.

"You really are something, you know that? Look more closely, Durden. That's *Down-TON Abbey*. It's a very proper and popular British series on the order of *Upstairs, Downstairs*."

"Never heard of either of 'em. Besides, I never was much on Brits mumbling incoherent things and calling it culture."

"Yes, well, maybe we're stretching things a mite in putting copies in the teen room, but you never know what will actually trigger someone's interest in exploring new ideas and new settings. Some high-schoolers need to be stimulated in a positive way. That's what a good library should be about for everyone, actually. At any rate, I just want you to understand that you're getting your money's worth with everything we buy. After all, your name is on the building."

At last there was a sigh of resignation. "Okay, okay. I wave the white flag." He shook her hand limply. "Here's an imaginary olive branch. You've won me over 'til the end of time. I'm officially impressed."

Jeremy had the last word on the exchange. "I told you, Councilman. It's useless to resist a librarian on a mission."

Maura Beth had high hopes for this particular meeting of The Cherry Cola Book Club, coming as it did a couple of days before the Grand Opening of the new library. The truth was, there had been such incidents as family quarrels, walkouts, a heart attack, false labor pains, and a direct lightning strike to the roof in previous gatherings that had been all too disruptive, ending everything prematurely. When this evening was all over and done with, would she have stumbled onto something by allowing the members to rave about their favorite, outside-the-box novels instead of having everyone review the same dignified classic? Would it even be popular enough to become the new format out at the lake?

Before the group could help themselves to the buffet table after everyone had arrived, however, Maura Beth took the floor to introduce her new staff members to the group. Miriam Goodcastle, the library's first true children's librarian, stepped to the podium first and said a few words about herself.

"I was born in Natchez and got my library science degree at Southern Miss," she began, making good eye contact with her audience. That was something Maura Beth had noticed on the job interview. The pleasant-looking young woman who wore her blond hair in pigtails—in deference to fairy tales or nursery rhymes, perhaps?—had no trouble looking her in the face that particular afternoon. In addition, her voice was very warm—even had a playful quality to it. That would be very appealing to children, who would be listening to her intently during her story hours. "I'm thrilled to say that this is my first job out of school, and I will always be grateful to Maura Beth McShay for giving me this opportunity. I look forward to getting to know all of you veteran Cherry Cola Book Club members better in the future . . . oh, and getting your children involved in the wonderful world of the library."

After polite applause, Agnes Braud, the tech services librarian, was next up. She was much older than Miriam with a bit of gray in her hair and the results of enjoying her favorite South Louisiana seafood dishes too much hugging her midriff. She, too, surveyed her audience with a smile and immediately put everyone at ease. "I'm from Lafayette, Louisiana, folks, but I was looking for a change of venue after my recent divorce. I have a sweet cousin over in Corinth who told me about the job opening, and I thought to myself, *Why not start over completely, me?* So, here I am, and it'll be my responsibility to get your books on the shelves so you can check 'em out. I've been doing that down in Lafayette for over twenty years."

Standing nearby, Maura Beth felt herself doing a mental backflip. "And let me just say that Agnes will be truly lightening my workload. I've been missing someone like her ever since I arrived in Cherico seven years ago and fresh out of library school just like Miriam."

Helen Porter was the final introduction as the library's third front desk clerk and general assistant, complementing Renette Posey and Marydell Crumpton. A very tall, slim, twenty-something whom Maura Beth had found through a Mississippi Library Commission lead, Helen revealed little more than that she was originally from Ackerman "down the road a bit" and was looking forward to "serving the public."

"And I know she'll do it well," Maura Beth added just as Helen stepped down to perfunctory applause. Then Maura Beth uttered the words everyone with their growling stomachs had been eagerly waiting to hear. "So, shall we attack the potluck buffet table, folks?"

No one had to be told twice, and soon they were lined up with their plates ready to choose among layered salad, pulled pork with barbecue sauce on the side, sliced ham—everybody's standby—tuna noodle casserole, green beans amandine, cheese grits, sweet potato fries, dill potato salad, biscuits, jalapeño cornbread, slices of watermelon, fruit salad, pecan pie à la mode, several different layer cakes, brownies, macadamia nut and chocolate chip cookies, with sweet tea and fruit punch to wash it all down. Here and there, the club may have missed the mark with its book critiques, but it never faltered where the food was concerned. Tonight was no exception, and a good half hour passed before everyone had had their fill.

Then the real business of The Cherry Cola Book Club began on this free-for-all night. Voncille Nettles Linwood took the podium first and began delivering a paean to Dennis Patrick's *Auntie Mame*, insisting that she had always seen something of herself in that madcap woman of means.

". . . and there was always a part of me that wanted to travel the world, give the most outlandish parties, hobnob with the most eccentric people, color my hair a different shade every year, and wear the most outlandish fashions that Paris could offer every season," she was saying. "I had no idea where I would get the money to do all that on a schoolteacher's salary, but I didn't worry about it too much. As things turned out—especially after my fiancé went MIA in Vietnam—I just retreated from that adventurous side of me and settled for safe, which meant teaching history in high school until retirement. It was a dependable living, but, alas, I never left the city limits of Cherico. That's just about as un-Auntie Mame-like as you can get."

"We'll make up for it, since money's no object now," her husband of less than a year, Locke Linwood, said with great animation. "You'll put Auntie Mame to shame by the time we've finished our travels together. I'm quite sure you won't suffer by comparison."

Maura Beth giggled softly from her seat on the

front row. "Will we ever see the two of you again?"

"We'll send postcards from all over," Locke said with a wink and a nod of his snowy-white head of hair.

"Locke and I plan to visit every continent before we're through. Just like Auntie Mame and Beauregard Burnside did. In fact, we've already planned our first trip. We're going down under to Australia and New Zealand in the fall."

To no one's real surprise, Voncille's childhood rival and the insufferable diva of Cherico, Mamie Crumpton, weighed in with a contemptuous chuckle. "You could never have pulled off being an Auntie Mame—not for one instant—even if you'd had the money to do so. I think we all have to admit that if we're talking reality here. Why, the very idea is ludicrous beyond belief."

"I wholeheartedly disagree. I suppose you fancy yourself the real thing, Mamie Crumpton?" came Voncille's tart reply.

"Far more than you, dear."

"Oh, really now? Your gloomy parlor parties with the portieres drawn and those eternal weekly bridge games of yours on Perry Street where you serve nothing but mixed nuts are every one as dull as dishwater, and your sense of fashion is strictly tacky and off-the-rack; that is, if you can find anything in your size without the sequins and beads falling off of it. You'd be easy to track if you ever got lost, Mamie. The police would just follow the trail of your missing accessories."

"Oh my. You've absolutely wounded me with such devastating repartee." She clutched a hand to her bosom. "Whatever shall I do?"

Maura Beth finally decided to intervene, as she had many times in the past between the two. "Shall we stick to the plot of the novel, ladies? We did not sell tickets to a catfight."

"Thank you for that," Voncille said, shooting daggers at her rival. Then she took a deep, cleansing breath and stood tall. "The thing I admire most about the character of Auntie Mame is that she answers to no one. She may bend the rules a bit, but her heart is always in the right place. I've always adored her 'life is a banquet' comment. And the second part of that is 'and most poor fools are starving to death.' Isn't that the God's honest truth?"

"Would anyone care to make an *adult* comment on that?" Maura Beth said, staring in Mamie's general direction.

But Mamie was having none of it, glaring back with a heave of her generous bosom. "I suppose that remark was aimed at me?"

"Not at all. What I meant was that Auntie Mame is the ultimate adult in the realm of fiction. If most fiction is the orange juice, she's the vodka in the screwdriver. Let's discuss the novel in those terms."

Voncille's voice was triumphant as she nodded enthusiastically at Maura Beth. "That's precisely why she appealed to me. I thought to myself while I was reading the novel for the first time, *I want to be just like her when I grow up.* Who wouldn't want to be that free and devil-may-care? Maybe we all start out wanting to be like that and believing it's possible. But then real life happens, and it's just not like the pages of some novel that makes you feel brave when you're young and naïve. I remember the time when I thought nothing bad could ever happen to me. But it did when my fiancé, Frank Gibbons, never returned from Vietnam."

The last sentence seemed to linger with the gathering for a bit as they reflected, but then the club's newcomer, Ana Estrella, raised her hand and joined the conversation for the first time. It was immediately clear that her public relations skills were enabling her to express herself cogently in a strange new environment, and everyone listened to her attentively.

"I've read the book, of course, and I have to admit that Auntie Mame's a role model for women who make up the rules as they go along; and I agree with Mrs. Linwood because I, too, have played it on the safe side. I went right into public relations for Spurs 'R' Us straight out of college, and I've stayed there ever since. To be honest with you, moving here to Cherico is the first time I've ventured away from Nashville where I was born after my grandfather moved from Puerto Rico. It may not seem like a big deal to some of you, but I consider my job here a real adventure for me, and I can't wait to get started in earnest."

"Thank you for sharing a bit more about yourself with us, Ana," Maura Beth said, seizing the opportunity to make her feel even more at home. "We've all found that our little club is a very efficient way to get to know one another, and I want to tell you again how much I appreciate you taking my advice and coming to our meeting. You have no idea how pleased I was to see you walk through the door this evening. I almost gave you a round of applause."

"The pleasure is all mine. I hope some of you liked my *bizcocho de gandules* I put out on your splendid buffet table. That's pigeon peas cake in English. That's the secret ingredient. Mine was the one with the powdered sugar dusted all over the top, and it's one of my family's prized Puerto Rican recipes. As a matter of fact, I have decided to feature it at the food tent I will be operating at the Grand Opening. You can't miss me—I'll be the one with the big HOLA! sign on my tent."

It was Connie McShay who began to rave about Ana's dessert. "That's wonderful news. The more, the merrier. And I would never have guessed your cake had pigeon peas in it. I absolutely loved it. I had an enormous piece. It tasted like cinnamon and coconut."

"Good. Then I made it right. It's not as heavy as some other desserts," Ana explained.

Connie quickly pointed to her waist and shook her head slowly. "Truth is, I could've eaten two pieces, though heaven knows, I shouldn't."

Maura Beth took advantage of the lull that followed to return to the literary discussion. "Does anyone have any further thoughts on *Auntie Mame*? Come on, now. A free spirit like that has got to inspire more commentary. Cherico has more than its share of such types."

This time, Becca Brachle spoke up. "Well, since my Justin and I have become a family of three recently with the birth of our son, Mark, the plot of the novel makes me think a bit about the definition of family. When little Patrick comes to live with his aunt, he really has no one else in the world to look after him after his father's death, as I recall. But fortunately for him, he ends up with Auntie Mame and her servants—I forget their names now—"

"Ito and Norah," Voncille put in crisply. "They all look after Patrick as if he were their own. None of them miss a beat."

"Yes. Well, the point I was going to make is that all the while Patrick is growing up, he has a truly loving family supporting him. They may be unconventional people like that actress, Vera

Charles, or that secretary, Agnes Gooch, but they all encourage him to take advantage of his Auntie Mame's free-for-all universe. Today, I think we've come to understand better that families come in all configurations, and as long as there's love and responsibility in the home, we shouldn't be fretting so much about those configurations." Becca gasped and briefly covered her mouth with the palm of her right hand. "Will you listen to me? I hope I didn't sound like I was on a soapbox, but those thoughts really did come to mind just now."

"Didn't sound like you were preaching to me," Jeremy said. "You made a great point that I never even considered. I guess I concentrated so much on Auntie Mame's antics that I lost sight of what you just said."

"So you've read *Auntie Mame*?" Voncille wanted to know.

"Sure. I think I was about fourteen, which is when I read the novel I wanted to talk about tonight—*The Catcher in the Rye*, by J. D. Salinger. I remember how excited I was to be checking it out of the Brentwood library. So, could I be next?"

Maura Beth immediately put the question to the group. "Are we through with *Auntie Mame* yet? Anyone?"

When no one answered as Maura Beth surveyed the room, she said, "Then I guess we're ready to discuss *The Catcher in the Rye*."

Jeremy allowed Voncille to take her seat and

then moved to the podium quickly, assuming his most professorial demeanor. "First, I don't think it's an overstatement to say that Holden Caulfield, the protagonist of the novel, is probably every high school boy's hero. He runs away from the restraints of the private school he's attending, which he despises, and every teenaged male at one time or another has wanted to tell his teachers and those tests and grades and the peer pressure and all the rest of it where to go. When I read the novel, I thought it had been written just for me. I mean, once he leaves school, Holden explores New York City and his sexuality fearlessly in a compressed amount of time, and I remember thinking what an adventure that would be going after girls that way. You have to remember how daring this all was, since J. D. Salinger wrote the book in 1951, which was years before the sexual revolution. Later on, when the movie *Ferris Bueller's Day Off* was made, I couldn't help thinking that *The Catcher in the Rye* might have been the inspiration for it. The plots do have a certain amount in common."

"I read the book when I was a teenager, too," Douglas McShay said. "All us guys thought it was the cool thing to do. But I also seem to recall that it ended up on a few banned book lists. It was considered too racy for the times. Am I remembering that right, Jeremy?"

"You are. It probably still does get banned in

today's hot-button political climate. Too much does, as far as I'm concerned." He nodded at Maura Beth with a smile. "But I'm proud to say that librarians like my wife there work very hard to make sure censorship doesn't happen at the local level. And I swear, she didn't pay me to say that, either."

After some muted laugher had died down, Connie McShay's hand shot up, and Jeremy pointed in her direction. "I was just curious. Being the English teacher that you are, do you think there's a novel out there that speaks to girls in the same way? Is there a female Holden Caulfield?"

Jeremy threw his head back and laughed. "Brilliant question, my dear aunt. I can answer it by saying that *The Catcher in the Rye* also speaks to girls in an overwhelmingly positive way if they're particularly discerning. I'm not referring to Sunny, the prostitute, or any of the other girls that Holden gets involved with on his tear around New York—but his little sister, Phoebe, who is wise beyond her years and is almost as ground-breaking as he is. She has a forty-year-old head on her ten-year-old shoulders. Holden definitely looks up to her and is always asking her advice. At times, he even seems to be reporting to her the way he would never do to a parent. I think their unusual relationship is one of the most amusing aspects of the novel, and it proves that good things can definitely come in small packages."

Becca spoke up with a great deal of enthusiasm, sliding forward in her seat. "I can't believe you just said that, Jeremy. That's exactly how I'd describe the character of Idgie Threadgoode in *Fried Green Tomatoes at the Whistle Stop Cafe*. She's small, feisty, and a tomboy, but she knows what she wants and goes after it. That's the novel I wanted to talk about tonight. It always appealed to the Becca Broccoli side of me that had to keep coming up with all those recipes for my radio show five days a week; and there those two brave women were—Idgie and Ruth, operating that small-town café serving up fried green tomatoes during the Depression in Alabama and making a success of it against some stiff odds. Running a business back then was supposed to be man's work. Women had to stay in their place. If it happened to be in the kitchen, it was as the cook, but not as the owner of the restaurant. Now, if that's not something to admire, I don't know what is."

"I like Fannie Flagg's writing, too," Jeremy added. "Her voice is authentically Southern and historically accurate. It ought to be since she's from the heart of Alabama—Birmingham, I believe."

Suddenly, Becca started giggling and couldn't seem to stop.

"What's so funny, hon?" her Stout Fella wanted to know, a hint of concern creeping into his face.

Finally, Becca was able to gather herself. "I just had the most perverse thought. I mean, in the novel, the faithful Sipsey hits Ruth's abusive ex-husband, Frank Bennett, over the head with a spade and kills him. Then Idgie and Big George dispose of the body by cooking him up as a Whistle Stop Cafe barbecue special, and no one has any idea what they're being served. They just all say it's lip-smacking delicious, and they've never tasted anything better as they gobble it all up. I just kept thinking about all the food tents we're going to be having at the Grand Opening, and somehow it struck me as funny."

"You had it right the first time," Mamie Crumpton said with a sneer. "That's more than perverse, it's downright grotesque."

"Lighten up, Sister dear," Marydell added. "It's all just creative fiction. I trust no one we know will be served up out at the lake on the Fourth of July. Though knowing you and your propensity for holding grudges, there are probably more than a few you wish would be."

A wave of laughter broke the tension in the room, and then Maura Beth said, "Well, I have to admit that this conversation is about as free-for-all as you can get. Meanwhile, does anyone else have any other comments about either *The Catcher in the Rye* or *Fried Green Tomatoes at the Whistle Stop Cafe*?"

"They are two very different novels, of course,"

Jeremy began, sounding once again like the English teacher and lover of good literature that he was. "But they do have something in common. They tackle human sexuality somewhat openly and without apology. Holden Caulfield doesn't know how to treat and handle women yet, but he's not afraid to explore such virgin territory—oops, no pun intended, folks." He paused to wag his brows, waited for the chuckles to die off, and then resumed.

"Sexuality of any kind was considered definitely taboo and out of the mainstream to discuss in the early fifties in America. There are those who would say it still pushes the buttons of way too many people today who ought to just mind their own business. But they don't, of course. Meanwhile Idgie and Ruth clearly love each other and try to build a life together after Ruth's failed marriage to her bully of a husband. That would have been a very courageous thing to do back in the twenties, but Fannie Flagg was pretty courageous herself in bringing these two Southern women to life with real wisdom and emotion for the reading public of modern America."

"Why does everything you say sound like a lecture?" Mamie Crumpton said, drawing herself up in her seat and fussing with the magenta scarf around her neck. "Or a stuffy review."

But Maura Beth was not about to let the snarky comment stand. If she could deal with

Councilman Sparks and render him harmless, she could deal with the Diva of Perry Street, who needed to be the center of attention every five minutes or so. "But may I respectfully remind you that that's why we're here, Miz Crumpton. Our book club reviews books, and we all express our opinions. Our purpose is both social and literary, of course."

"Don't forget how much we love the food, though," Becca added. Then she just couldn't seem to resist. "I only hope no one decides to fix barbecue at the Grand Opening."

"Hon, if you keep that up, we'll all lose our appetites and all those tents will be a big bust," Justin said to his wife, nudging her playfully.

"Okay. No more jokes, then. But I would like to remind everyone that I'll be signing my *Best of the Becca Broccoli Show Cookbook* from eleven to two tomorrow in the lobby of the new library, even if I have to sit in a folding chair. If you've lost some of the recipes you wrote down while listening to my radio show, here's your chance to get them back. The cookbook covers the entire ten-year run of the show, so I hope you'll all come out and support me. I've never done anything like this before, so I'm a bit nervous about it."

"You don't have to worry about a thing, Becca. I wouldn't miss it for the world," Voncille said. "Locke would just never forgive me."

He had the biggest grin on his face, looking just

like a little boy who had been given an extra dessert after dinner. "We swear by your recipes at our house, Becca. We never missed one of your shows, did we, sweetie?"

Voncille was counting on her fingers almost absent-mindedly. "Well, there might have been one or two times when I was conked out in bed with the flu or went to visit relatives out of town or something like that, but I know I didn't miss many. By the way, Becca, will you be having a food tent for us?"

"I've gone back and forth about it. Justin wanted me to in the worst way, but I've decided not to," she said with a shrug of her shoulders. "I've had more than my share of success, so I wanted to give someone else a chance to win those prizes. Goodness knows, Justin and I certainly don't need the money."

Then Periwinkle spoke up. "I won't be having one, either. My prize is all the business The Twinkle gets from all of you throughout the year. But I will be casting my ballot for Best Appetizer, Entrée, Dessert, and Queen of the Cookbooks. Oh, and Parker won't be entering the dessert category, either."

"Might be easy as my grasshopper pie to win," he told the gathering with a gleam in his eye. "Not an evening goes by that our Barry Bevins doesn't have to hop in the van to deliver a piece to someone out there in Greater Cherico. Heh. I just got this image of Barry hopping around like a grasshopper."

Periwinkle gave her husband a playful slap on the thigh. "You're too corny for words, Parker. Meanwhile, back to our book review, I have to say that I've never read *Fried Green Tomatoes* or even seen the movie, but I'm definitely gonna have to, now that I know it's about running a restaurant." She suppressed a giggle. "But I just wanted all of you to know that you can trust the contents of whatever I will be serving you down at The Twinkle."

"That goes for the desserts, too. No insects in my pies," Parker added quickly, and the remarks brought down the house.

Would wonders never cease? At last, a meeting of The Cherry Cola Book Club that had not been disrupted, start to finish, even with a flare-up or two from Mamie Crumpton. Was it the new format, or had the stars and planets merely been properly aligned? Whatever the case, Maura Beth felt good about asking all the members for a special favor after discussion of everyone's novels had been exhausted.

"As of this evening," she began at the podium with some gravity in her tone, "our new library's furniture has not arrived. I won't go into what's happened because it's too aggravating for words and won't be good for my digestion. But suffice it to say that if it does not arrive tomorrow, the carrier has informed us that they will not be delivering on the Fourth of July since it's a holiday. Therefore, the very real possibility exists that we will have our Grand Opening with just these old, uncomfortable folding chairs we have here for people to sit on if they want to browse and read, or use our new computer terminals. Which, I might add, the patrons of Cherico have been waiting on since the invention of the abacus."

A wave of laughter broke across the semi-circle. "So I wanted to ask each of you to consider temporarily donating any comfortable seating you might have around the house or even in the attic. Anything will do. A couch you don't use, maybe patio furniture that we could put out on the deck overlooking the lake because I know people will want to take in the view—you get the idea. Of course, it needs to be fairly presentable. We don't need something that Fred Sanford would have sold in his junkyard. Just think of this as the Great Chair Emergency Roundup, and I'm sure the library gods will smile down upon us for it."

"Well, we have a few things in the attic that might do," Mamie Crumpton said, for once sounding a positive note.

"Yes," Marydell added. "There's a grand old sofa up there, and we could have our Jellica vacuum it good to get out all the dust mites. And

103

there are a couple of easy chairs we haven't used since Father died. Now, I wouldn't say they were the latest style, but I can guarantee they're both comfortable since Father and Mother would fall asleep reading in them all the time."

"They're butt-sprung," Mamie said offhandedly.

Marydell's jaw dropped. "My goodness, Mamie, was that necessary?"

"Now who's being stuffy, Sister dear."

Maura Beth stepped in as peacemaker once again. "I suspect it's perfectly fine if no one has to break them in. I think the Crumpton family has us off to a very generous start. Anyone else want to offer something?"

Becca spoke up next. "We've got some lovely chair cushions that we could contribute, don't we, Stout Fella?"

"Uh, well, if you say so. The only thing I've been keepin' track of lately is how much money we've spent on baby furniture and stuff. Man, it's an eye-opener what all this paraphernalia costs."

"For heaven's sake, Justin, the library doesn't need cribs or basinets. This isn't a day care center." She paused as everyone snickered. "And we could also lend some of our patio furniture. When the weather's nice, we have our coffee and biscuits out there every morning by the rose garden. Wouldn't that work for your deck?"

"It would be perfect," Maura Beth said.

Douglas raised his hand next. "Connie and I

could spare a little divan in the guest bedroom upstairs that no one ever sits on. Honestly, I think it's in showroom-new condition. Even dust won't settle on it."

"I think the reason nobody sits there is because I've put too many throw pillows on it. It's all covered up. Tastefully, of course, but still covered up. I'll be the first to admit that there is such a thing as overdecorating and going crazy with fabric swatches," Connie added. "So, do you think you might be able to use some throw pillows, too, Maura Beth?"

"At this point I'm not turning anything down. It's the comfort of the patrons that concerns me."

After the input of a few more volunteers, Maura Beth relaxed just a tad bit. If they had to have an emergency move-in tomorrow evening, she knew everyone would pitch in and get the job done. Whatever else her Cherry Cola Book Club was, it had never failed to be supportive of what was best for Greater Cherico. As much as the new library would be, it was also part of her legacy to the little town.

4

Couches and Cushions and Chairs, Oh My!

Jellica Louisa Jones had been in the employ of the Crumpton family since she was sixteen, a period going on twenty-five years now. Before that, her mother, Surleen, had gathered up all the courage she could muster and just shown up one morning from the "shanty side of town," asking if the family needed any extra help. On an impulse, she had carried a small bouquet of sunflowers she had stumbled upon and picked by the side of the road for what she hoped would be the job clencher. Flowers never hurt anybody or anything, she had reasoned.

"I need me some work bad to keep my family fed," she had said, careful to keep herself calm and her dignity intact.

As it would happen, her ploy succeeded, and she had begun cooking and cleaning for Myrna and Winston Crumpton, parents of Mamie and Marydell—staying on for forty years until her death from natural causes. Both mother and daughter had made a specialty of tidying up the dark, magenta-drenched Victorian parlor with its ball-and-claw furniture in which Jellica was now standing; so it would probably have been a safe bet that the Jones women knew every nook and cranny of the Crumpton household on Perry Street.

Except it so happened that Jellica had never actually been in the sprawling attic before. How that could be was impossible to say, but nonetheless, there it was. And around four-thirty on the afternoon before the new library's Grand Opening when she was ordered by Mamie Crumpton to venture "up there" and "retrieve Mother and Father's easy chairs and *that* couch," she had the backbone and good sense to balk. Her mother had often said to her over the years, "Don't take no nonsense offa those people jes' 'cause they have all that money to throw around the way they do. They'll be judged like the rest of us when that time come. You cain't guarantee a seat in Heaven with a wad a' money."

Taking her faith-driven mother's advice to heart, Jellica faced Mamie Crumpton and made a ridiculous excuse of a bicep with her skinny brown arm. Then her long, narrow face with its high cheekbones from the touch of Native American in her genes took on a no-nonsense scowl.

"Now, Miz Mamie, do I look like one a' them disgustin' bodybuilders with all the veins you see on TV all the time? I weigh all a' one hundred and fifteen pounds when I'm soakin' wet right outta the bathtub. Mama Surleen always said I was the runt of the litter. Now, how'm I s'pose to drag heavy furniture like that down from up there all by myself? You don't pay me near enough money to even try. I say no thank you to that. I know you know I need me some help and lots of it." She pointed to the ceiling. "I go up there on my own, you be waitin' for the thud when I drop dead."

Mamie bristled at first, but the truth of the matter quickly dawned on her. "Hmmm . . . I guess I wasn't thinking."

"That happens quite a lot these days," Marydell said, knowing full well she would draw her sister's ire. She realized too late that it had been a mistake to let Mamie know about Maura Beth's phone call in the first place.

"Don't you start up with me, Sister dear. You have just gotten so out of control since you decided to become a lowly front desk clerk at the library. I shudder to think what Mother and Father would have said about you catering to whomever comes in off the street to order you around like a servant. 'Get me that book off the shelf, find me this one, here's my fine because this book is overdue.' Why, the very idea of a Crumpton groveling and collecting petty cash like some dime-store clerk makes me ill. We don't take orders from anyone in this family. We give them."

Marydell completely ignored her and turned to Jellica, who was obviously trying to keep her temper in check. "Don't worry, dear. I was way ahead of my sister on this one. I've got three strapping young men from out at the high school coming to pitch in and do the heavy lifting. Maura Beth's husband, Jeremy, recruited them for me. I've already called them up, and they said they'd be right on over. That muscle power you need is on the way."

Jellica raised an eyebrow, meticulously smoothed the apron of her maid's uniform, and then exhaled noisily. "Amen to that!" Then the scowl on her face changed to puzzlement. "Tell me somethin', though. Whadda y'all want that old furniture drug all the way down here for anyhow? It's 'bout a thousand years old, I reckon. Maybe older than that. Prob'ly got the dust of the first day of creation still on it. No tellin' what'll fly out if you beat it long enough. You best take my advice and let that old thing lie in its grave."

"I do not appreciate you saying awful things like that in front of me, Jellica. It was fine, expensive, serviceable furniture in its day. Mother and Father swore by it," Mamie said, striking one of her patrician attitudes. "I'm quite sure I don't need your opinion in the matter, or anything else when you come right down to it. I don't pay you to comment on the décor. You are here strictly to cook and clean and make the house presentable for guests."

"Be that as it may," Marydell added quickly

before Jellica could really get her dander up, "I'll remind you again that we've passed the deadline my boss set for emergency furniture for the new library. The new furniture simply hasn't made it to Cherico yet, so naturally we've gone ahead and set our backup plan in motion. It's just part of being a Cherry Cola Book Club member."

While Jellica nodded approvingly, Mamie continued to try to pick a fight. "Sister dear, I just wish you wouldn't refer to that Maura Beth as your boss. It makes you sound so . . . well, so working class, and the Crumpton family was one of the important founders of this town. We were practically the first family to build a house on Perry Street. We led the way, and the others just followed suit. The rest is history, of course. It became the street where everybody who was anybody wanted to set up residence. Sometimes I think you are dead set on throwing away our proud heritage like it was a leaf in the wind."

Marydell folded her arms, shot Jellica a knowing glance, and stared down her sister. "For heaven's sake, that's such old, tired news. You're stuck on one note. Why don't you tell me something I don't know for once? And, by the way, last time I looked, there was nothing in this big wide world wrong with doing an honest day's work, is there, Jellica?"

"Not if you wanna put you some food on the table erry day," she answered with a lopsided grin and a slight thrust forward of her neck, like a turtle briefly venturing out of its shell to take a look around. "Call me crazy, but I swear by it and so do all my chirren."

Mamie threw up her hands with her nose pointed toward the elaborate frieze on the ceiling. "I absolutely give up. This is hopeless and the absolute end. You two have become so chummy of late, I can hardly tell who's the help and who's the master anymore. And besides that—"

Marydell interrupted, sounding completely incredulous. "Master?"

"Don't you dare bandy words with me, Sister. Not at this late date. You know how I feel about everything under the sun. I can't believe this is what our family has come to. I certainly never thought I'd see the day. Marydell, you are a disgrace to old Southern families everywhere."

"Well, I just happen to think what I'm doing is a big breath of fresh air for us Crumptons."

Mamie bristled. "If I could disown you, I would."

"I'd like to see you try."

At which point Mamie had apparently had enough, walking off mumbling something to herself.

Marydell and Jellica were chuckling together at Mamie's exit, but then Marydell grew serious, bringing her hands together prayerfully. "You know, Jellica, you should come to the library sometime—maybe on your day off next week. I'll be right there at the front desk to check out anything you find that you want to read. Are you much of a library user? I know I haven't ever seen you there since I started working and annoying my sister no end."

Jellica didn't have to think twice. "Never been a library user in my life, to tell the truth. You know, my mama couldn't use the library back in her day, so she never had anything good to say about it to me. She always told me the truth 'bout everything. 'They don't let us black folks get cards,' she'd tell me. I guess I still got it in my head that things is still like that around Cherico. Sometimes, you gotta let go to keep from goin' crazy. If you don't mind my sayin' so, that's how I've kept this job all these years."

"Well, things are not that way anymore, believe me. Haven't been that way for a long, long time. You should even consider joining The Cherry Cola Book Club and bringing some of your good food with you at our next meeting. We'd love to have you. But even if you don't do that, you should definitely come out to the lake tomorrow for the Grand Opening. Had you planned to?"

Jellica shook her head, saying nothing and waving Marydell off as if she were swatting at a gnat.

"No, really, you ought to. There'll be some food tents and later on in the evening some fireworks and then a country music concert by Waddell Mack. Maybe you don't care for country music, but the man single-handedly brought the new Spurs 'R' Us cowboy boot plant to Cherico. I'll give him a listen for that alone, and I'll even help you get your first library card since that's part of my job now. Come on, now, it'll be a lot of fun, you'll see. And you ought to bring your children out, too. They like to eat, don't they?"

"Lord, you should see how much they like to eat. I keep thinkin' my boys'll stop growin' one a' these days and gi' me a break. They both over six feet now and still in high school. All right, then, maybe I will come on out, Miz Marydell, and bring Carver and Narvelle, too. And maybe the three of us'll even take a seat on that old couch from the attic."

Marydell laughed. "If I don't beat you to it. But don't worry, I promise to scooch on over for all of you."

"You been doin' lotsa scoochin' lately, if you ask me. It's tickled me."

"Drives my sister crazy," Marydell said out of the side of her mouth. "Which makes it all worth it."

Jellica was all smiles. "Wusht Mama Surleen coudda lived to see this that just played out right here in the parlor. She woudda got such a kick outta it all. I don't think she woudda stopped laughin'."

"I'm sure you're right."

Jellica patted her employer on the shoulder. "Yes, indeedy. Mama Surleen used t'say all the time that if you waited long enough, you'd see just about errything that go around, come around."

Becca had been trying desperately to remember ever since she'd gotten the call from Maura Beth to execute the emergency furniture plan, but she was drawing a blank. "Justin, what on earth could I have done with them?" She continued to wring her hands over it all, but he didn't have the answer, either. His job was to sell houses to other people, not keep up with the whereabouts of the decorative items of his own. That was women's work.

"Beats me," he told her, standing in the middle of the master bedroom in their lavishly furnished, white-columned mansion outside Cherico. The manse in the country, they sometimes called it. "Are you sure you didn't give 'em away to the Salvation Army or something like that? You're always doin' things on impulse and then later on, you wanna take 'em back."

She gave him a derisive glance, moved away from him, and plopped down on the edge of their antique four-poster bed. "Justin, please. They were wedding gifts from Mama. I would never have done something like that with them. The monarch butterflies in the design were to die for.

Those chair cushions were my favorites until I decided to change the color scheme from royal blue to aqua. They'd come in handy now and make it more comfortable for people who have to sit in those folding chairs that Maura Beth is stuck with until the new furniture finally arrives. I'm just trying to help her out as much as I can."

"And you've checked every closet and the attic?"

"Yes."

He couldn't help himself. "Then I guess we have one a' those paranormal experiences goin' on in this house. We should sell tickets, or notify one a' those TV shows that chase after ghosts and always claim to have captured them on film." He made a low-pitched, spooky noise and screwed up his face.

"You're no help at all." She wagged a finger at him halfheartedly. "This isn't funny, and I'm not going to rest until we find them."

He trudged over and sat beside her, putting his muscular, ex-quarterback arm around her shoulder in his most protective of gestures. "Please, hon. We've gotten too little sleep as it is with Markie. Now we're gonna stay up half the night lookin' for those cushions?"

The mention of their six-month-old son softened Becca's attitude. At the moment, their pride and joy was "down," and she was thankful for that. Those "baby breathers" were few and far between.

Even though she and her Stout Fella had taken turns with the bottles and changing diapers in liberated millennium fashion, it had been a while since either of them had gotten a decent night's sleep. Perhaps she wasn't thinking clearly these days as a result. "I know I sound unreasonable, but I just don't want to disappoint Maura Beth."

"Hon, we're letting her use all our patio furniture for the deck. Isn't that enough for you?"

"But that cast iron is even harder than the folding chairs. I was just thinking those cushions would be the perfect touch for people's bottoms."

"Nah. Your cookbook signing will bring in plenty a' people, and they'll all be standing around in line for you. They won't even be worried about the chairs. No telling how many fans you still have from your radio days. Nobody in this town can say you're not contributing."

Becca bit her lip, clearly unsatisfied. Her attention to detail, always a source of pride for her during the long run of her radio show, had soared to new heights since becoming a mother. She was determined to become the best mother ever after waiting so long to have her first child. "Let's just make the rounds of the closets one more time. This is an enormous house. Maybe I overlooked something. I'm good at putting things away in safe places and then forgetting where those places are."

"You should never do that without telling me. I'm your backup, hon."

"Maybe there are some things I'd like to keep hidden from you. That's a woman's prerogative."

Justin snorted. "You know good and well you'd throw a fit if I tried to keep something from you. Women!"

"Don't say something sexist like that to me, Justin Brachle. After all, I am the mother of your child," she said, playing at chastising him.

Nonetheless, he looked somewhat embarrassed and averted her gaze. "Well, when you put it that way, I'm all in. So, which side of the house do you want me to take this time?"

Periwinkle and Mr. Parker Place were busy doing a quick inventory in her office down at The Twinkle. At the moment they had come to the conclusion that they could spare a dozen of the cushioned chairs that were used regularly for customer dining. She had rightly pointed out that the evening before the Fourth of July, now nearly upon them, was never one of their busiest times. People were too busy at home preparing their own holiday picnic food such as potato salad, peach ice cream, and apple pie to even consider eating out.

"We'll just get Barry to take the chairs on out to the library in the delivery van," Periwinkle continued.

"He's out on a delivery right now, but as soon as he gets back, I think I'll ride with him to help. I mean, there's a difference between delivering tomato aspic and a load of furniture," Mr. Place said. "Barry's a hard worker, but he's a bit on the short side. Might as well do this up right, Peri."

"I agree. You know, at first, my girl Maura Beth sounded nearly panicked when she called. Knowing her like I do, I can tell you it bothers her that she'll have such a patchwork quilt of furniture out there tomorrow for the opening. I told her she just needed to relax and trust her Cherry Cola Book Club people to get the job done. I think she put her head on straight after that." Then came a soft intake of air. "You know what, Parker? I just thought of something that'll fancy up her library opening a little more. Remember those two silver star mobiles we replaced and took down last month? They're still in the storage closet."

He looked slightly baffled and pointed at the mobile directly above them. "Yeah, I ought to know where they are, Peri. I put 'em there not all that long ago. But if you don't mind, please satisfy my curiosity—how are they gonna improve the library's seating arrangements?"

She elbowed him playfully. "No, silly. You've got it all wrong. People won't sit on 'em. They'll see 'em first thing when they walk into the lobby—all glittery just hanging from the ceiling right over the circulation desk. Why, Maura Beth may like 'em well enough to let 'em stay there permanently. That way, The Twinkle will always be a part of the library's ambience."

"And you want me to hang 'em for you?"

"I think you and Barry could get the job done just fine. He can steady the ladder for you."

His laughter was forceful, ending in a couple of coughs and finally a clearing of his throat that sounded like gears being stripped. "Did you take out an insurance policy on me that I don't know about? If you did, I predict the last thing I'll see will be stars before I fall to my death on the library floor."

"Trust me, Parker. You won't fall, and the patrons'll be reminded of how many delicious meals they've had at The Twinkle over the years when they spot those mobiles. And we won't even tell Maura Beth we're gonna do it. We'll just let it be a nice little surprise."

He was clearly lost in thought for a while. "I sure hope everything goes the way Maura Beth expects tomorrow—no glitches or anything unexpected. She's been waiting for years to show Cherico what a real library looks like. This is her big moment in the sun."

5

Great Day in the Morning

As the sun came up on the Fourth of July Grand Opening, Maura Beth opened her blue eyes, knowing that her long journey out of darkness was nearly over. Waiting for her on the willow-lined shores of Lake Cherico was the library of her dreams—shiny, spacious, and eager to please her long-suffering patrons. Skylights above the long central corridor would forever be illuminating the way for those who walked in looking for a casual read, or a job lead on one of the computer terminals, or résumé help, or keeping up with national and world affairs browsing newspapers and magazines in the periodicals section. Or even just having a place to spend the day if they were homeless—a sad reality but one that definitely existed. At last, Maura Beth's days of being practically imprisoned in the claustrophobic, windowless room that she had called her office for nearly seven years were thankfully coming to an end; and she couldn't help cheering the moment her brain cleared.

"Wow, great day in the morning, and hallelujah!" she shouted as she sat up, stretched, and lifted her arms heavenward.

Jeremy sprang to life like a jack-in-the-box on his side of the bed, his eyes blinking in disbelief. "What?! What's the matter, Maurie?!"

She leaned over, gave him a kiss on his scruffy cheek, and then drew back, studying his handsome but startled features. "Now don't be so dense. It's finally here, that's what's the matter. The Charles Durden Sparks, Crumpton, and Duddney Public Library opens its doors to the world out there on this wonderful day of our country's independence. So, let there be light!"

Despite her stirring patriotic tribute, he feigned displeasure while wiping the sleep out of his eyes. "Geez. I thought we might be in the middle of a home invasion or something."

She reached over and pushed against him playfully, knocking him down like a pesky spare pin at the bowling alley. "You're smarter than that. You do not offer up praise for criminal activity of that sort."

"That may be," he told her, recovering from her feisty display and bracing himself against his pillows. "But I was having a remarkable dream, and you pulled me up out of it rudely. At long last, I was taking one of my English classes on a field trip to Rowan Oak over in Oxford, and William Faulkner himself greeted us at the door, saying that we had taken way too much time getting there on the bus. 'I've been waiting patiently for you,' were his exact words, as I recall. I was so flattered. Can you imagine being able to pick his brain on the subject of writing? It would give me such an edge for my Great American Novel. In fact, I had gotten to the point in the dream where I pulled out my manuscript and asked him to read it, and he said he would."

Maura Beth giggled like a schoolgirl. "Oh, yeah? Well, how is he doing these days? Working on any new manuscripts? Something about the accommodations, I suppose—*The Long, Hot, Heavenly Summer*?"

"Very funny and totally disrespectful. Anyway, I was about to have an honest-to-goodness audience with him when you woke me up."

"An audience? That's a new one—you adding religious overtones to your everyday banter."

"Literature is my religion, you know that."

"It's just as well I woke you up, though. We've got a long day ahead of us out at the lake, and I need you to be my right-hand man."

He considered for a moment and then squinted. "I thought Renette was your right-hand man—err, woman."

Maura Beth pulled back the sheets and swung her legs over the side of the bed, wedging her feet into her fuzzy purple bedroom slippers, the very last holdover from her college days. "Not so much right now. That ongoing infatuation of hers with Waddell Mack I told you about has continued to fester. That's all she talks about on the job.

Marydell says it's driving her crazy, and she's just not one to complain about much. At any rate, I'm hoping this concert tonight will let Renette get it all out of her system. It's the prospect of seeing him again in person that's got her going. Well, not up close and in person. I told her that wasn't going to be possible. His schedule is just too hectic, and he's got all those people surrounding him. But maybe seeing him from afar and hearing his music will do the trick."

"Or she could become even more obsessed and go off the deep end. Have you thought about that?"

Maura Beth froze. "Now, why did you say that? I'll just be even more worried about her."

"Because it's possible. You just can't predict the behavior of someone who's truly obsessed."

There was a long sigh of resignation. "Well, I'll just have to hope for the best. I'll just put that completely out of my mind. Meanwhile . . ."

After an extended period of silence, Jeremy said, "Meanwhile, what? Please finish your sentences, Maurie. It's become a bad habit of yours. I've decided to call it *hesi-talking*."

She briefly indulged him. "So, the English teacher is now making up his own words, is that it? Never mind. What I was going to say was that it's all that mismatched furniture in the new library. Please don't get me wrong. I'm grateful the book club came through—bless their hearts, each and every one of them. There's at least something for people to sit on and get off their feet. But after we all got through lugging it in and moving it around . . . it looked like . . . well, it looked like we had bought all our furniture at a yard sale or a flea market. I guess I really didn't think things through the way I should have."

His eyes widened. "Come on now. What did you expect? A designer showroom?"

"I know, I know. And, of course, you never heard me say that. My Cherry Cola Book Clubbers are the best friends I've ever had, and that includes some mighty good ones when I went to LSU."

"That's more like it. Hey, it's just temporary, Maurie. You really need to get over being the ultimate perfectionist. It's always going to leave you disappointed in people and things."

She padded across the room with determination, shrugging him off. "Part of my mission, I guess. No librarian worth her fines wants even one book out of place on the shelves. Our universe is always perfectly ordered according to the gods of library science. End of lecture."

"Hey, I'm just glad you're not like that in bed," he called out after her as she disappeared into the bathroom. "You're as different as night and day when we make a mess of the sheets and that fiery red hair of yours is all out of place and wild on the pillows—just like you are."

There was a wicked grin on her face when she

suddenly popped back into view for another round. "I'm afraid I do resemble that, you devil, you. Last night really was fantastic, sweetheart. Kudos. You melted me like butter in a hot skillet. My stress levels needed it."

"Anytime," he told her, getting out of bed at last in all his splendid nakedness. "I just want you to remember that making love should be dreamy and never by the book, Miz Librarian."

"Speaking of dreams," she said almost as an afterthought as he approached, "I had that strange one again about wandering around forever in the mist, feeling all lost and abandoned, until this ray of light appeared ahead of me. Each time I have this same dream, I keep thinking if I can just walk faster and get to the clearing where the light is, I'll find out what's going on. But I always wake up before I get there, and I just have no earthly idea what it could possibly mean. Maybe I should check out one of the books we have on the shelves about dream interpretation."

He embraced her tenderly in the doorframe of the bathroom. "I don't know about that, but I've had a recurring dream myself for years that I've never told you about. Didn't think it was worth mentioning. I was always being pursued by a tornado in it, and I'd always wake up just before it got to me and sucked me up like Dorothy inside that farmhouse in Kansas. But for some reason I haven't had it in years. It seems to have disappeared as fast as a tornado does. Go figure."

"Maybe it's just as simple as I've been a calming influence in your life."

He kissed her softly. "That's a thought, and I guess what we're doing right now is the proof."

But Maura Beth wasn't inclined to dismiss her dream the way Jeremy had. Something kept telling her that a message of some kind was being conveyed to her and that eventually she would discover what it was. In any case she clearly had something on the brain that was struggling to surface.

The entire town of Cherico had been hoping and praying for good weather on the Fourth and that the Grand Opening of their new library would not be marred by thunderstorms to keep people away. When they all awoke that morning, there was not a cloud in the July sky—only the torrid heat of midsummer awaiting them. So far, so good. Even if that meant a lot of sweat went into pitching the patriotic-looking food tents in the green space between the library and the temporary bleachers that had been set up for Waddell Mack's concert that evening. These impressive and colorful canvas structures—some red, some white, some blue as befitted the Fourth—were the type used primarily for tailgating at football games, and gradually the makeshift venue took shape, complete with tables and folding chairs for alfresco dining both in and out of the heat. Of course, there were American flags everywhere—on lapels, on sticks in jars, pinned to the sides of the tents, on the awnings, and in the hands of many an interested onlooker. Best of all, there were any number of eclectic and mouthwatering choices for sampling. To be sure, a few local fast-food places serving pizza and hamburgers were up and running to make a quick buck, knowing full well that they would likely not win any prizes. But it was some of the individual chefs who made the lineup truly interesting and worth the price of admission.

Bit Sessions had chosen to concentrate on two items only—her ham and butterbean soup, along with her famous fried chicken—and her signage proudly proclaimed: CORINTH'S BEST HERE IN CHERICO. At first she had been reluctant to reference Corinth when she was smack dab in the middle of Cherico, but she thought better of it after she had phoned all of her most sycophantic friends and told them they must put in an appearance on the grounds of the new library and vote for her as Queen of the Cookbooks. Calling in every favor she could recall, her conversations had always ended with a very emphatic, "Remember, you owe me big-time. I darn well better get your vote."

On the other hand, Gwen Beetles had disdained any reference to Corinth and instead had opted for a banner that read: GWEN'S FOURTH OF JULY PICNIC. To back that up, she had settled upon foot-long hot dogs made with andouille sausage— a tribute to her Cajun heritage as a Leblanc before marrying a Mississippi boy, the late Hyram Beetles. There was nothing more American than hot dogs on the Fourth of July, but she saw no downside to selling her version of them with a little kick.

Then she, too, had called up her troops to duty with an appearance at her church's Wednesday night potluck where she had pleaded with the regulars to support her in Cherico. "I promise I'll tithe to the church if I win anything," she had told them all. Both Bit and Gwen were pleased to discover that their tents were widely separated from each other, making it difficult for them to indulge their rivalry and báser instincts by getting into each other's business.

Dressed in a bright yellow frock that contrasted beautifully with her shiny black hair, Ana Estrella had set up shop midway between Bit and Gwen as a dessert specialist with her HOLA, AMIGOS! sign and five pigeon peas cakes ready to slice up. Perhaps she might increase her chances of winning the top prize if she offered only one thing and did it very well, she had reasoned. Plus, she was counting on the novelty of people taking a chance on a recipe with such unusual ingredients and coming away pleasantly surprised, if not raving. Why, everyone and his brother had tasted the brownies or peach cobbler with homemade ice cream or Dutch apple pie that some of the others were offering—but pigeon peas cake? Since moving to Cherico, she had come to the conclusion that she might very well be the only Hispanic citizen in the Mississippi mix, and that, she decided, was not a bad thing at all on a day like today.

She soon became slightly concerned, however, when the plump, elderly woman wearing a big straw hat and a fanciful dress dotted with red, white, and blue stars put up a hand-lettered sign in the tent next to hers: GET YOUR NO-SUGAR-ADDED DESSERT HERE.

Ana reflected briefly. Anyone with a passing knowledge of the Deep South was well aware of the epidemic that diabetes had become in recent years. Everyone could recite the litany: the overeating, the sugar and carbs consumption, the resulting obesity—all of them linked together as the culprits behind the disease. Thus, it was barely possible that the neighboring tent might just steal Ana's thunder by focusing on such an important health issue while she offered something tempting and exotic. What bad luck to be positioned right next to her!

So Ana decided to be proactive, introducing herself quickly with the friendliest smile she could muster. Being the public relations professional she was, perhaps she could earn her salary and figure out a way for the two of them to coexist.

"Nice to meet you, too," the woman said, extending her hand. "I'm Maribelle Pleasance. My family was originally from Jonesboro, Arkansas, but we moved here near 'bout fifty years ago. Guess that makes us practically natives. Now, who's to say different? Are you from Cherico? I don't believe I've ever seen you around town, and I may not look it, but I do get out quite a bit."

Ana explained who she was and why she had come to Cherico but then lost no time in pursuing the strategy she had just concocted on the spur of the moment. "Tell me about this no-sugar-added dessert of yours. You don't often see that sort of thing on the Fourth of July. It's one of those holidays where everybody splurges and has to let out their belts a notch or two. I'm completely fascinated."

Maribelle's fleshy face lit up as her lips drew back in the broadest of smiles. "I'm flattered you would ask, and I hope everyone will be as inner-rested as you are. You see, I developed type two diabetes a while back. Now, I know it was my fault, and I could have avoided it if I'd had me any sort of willpower. I'm not sure I believe it, but Mississippi just got the title of the most obese state in the union. Like the minute you cross the border, everybody starts stuffin' their faces and can't stop. But, anyway, I just got so tired of not bein' able to eat sweets anymore when my doctor laid down the law. At least not any sweets that would really taste good. I mean, great day in the mornin', the aftertaste some a' those sugar substitutes have would drive you to drink. Not that I would ever imbibe, mind you. I'm a devout Southern Bab-dist, and we never touch the stuff."

"I love your accent," Ana told her. "It's charming. Some people turn up their noses at Southern accents, but I just love hearing them."

"Do ya? Well, I nearly fainted when I heard a recording of myself once. 'Who on God's green earth is that?' I remember sayin' to myself. Had somethin' unholy took possession of my soul? But, anyway, I found me one a' them substitutes I could tolerate and finally got just the right mixture of it and some cherries and walnuts and a buttery crust, and I come up with my No-Sugar-Added Cherry Cake with Walnuts. It makes you feel like you've just sinned, but really, it's not a diet breaker. Now, I'm not sayin' it doesn't have a few calories. Calories is calories. If it tastes good, you know it does. But let's just say you don't feel deprived after you've had a piece. You feel like you've had uh honest-to-goodness dessert. Will you just listen to me? I've prob'ly bored you goin' on and on about my problems."

Ana could not help but warm to the woman. Her lack of pretension was endearing, and the lines in her face seemed to demand a certain respect. In

131

her own family, elders were always revered, and she was not about to go against her training.

"You've done no such thing. I've loved hearing about your process."

Maribelle scowled, cocking her head. "My what?"

Ana chuckled and gently patted Maribelle's hand. "I'm sorry. What I meant to say was I loved hearing about how you invented your recipe. Sometimes I get caught up in public relations talk."

Maribelle leaned in and lowered her voice, pointing to her scalp. "Well, I thought for a second there, you might be talkin' about the way my hair gets all frizzed up in this humidity. Seems the worst months is July and August. I can look like a briar bush at times."

"Aren't you the cutest thing this side of the Mississippi River? Anyway, I have a specialty, too. I'm Hispanic, and I'm selling my pigeon peas cake. It's a favorite down in San Juan where my family is originally from, you know."

"You mean like down on the island of Por-da Reek-oh in the middle of the Carry-bee-un?"

"That's the spot. Somewhere down there in the tropics," Ana said. "And I was thinking that you and I might team up today. You steer the ones who don't have to watch their sugar to me, and I'll steer the ones who do to you. We'll catch everybody that way. What do you think? Is it a deal?" Ana offered her hand once again, and the two women shook on it.

"Well, I guess there might be a market for both of us when you put it that-a-way," Maribelle said, keeping the smile in her voice. "Although like you say, people usually don't pay too much attention to their diets on the Fourth of July. I know I never did until I got this dad-blamed diabetes."

"That's why my putting in a good word for you might work wonders. It's worth a try."

"Well, if you can sell customers as good as you just sold me on your idea, I think it definitely will work. Meanwhile, would you like a little bitta taste a' my cake? I'd be right proud to have you tell me what you think of it, bein' as you're a baker yourself and all."

"Sure. If you'll taste mine."

"You got yourself a deal."

And with that the two women sampled slivers of their cherished recipes on paper plates, rolling their eyes and praising each other effusively afterward.

"You weren't kidding, Maribelle. I feel like I've just indulged in a thousand sinful calories. Your crust is so rich, and I love the crunch of the walnuts. My compliments to the chef. I just think it's genius."

"It's right tasty if I do say so myself," Maribelle said, the color rising in her cheeks. "And I'da never thought your cake had peas in it as uh ingredient. When you first told me about it, all I could think of was it had to be somethin' savory comin' down the pike. Actually, I thought somethin' crazy was comin' down the pike. But all I tasted is coconut and cinnamon, and I'm just as satisfied with yours as you were mine. Now, aren't we a pair?"

"That we are."

"Maybe we'll both win us a prize."

Ana crossed her fingers. "Let's hope so."

After the spontaneous mutual admiration society had ended, Ana relaxed and reflected further. Maribelle Pleasance might be competition, but in the larger scheme of things, she was also a citizen of Cherico who ultimately would benefit from the economic boost that Spurs 'R' Us would bring to the economically depressed town. Ana Estrella was first and foremost a public relations expert and then a baker in her spare time; and if she didn't win any money today, well, it hardly mattered. She was well-compensated by Spurs 'R' Us for her work, and she now genuinely hoped Maribelle Pleasance would win the top prize.

She checked her watch. They were only fifteen minutes away from the brief, perfunctory ribbon-cutting ceremony presided over by Maura Beth McShay, Councilman Sparks, the Crumpton sisters, and Nora Duddney. Then the library doors would open, and the public would also start sampling the tastiest food Cherico had to offer.

Maura Beth had told Ana there was something special about this little town and its people tucked away in the extreme northeast corner of Mississippi, and she was truly beginning to feel it.

Renette Posey was already growing restless. No, it had nothing to do with Councilman Sparks and his pompous, self-serving, ribbon-cutting oration during which he was careful to point out more than once how much the new library had "always been his baby."

"Legacies are important to our little town, and the new library is mine. I have always been aware of Cherico's need to move forward with facilities like this," he had concluded.

Renette and Maura Beth had exchanged furtive glances at that misrepresentation. Nor had the more self-effacing speeches by Mamie Crumpton and Nora Duddney, two of the other benefactors who had helped to finance the library, been all that much of a trial to bear.

"We always want to do what's best for Cherico," Mamie had begun, hogging the microphone and successfully preventing her sister Marydell from taking her turn and fulfilling the "we." "The Crumpton family, being pioneers in Cherico, are more than proud to have this facility bear our name. Generations from now, people will recognize our contribution. It is important to leave something worthwhile behind, especially since we live in an age of such disposable things. . . ."

"I know my father, Layton Duddney, would be proud to know I've done this," Nora had said when Mamie had finally relinquished her self-serving spotlight. "He's still hanging on out there at the nursing home as he has for years, now pushing one hundred, but I'm sorry to say he doesn't recognize me or anyone else anymore. Nevertheless, I believe this is the Duddney family's finest hour."

Beyond that, once the tours had begun inside the new library, Renette had more than enough to occupy her. Maura Beth had put her in charge of overseeing the computer terminals, making sure the patrons signed up properly and understood that they were limited to an hour's use on opening day. The goal was to allow as many people as possible to experience the library's new toys, and there was no scarcity of questions for her to answer.

"How do I print out this document, miss?" said an acne-faced, male high school student wearing a T-shirt that read FIRST-CLASS GEEK—but whose "geekdom" at the moment was letting him down.

At the neighboring terminal: "This e-mail I just sent to my son at the University of Texas bounced back. I know he's out there. He told me over the phone he wanted me to send along a care package so he can nibble late at night in the dorm. You know how these college kids are. So I thought I'd try out these nice new computers you got here. Can you tell me what I did wrong?" an agitated older woman wearing a burnt orange, LONGHORN MOM T-shirt explained.

And then there was the young man with a nose ring and a T-shirt that read I LUV THE DARK SIDE who was quite adamant about connecting with "alternative rock" Web sites.

"Uh, miss, I can't seem to pull up Well-Done Stake on here. I know they've got a Web site."

Renette was completely at a loss but smiled gamely. "Uh, is that one of those food sites? Do you like to cook?"

He had snorted and shaken his head. "No, not S-T-E-A-K. It's S-T-A-K-E. It's a rock band. They dress up like awesome vampires and make up their faces with fake blood. They are beyond way cool. Don't you know about their big hit 'Blood in the Coffin'?"

Wide-eyed and somewhat tentatively, Renette said, "I guess I must have missed it somehow."

"Bummer."

As it turned out, the band's Web site had been blocked, and the young man shot up out of his seat in disgust when that fact came to light, leaving Renette to call out after him as diplomatically as she could: "Come back soon. We'll be more than happy to help you find something else anytime."

As busy as Renette's duties were keeping her, however, her restlessness was the result of her secret focus on Waddell Mack, whose concert she could not wait to witness right after the fireworks display at dusk. She longed to rush home to her apartment when the tours were finally over at five and change clothes. This standard-issue, library workplace outfit she was required to wear that consisted of a much-too-large beige shirt over khaki slacks did absolutely no justice to her shapely young figure. Even if she was somehow unable to reach the stage and talk to Waddell Mack again, as she had at The Twinkle when he and his band had come through Cherico just before Christmas last year, she was determined to look good for him in the stands.

She would pull this off, she had decided, by venturing into the forbidden land of makeup. It was all for a good cause—which was being near all that dark, curly hair and those intentionally scruffy cheeks and those tight jeans and cowboy boots. Why, he was the man of her dreams, and she had spent the last six months or so circling the days on her calendar until his return to Cherico.

Her warnings about makeup from Hardy and Lula Posey had been frequent and elaborate from before she hit puberty. "It's something those with idle hands use," her mother had insisted. "It's nothing but temptation for a man, and smeared lipstick means a forbidden kiss. You never let a man kiss you that-a-way unless you are married and trying for a child. And, mind me well, your husband must be the one to initiate. That's the righteous way."

But Renette couldn't wait to apply her newly bought foundation and mascara and lip gloss and all the rest of it in defiance of her strict childhood. She was doing her own makeover. She envisioned a scenario where she would walk up to the makeshift stage after the concert, and Waddell would somehow notice her among the waving, cheering throng.

He would say to her, "Aren't you that right pretty young librarian I met last year at The Twinkle, Twinkle Café? You're . . . wait, let me jiggle my brain cells just a tad bit . . . you're Renette, right? Musta made a mental note 'cause the name sounded so different."

"You remembered, Waddell," she would answer all aflutter. "That means so much to me—you just can't imagine."

"How could I forget a fan like you? You know, I even spotted you out there in the audience. Why, who wouldn't with that pretty smile a' yours, darlin'. You're knockin' the strings off my git-tar."

Renette's fantasy would continue as the exchange would somehow ring true in her head. How demure she would be in fishing for compliments! "You're just way too kind. I'm just your average small-town girl when you come right down to it. Nothing special."

"No way. You look like Miss America. In fact, I

think you should try out for it. First you'll win the Miss Mississippi contest, and then I'll bet you'll go on television and win the whole shebang."

"You think so?"

He would nod, touch his thumb and index finger to the tip of his cowboy hat, and give her that sexy smile of his. "Great day in the mornin', little Miz Renette, I shore as heck do."

"Really? I didn't even think you'd notice me with all the thousands of pretty girls out there that you see on tour."

"None as purty as you, though."

She would, however, stop short of saying, "Oh, shucks!"

Then, Waddell might even start serenading her with his git-tar. She had almost swooned when he had pronounced the word that way at The Twinkle last year, feeling it as a rush in her blood. The way of the world was this: There were "bad" good ole boys like Councilman Sparks, and then there were "good" good ole boys like Waddell Mack. His long, talented fingers would go to work making his music, stroking those strings, the light from his eyes penetrating her like a laser beam, and before either of them knew what was happening—

"Renette!?"

Was her imagination playing tricks on her, or was that Waddell actually calling her name in the real world?

"Renette!?"

There it was again.

Then she came to and realized that she had drifted off into a daydream deluxe, ignoring her duties to the extent that Maura Beth was standing next to her at the computer terminals and nudging her gently. "Renette, the man on the end down there with the gray beard needs your help. He's been waving at you for a while. We need to pay a little more attention."

Renette's sweet little face blushed. "I'm so sorry about that, Miz McShay. I guess I was doin' a little daydreaming. I certainly didn't mean to be ignoring our patrons."

"That's all right, sweetie. It's all going well, isn't it? They just keep pouring in and asking questions. I never knew we had this many people in Cherico, and we certainly never had this many come into the old library in one day. Maybe not this many in six months. This is the day I've been looking forward to for so long, and I have to keep telling myself that it's finally here."

"We've been swamped since we opened. Not an empty seat in the terminals any time, and I've seen you and Mr. Jeremy busy as bees showing everyone around. I think we're a real big hit, Miz McShay."

Maura Beth leaned against her and inhaled the smell of the new library's fresh paint. Was there a sweeter perfume in the world? "Yes, indeedy. I keep wanting to pinch myself, but I hope this wonderful day never ends. It's the keeper of all keepers in my book."

As Renette headed toward her patron, however, she felt exactly the opposite. The sun couldn't go down fast enough for her, bringing with it the fireworks display and then Waddell singing his greatest country hits. Who knew what romantic adventure might be in store for her?

6
Food Fight

Decked out in a white bonnet, gray wig, red floral granny dress, and spectacles as The Old Woman Who Lived in a Shoe, Miriam Goodcastle was in the midst of her very first story hour on the stage of the sprawling, imaginative Children's Room. She had just recited the venerable, eponymous nursery rhyme for what was a packed house full of mesmerized youngsters and their obviously delighted mothers. In fact, there was standing room only.

One little girl in pigtails and a red gingham frock raised her hand. "Why did that old woman live in a shoe? There's not very much room in a shoe. Sometimes I can't get my foot in mine without squiggling it around lots and lots, and my mommy has to come in and help me with it. You ask her, and she'll tell you."

A wave of laughter moved across the audience, and Miriam said, "You're absolutely right, you know. Sometimes I have trouble getting my shoes on, too. Well, I think the answer to your question is that the shoe might have belonged to a giant and was big enough to hold her entire family. That would have made her very happy to find a place to live like that."

"What happened to the giant?" the little girl continued. "I think giants are really scary. Did the giant go, 'Fee, fi, fo, fum'? That's what all the giants in the storybooks say."

Miriam thought on her feet, as all good children's librarians must do. "He may very well have said something like that. As for my theory on the giant and his shoes, well, I think he probably outgrew his old ones and got a new pair. Then he probably left the old ones behind in the forest one day, and that's where the Old Woman found one of them when she was wandering about looking for pecans to make into a big pie to feed all her children. Quick, raise your hands right this minute: How many of you children like pecan pie?"

There was a forest of little hands and a few giggles, along with an enthusiastic "I do!" or two.

"Good. Who doesn't? I'm afraid I like it too much, and it really ruins my diet, especially when I put vanilla ice cream on top. Now, have any of you ever eaten it like that?"

There was another display of little hands and voices.

"So, to get back to the Old Woman finding the giant's shoe in the forest—she probably thought to herself what a wonderful home it would make for herself and her family. Not only that, but she could lace it up tight to keep out the rain and the wind and the animals of the forest."

The little girl spoke up again with a sense of awe in her voice. "You mean like bears and wolves? They could eat little girls up."

"Yes, like bears and wolves, and who knows what else might be prowling around out there?"

"But where were they all living before she found the shoe? You have to have a place to go to sleep at night."

Miriam was not rattled in the least as her training continued to kick in. This was what she was being paid to do. "You know, I can't say for sure. Perhaps they all lived in a big oak tree before they lived in a shoe. Maybe every one of her children had their own branch to live on."

The little girl wanted still more. "Like birds?"

"Yes, like birds."

"Was that the same mean giant that was in *Jack and the Beanstalk*, or was it a good giant?"

"Well, it might have been either one. All giants wear shoes."

"Are you sure? What if they went barefoot? I like to go barefoot, but sometimes I step on something and it hurts."

The little girl's mother finally stepped in. "Now, Wendy, Miz Goodcastle has given you her best opinions, and you're not letting any of the other children ask her questions. You're wearing her out."

"Don't you worry about that in the least, Mrs.—?"

"Mrs. Grant. And this is my daughter, Wendy."

"Happy to have you both with us this morning. Well, Mrs. Grant, I just love Wendy's questions. It's why I'm here," Miriam added, her disposition as sunny as the weather outside. "It's the curiosity that gets them reading in the first place, and that's our ultimate goal. I've been very pleased with how all of you parents have responded to our summer reading program. Next week, I've decided to move from depiction of a nursery rhyme to Roald Dahl's *Charlie and the Chocolate Factory*. Mothers, I just know your children will have a lot of fun with it, and I'm sure you will, too. You're welcome to go online and find out more about it."

Maura Beth and Jeremy were watching the proceedings from the back of the room, taking a short break from their guided tours. "Miriam really is very talented," Maura Beth whispered. "She has the patience of Job. I knew I had the right person the second she walked in the door for her interview."

"And how did you know that?" he whispered back. "You mean before she even opened her mouth?"

"Yep."

"This I gotta hear."

"Well, she showed up in costume as Mother

Goose. She totally blew me away. None of the others thought to do something like that. They were all about street clothes and pointing to their résumés."

Jeremy gave her a thumbs-up. "Ah, I see. Very creative. She was living the part in the real world. She would've gotten my vote."

"All you need to do is look at those angelic little faces. They're soaking it all up like sponges. I was never able to do anything on this scale in the old library because I just didn't have the space or the time. Or the budget. Now, Miriam has her own little universe to play with."

He patted her on the shoulder. "And you'll have a new generation of taxpayers to support the library somewhere down the line."

"That's the plan."

Bit Sessions had never liked the curly blond Garber twins—Lisabeth and Isabeth. It wasn't just that their personalities were the most cloying in all of Corinth and possibly the rest of Mississippi to boot. Nor that they truly did mimic each other down to the fake beauty marks they applied to their right cheekbones with eyebrow pencil—a fact that had been embarrassingly revealed when they were once caught in a thunderstorm and the little dots had washed away, much to their horror. Nor even that their wardrobes were age inappropriate: They were now in their early twenties and dressed more like they were Shirley Temple moppets. Just way too cutesy for words. What sort of *Whatever Happened to Baby Jane?* world did they live in?

No, the real rub was that they were such fast friends with Gwen Beetles. Everyone knew that the Garber and the Beetles families were thick as thieves, and Bit had always regarded it as one unholy alliance for social and financial purposes. Thus, it was with great suspicion that she regarded Lisabeth and Isabeth approaching her food tent with the customary sickening smiles on their faces.

"Oh, Miz Bit," Lisabeth began in that syrupy way of hers, "we're just dyin' to try your ham and butterbean soup. Everyone back home always raves about it. They say it's the best thing they've ever put in their mouths, and you know how picky people in Corinth are. They all swear by you."

"Do they?"

"Why, yay-iss," Isabeth added, sounding even more syrupy than her sister. "They really do."

Bit squared her shoulders, adopted her most distant demeanor, and pointed to the big steaming kettle on the table behind her. "Well, I'm charging a dollar for a cup and two dollars for a bowl. Which do y'all want?"

The two turned away, huddled for a moment, and then said in perfect unison, "We'd like one cup. We'll share."

Bit looked disgusted. "Do you two have to talk like that? Such an act! Anyway, I mighta known you'd be cheap about it."

Lisabeth batted her eyelashes and cocked her head. "Why, Miz Bit, whatever do you mean? We don't wanna get too full at one tent. We have to pace ourselves. Besides, it's not cricket for young ladies to stuff themselves. It'd be bad news for our girlish figures, you know."

"Never mind all the precious playacting and the butter-wouldn't-melt-in-your-mouth routine. That'll be a dollar, please." She held out her hand expectantly, her nose in the air.

It was then that Lisabeth fumbled around in her purse and somehow managed to turn it upside down, dropping it to the ground and spilling all the contents everywhere. "Oh, no," she said, clutching a hand to her shapely chest, "will you just look at what I've done? Come help me pick all this up, Izzy. I've made a big mess. We need to track everything down, or I'll have to spend a fortune on cosmetics. Or borrow yours, and that would drive us both crazy."

"Look, it's gone everywhere, Lizzy. And your lipstick rolled all the way over there by the table, and I think I see your mascara nearby. You may even have to crawl underneath on all fours. It'll take us forever to track everything down. Can you please help us, Miz Bit?"

Bit was extremely aggravated but reluctantly

decided to pitch in. The sooner she got rid of them, the better. Truth to tell, she didn't even want to be seen in their company, she was that disgusted by them both. Plus, her foul mood, which was certainly showing up on her face, couldn't possibly be good for business. Nothing turned customers away like a scowl.

After a few minutes of scouring the grass, bending over, and a little unladylike grunting here and there for good measure, the three of them finally got the job done, but Bit's annoyance continued to flare. "Do you two still want the soup, or are you both too pooped to pay up?"

"Why, of course we still want it," Isabeth said. "Don't you want us to vote for you as the Best Appetizer? There's no way we can do that if we don't have a little sip, you know."

Bit's laugh was loud and derisive. "Give me a break, honey. Like you're gonna actually vote for me. I didn't just fall off the turnip truck. Listen, you two, I'm halfway convinced that Gwen Beetles sent y'all over here, though I don't know why. I'm sure you know we've never been the best of friends, so my suspicion is she's prob'ly up to no good."

"Why, no indeed, she didn't send us, Miz Bit," Lisabeth added. "We came over here of our own accord. We're just tryin' to cast an objective vote this afternoon after we've made the rounds of all these food tents." She raised her hand as if she were swearing an oath on the Bible. "Honest."

Bit managed to restrain herself, offering up a skeptical smile. "Now that's a likely story if I ever heard one. Just go ahead and gimme your money, and I'll give you your cups a' soup. There are other customers milling around, and I don't want to lose them by taking up all my time with you two."

After that testy exchange, the twins paid up, and then it happened. They held their cups of steaming soup high in the air and poured the contents onto the grass below, sticking out their tongues in unison as a finishing touch. It was childish choreography of the highest order.

"You little smart-ass prisses. I knew you were up to no good. You've wasted my time, and more to the point, you've wasted some of my precious ham and butterbean soup."

"Ham and butterbeans mushed all together? How common, and how disgustingly chunky!"

"You better git outta here with your mischief, you two!"

As they began backing away, Lisabeth had the smirk of all time on her face. "You don't know the half of it."

Bit was getting angrier by the second. "I'll tell you one more time. Get on back to Corinth where you came from."

"We will. All in good time," Isabeth said, elbowing her sister as they scurried off full of high-pitched giggles.

Bit was worried now. She could definitely smell Gwen Beetles all over their obnoxious little visit.

Maura Beth and Jeremy had just finished a tour of the Tech Services Room where Agnes Braud had held forth for about ten minutes on the subject of processing books and getting them ready for the shelves. Though her presentation had been a bit on the dry side—particularly when she had ventured into a detailed explanation of MARC records—she had livened it up by showing the small group how a scanner worked on the bar codes. "In today's technological world," she had told them, "most people are fascinated by things that light up and go beep." For the topper, Agnes had let some of the patrons scan for themselves, much to their delight.

"The more y'all understand the inner workings of the library," she had continued, "the more you'll want to support us all year-round."

"The tours couldn't be going any better," Maura Beth said to Jeremy as they headed back into the central hallway.

No sooner had she said that, however, than Renette came racing over to her, flushed and out of breath. "Miz McShay, you and Mr. Jeremy need to go over to the tents real quickly. Someone just came in and said they're shouting at the top of their lungs at each other out there."

"Who's shouting at each other?"

"Two women by the food tents," came the reply. "I don't know what their names are, but they're supposed to be really mad at each other."

Once she was out the front door, it came as no surprise to Maura Beth to see even from a distance that the two women engaged in a shouting match of epic proportions were Bit Sessions and Gwen Beetles, and right in front of Bit's tent with a crowd gathering quickly by the second. Maura Beth and Jeremy could not get there fast enough to break it up.

". . . and I can't help it if your food's gone bad!" Gwen was shouting, wielding one of her foot-long, andouille sausage hot dogs—her Fourth of July specialty—in her hand like it was a sword.

"It's no coincidence that people started throwing up not long after those nauseating Garber twins left here. Admit it, you sneaky, miserable, old hag. You had them put something in my soup, didn't you? You'll prob'ly never admit it, but I just know you were behind it."

Gwen brandished the sausage high above her head, causing widespread snickering among the onlookers. "You are paranoid beyond belief, Bit Sessions . . . and you can't prove it anyways . . . I'd like to see you even try. What are you gonna do . . . call the police?"

"Ladies, please," Maura Beth said, stepping between them as soon as she could. "This is no way to act in public, and I'm sure you are not endearing yourself to your customers with all this fighting. You've drawn a crowd for all the wrong reasons. Let's end this right here and now."

Bit pushed her aside and glared at her rival. "This is between the two of us, Miz McShay, if you don't mind. What did you have them put in my soup, Gwen? I'll bet you anything it was syrup of ipecac. Why else would some of my customers come up to me after buying my soup and tell me they were throwing up right and left? You think that was a coincidence? I know you've sabotaged me. I thought there was something fishy about that purse-dropping foolishness. That's when they did it, wasn't it? When I was helping them look for things on the ground, one of 'em slipped it in, sneaky as you please. I just know it, sure as I'm standin' here. I shoudda known better than to let those little Barbie dolls into my tent."

"You are talkin' nonsense . . . and you well know it, Bit. I didn't even know the Garber twins were here today. . . . You musta left your soup out in the sun too long, that's all. Ever heard of botulism? But then, I wouldn't put it past you to grow some germs in your swill."

"How dare you call my delicious food swill. It is always properly refrigerated, and my kitchen is spotless to a fault. Why, you could eat off my floors, and for God's sake, stop swingin' that obnoxious hot dog around before I haul off and hit you upside the head!"

Jeremy tried his luck as the conversation escalated. "Ladies, we don't want to have to call the security guard on you now, do we?"

"I'm tellin' you sure as I'm standin' here, she started it," Bit said, sounding every bit as juvenile as Miriam Goodcastle's story hour audience. But perhaps nowhere near as well-behaved.

Then, before Jeremy or Maura Beth could do anything further, Gwen rushed past the two of them, ripped the sausage out of the bun, and gleefully rapped Bit on the head twice with it with as much force as she could muster.

"Take that in the name of all that is holy, you four-times-married sinner!" she shouted, puffing herself up triumphantly.

Bit's jaw dropped and remained wide open in disbelief. "You holier-than-thou heretic. You're always sermonizing, and you're a fine one to do it. You can't baptize people with sausage. The very idea is sacrilegious."

"I wasn't baptizing. I was exorcising. You've always had the very Devil himself in you!"

Then in what was a magnificent blur, Bit hurried over to her ladle, scooped up some of her soup, and flung it in Gwen's general direction. Her aim was way off, however, and she ended up splashing some of the crowd gathered around instead.

Gwen made a monstrous face, brandished her sausage high above her head, then lowered it in the most classic of fencing moves, and shouted, "En garde!"

"Don't you dare come at me with that nasty-lookin' thing again, Gwen Beetles. Why, the very idea!"

"I'll put it down if you'll stop stirring that cauldron you've got back there on the table, you witch!"

"Go run real quick and get the security guard, Maurie," Jeremy said, pointing toward the library with urgency. "Mr. Peters will earn his keep and put an end to all this nonsense."

While Maura Beth hurried off, Jeremy did his best to keep the two women separated until help arrived; but it was anything but easy. Gwen kept threatening further bodily harm with the sausage, but she was pressing and twisting it so hard in her hand that it began to fall apart, leaving nothing but a squishy, greasy mess. Meanwhile, Bit kept trying to break Jeremy's substantial grip so she could reach her kettle and return with more soup to pour upon the scalp of the enemy. The reaction of the mesmerized crowd varied depending upon who had been splashed and sullied with hot soup and who had not.

Finally, the beefy, scowling security guard arrived with Maura Beth and read them the riot act. "Ladies, as long as you are part of this event, you will behave or leave the premises. I won't be telling you this twice. I'll call the sheriff's office and have you both hauled off to jail to cool down. Is that how you want to spend the rest of the Fourth?"

Bit recoiled. "You wouldn't dare treat me like that. Do you have any idea who I am?"

"I do not, ma'am. But I *would* dare to put you in jail if you don't calm down right this minute. Just try me."

A shrill woman toward the front of the crowd pointed a finger at Bit. "She threw that butterbean soup on my dress. It's brand-new, too. Can you arrest her for that? Can you at least make her pay for my dry cleaning?"

The guard continued frowning and shook his head in her general direction. "You'll have to take that up with her, ma'am, but I don't think throwing soup on someone is a biggie with law enforcement these days."

"You mean it's not considered disturbing the peace? I mean, she was definitely doing that."

Mr. Peters smirked. "That may be true, but it's certainly not assault with a deadly weapon. It's more like making dirty laundry for someone. If you want my opinion, I think it'll all come out in the wash."

Maura Beth followed up the guard's stern words with some of her own. "Mrs. Sessions and Mrs. Beetles, the library appreciates the effort you both made to come all the way from Corinth to participate in our Grand Opening. You both came to my old library to make sure you qualified, and we're sure the food tents are adding a lot to our celebration. But the library simply cannot endorse your outrageous behavior, and there does appear to be some hanky-panky going on between the two of you behind the scenes. I'm not going to get in the middle of it any further, except to say that I have made the decision to disqualify both of you from the Queen of the Cookbooks competition. Frankly, I don't think either one of you will be getting that many votes after this exhibition. Do you have any idea how you've come off to all these people? You should be ashamed."

"That lady with the soup won't get my vote," the shrill woman added. "No way, no how!"

Another female voice joined the shouting. "Mine, neither. She spilled butterbeans all over my cowboy boots. My brand-new Spurs 'R' Us boots. I just bought 'em 'cause they'll be coming to town soon!"

"And I got some ham along with the soup. And this was one of my best cowboy shirts!" a masculine voice chimed in loudly.

"Hmmph!" Gwen practically spit out the word. "The only reason I came was to make sure she didn't win."

"You see?" Bit answered, herself red in the face. "She's just practically admitted that she sabotaged me. There's the proof."

"I did no such thing. What I meant was . . .

I came here to make sure she didn't win by offering my superior food, that's all. Everybody says I'm the best cook in Northeast Mississippi."

"And when was that survey taken? That's a mighty big piece a' real estate to be braggin' about," Bit countered with her hands on her hips. "The truth is, you're just a legend in your own sad little mind."

Maura Beth drew herself up and spoke with great authority. "Neither of you is going to win anything because I have disqualified you both, as I just said. Please pack up your things and leave as soon as you can. I'll ask the security guard to keep an eye on you to make sure you do. I'm sorry to have to be so harsh, but that's my decision. I will not allow you to ruin our Grand Opening with these petty antics. We're here to celebrate, not fight with each other."

"Well, see if I ever come back to use your library," Bit told her with searing indignation.

"You have a perfectly good one in Corinth to use," Maura Beth reminded her. "I strongly suggest you do so."

Out on the perimeter of the crowd, Ana Estrella and Maribelle Pleasance had been watching the tail end of the proceedings with a great deal of interest, if not disbelief. They simply had been unable to resist leaving their tents for a few minutes to discover what all the commotion was about and had displayed their back in a minute signs that the library had graciously provided for their tables.

"Well, whaddaya know? There's two less competitors for us in this thing," Maribelle said out of the side of her mouth. "Just increases our chances of winnin,' don'tcha think?"

Ana was just shaking her head, somewhat at a loss for words. "Uh . . . maybe, maybe not."

"Cat got your tongue?"

"It's just that I would never act like those women did in public just now. Imagine hitting someone over the head with a sausage like that, no less. Assault and battery with a hot dog—now that's a new one."

"Not to mention slingin' hot soup around. I wonder if somebody got scalded. Seems like people file lawsuits these days at the drop of a hat."

"Well, those two may be gone, but that doesn't mean there still aren't some good cooks out there today," Ana said, regaining her perspective. "I've been keeping an eye on that woman all dressed up so fancy with the Chicken on the Sofa tent, myself. I tell you, they've been flocking to her, although I have no idea what chicken on the sofa is. Sounds like something a child spilled on the furniture to me."

"And how about that tiny little woman roamin' all around the place with samples of her cheese balls on toothpicks? Seems to me like she's givin' away the store, if ya ask me."

"There may be a method to her madness, though. Did you gather your courage and try one?"

Maribelle drew back at the question as if an unpleasant odor had just assaulted her nostrils. "No, I most certainly did not. It's my opinion that we should all stay on our own turf. I believe in lettin' the crowd come to me, although once they get within shoutin' distance, I'm liable to reach out with one a' those old-fashioned vaudeville hooks and snag 'em."

Ana had a good laugh over the image. "I actually took one of her cheese balls when she offered me one. I guess I was more than a little curious. I have to tell you, it was pretty tasty. Good thing I'm not up against her in the appetizer category. Good thing neither of us is."

Maribelle snickered as she started walking. "Well, I don't think we should be gone from our tents any longer than necessary. So how 'bout we go back, smile real pretty for everyone, and sell some of our great desserts to them that's got a sweet tooth? We'll stand out all the more actin' like adults after this knockdown drag-out with soup and sausage."

Ana followed, frowning as she thought about the spectacle of people wasting food that way. She had been brought up required to eat everything on her plate before finally being excused from the table. After saying grace over food, the Estrella family considered it impious not to finish it, and throwing food at one of her many siblings would have gotten her grounded for at least a week.

Ah, well—back to the task at hand and selling her delicious pigeon peas cake to all comers!

Ana and Maribelle had not been the only ones watching the food fight and Maura Beth's disqualification of the Corinth women out on the perimeter of the crowd, however. Hardy and Lula Posey had reluctantly ventured out to the lake to assess everything, particularly since their daughter was intimately involved in the Grand Opening. Although Renette had invited—no, practically begged—them to tour the new library, they had told her they would not do so under any circumstances, knowing that it was full of material they found objectionable and still wanted off the shelves. But Hardy had relented at the last minute.

"Elder Warren called me up and told me that he's just talked to God, and I think we need to document things for him and the church in case we go through with our picketing plans," he had told Lula. "Renette dudd'n even have to know we're there. If she spied us even for a second, she'd be full of questions and all that, since we've quarreled about this before. Our little girl is too headstrong for her own good. I don't know where that came from, since you've always been an obedient wife."

Once the two ladies had started assaulting each other with food and Maura Beth McShay had rushed out to stop them, the Poseys had had to move quickly to the back of the gathering to avoid being spotted in the midst of their espionage.

"We are on a mission," Hardy had reminded his wife. "We will have a nice little surprise for that bossy Miz McShay down the road, no matter what. We'll have our say in this."

After Maura Beth's dismissal of Bit Sessions and Gwen Beetles, the Poseys had walked back to their car with a self-righteous vengeance. "Now, you see, Lula, that woman acts like a virtual dictator. She picks out our library books with no accounting and picks the winners and losers in a contest like that. She hadn't oughta've kicked those women out like that. That was just way too harsh to my way of thinkin'. I'd just like to know who made her judge and jury of all creation. Everyone seems to be afraid to stand up to her these days—even Councilman Sparks—and the worst part is, she's got our little Renette in her tentacles and won't let her go. Seems to me she needs to be brought down a notch or two, and we'd be doin' the town of Cherico a service if we were the ones who did the deed."

Lula said nothing, nodding vigorously.

"We will bide our time and wait for the right moment. We'll get our point across one way or another."

This time, Lula spoke up with conviction. "We must save our sweet little girl, that's all I know. Since when do librarians have more rights than parents? Sometimes I think the world's been turned on its head."

Hardy made a strange little noise as if something had caught in his throat, halfway between a grunt and a gurgle. "After all, we only want what's best for her. What in the world could be wrong with that?"

7

Coronation of a Queen

It was now nearly one o'clock, and a long line had been forming for the last two hours just inside the front door of the library, extending all the way down to the computer terminals for Becca Brachle's long-awaited book signing. At the moment, there were nearly two dozen people waiting to snap up a copy of the *Best of the Becca Broccoli Show Cookbook*, and Becca sat at her table beaming as she wielded her pen masterfully and with great patience.

"And how do you want this signed?" she was saying to a very tall woman wearing pink capri pants and flats. It was a question she was happy to repeat, since it meant her sales were going well. In fact, they were exceeding all of her expectations, and she was going to run out of stock at this rate.

"Oh," the woman began, "could you write, 'To my best girlfriend forever, Shellie Raye Compton'? That's me, of course. Now, I know we're not even close to being that, but when my grandchildren see it someday, they won't know the difference, will they? So maybe you could fudge just a little?"

Becca remained pleasant and pliable. The customer was always right. "Good point." She quickly signed the title page and handed over the copy with a smile and a nod. "Mission accomplished."

Next in line was Douglas McShay, who had been partially hidden from view by the Compton woman's height, and Becca stood up, leaned across the table, and gave him a big hug. "You snuck up on me, you rascal, but I'm happy to see you as usual. Where's Connie?"

"She's out sampling all the food. She says she wants to cast an informed vote for best in show. Funny the way she puts things sometimes. So I've been assigned the task of getting a copy of your cookbook for us. But she still thinks you should have had a tent out there today, and I agree with her. We both swear by your okra and tomato gumbo stock, just to mention one recipe we love. Connie says she never would have thought of cutting the okra on the bias to soak up more of the seasonings. So simple, but also genius."

Becca put down her pen, wrinkled her nose, and shook her head. "Thank you both for the compliment, but I just don't think it would be fair to have a professional in the contest. I ran *The Becca Broccoli Show* on the radio for years for profit. Besides, all you have to do is look at this line to know I'm already a winner today. I don't say it to brag, but I do think I would have had a definite advantage with my expertise."

Douglas leaned in and whispered, "No matter

what, you'll still be our Queen of the Cookbooks." Then he forked over his money, and while Becca signed his copy, added, "Where's my little godson today?"

Becca handed over his cookbook and eyed him with amused skepticism. "You think I'd bring him along with me for this? No, Justin's watching Markie at home. You should see the two of them together. I never thought my Stout Fella would actually look forward to something like diaper duty, but he does. Being a father has really changed him, Douglas. He's finally slowing down for the first time since we were married. No more dashing off to the office to sell real estate at the crack of dawn until he has a heart attack like he did. He's got some much-needed balance in his life, and Markie's the reason. We should have become parents long before now, of course. For the longest time I thought we were never going to get there."

"That's all great news," Douglas said, glancing back over his shoulder. "When Connie and I had Lindy, it really changed our lives for the better. I've heard some people say that becoming parents tied them down and their lives were never their own again, but Connie and I always felt that it liberated us. It brought out the best in us. Maybe you have to go through it to understand what I mean."

"I already understand," Becca told him. "I can't

imagine our lives without Markie. That says it all."

"Well, I've taken up enough of your time," Douglas said, briefly looking over his shoulder. "These folks behind me are probably getting impatient, so I'll mosey on out to the tents and try to track our dear Connie down before she samples everybody out of business."

Becca laughed. "Good idea. I want to get out there myself with my taste buds and give everybody a fair shake."

It was a good thing that Voncille and Locke Linwood appeared near the end of the autograph line, since they took up more than their share of Becca's time getting their copy of her cookbook signed. The bond among all members of The Cherry Cola Book Club had only grown stronger with the passage of time, and they supported one another whenever and wherever they could.

"We meant to get out here much earlier," Locke was explaining at the table while pointing to his watch. "But Voncille held us up. She just couldn't seem to decide what she wanted to wear. She tried on about six different outfits, but she kept saying none of them would do. I thought she looked great in everything she tried on, as usual, but nothing I said seemed to make any difference to her. Used to be, she'd take my compliments as gospel, but not so much anymore. Are we turning into an old married couple?"

Voncille gave him a little shove and pretended to be annoyed. "We started out an old married couple! But you just don't seem to get it, Locke. I was just trying to be patriotic." She focused on Becca. "I was rummaging through the closet trying to find something that had a touch of red, white, and blue in it—all three. Well, it turns out I had something red, something blue, and something white, but they weren't all in the same dress. Now how I could've gotten by all these years without such a thing, I just don't know."

Locke managed a conspiratorial wink and a little nod as he rapped his knuckles on Becca's table. "And the Earth stopped spinning on its axis."

"You men have it so easy," Voncille said, tugging at his sleeve as if she were getting the attention of a disobedient child. "There you stand in your pressed seersucker suit without a care in the world. You didn't have to give your outfit a moment's thought. Same thing with your hair. You just brush it once or twice every morning, and you're good to greet the world. Show me a woman who gets away with that sort of thing, and I'll show you a scene from a horror movie."

"For heaven's sake, Voncille, I think the blue dress you have on is just fine," he told her, trying to calm her down. "I've always liked it. Don't you think it fits the bill, Becca?"

"I certainly do," Becca said, winking at Locke.

"And I love your little American flag lapel pin. That's about as patriotic as you can get."

"Well, we do have bunting draped all across our front porch on Perry Street," Voncille continued, somewhat placated. "I saw to that. Seems like all our neighbors do, too. And we all fly the flag proudly on our porches, too. Perry Street always gets spruced up like that, and I always want to do my part on the Fourth of July. It helps me honor my Frank's memory, and Locke has always been a perfect angel in understanding how I feel about his MIA status." She blew him a little kiss. "There's not a jealous bone in his body."

"Anyhow, we're here," Locke added, catching her kiss and then taking a deep breath after the crisis had passed. "We saw you talking to Douglas at the head of the line a little earlier. Has all the book club gang made it out here yet?"

Becca handed over their signed copy with a smile. "Just about. I'm holding out one copy for Nora Duddney and another for Audra Neely, though. I'm getting close to being sold out. Looks like I should have had a larger print run, but then you don't want to be stuck with a garage full of books, either."

Locke looked suddenly thoughtful. "You underestimated your popularity, Becca. As a matter of fact, Maura Beth ought to consider having all of us bring nothing but recipes from your cookbook at one of our future Cherry Cola Book Club meetings. I bet that'd be a smash hit, since everything we'd have to choose from would be one of your specialties."

Becca was beaming. "Well, as you know, I'm always in charge of assigning who brings what to the buffet table. I'll mention it to Maura Beth next time we talk. Meanwhile, you two should get out there and sample some of the great food everyone's raving about before it's all gone."

"I am the ultimate equal opportunity food sampler," Becca was saying to Mrs. Olla Bowman after taking a bite of the woman's orange and lemon meringue dessert.

A few moments earlier, Olla had pursued Becca aggressively with her carnival barker's pitch: "Come git yer meringue, light as a feather, sunny as a Florida afternoon, come and git it! What about you there with the blond hair and that cute figure? What's yer name?"

After Becca had identified herself, she thought Olla was going to faint as she fanned her face. "You mean you're the real Becca Broccoli—the one who was on the radio show all those years?"

"One and the same, last time I looked."

"Why, you look even prettier than I imagined while I was listening to you. I just got this picture of you in my head as a mite bigger than you really are. I mean, you're so petite. Wish I could be like that. Well, I was a decent size back in my twenties, but somehow, when you get over fifty, the calories just don't behave the way they used to. Know what I mean?"

They were now both standing in front of Olla's tent beneath a sign that read OLLA'S HEAVENLY MERINGUE, and Becca had not been able to resist the compliments. "Well, you got to me where I live. I do like to watch my figure, and I'm right proud it didn't get blown out of the water by my pregnancy. I've got a six-month-old baby boy to show for it all, and that's the most important thing—win or lose the pounds."

"Well, congratulations. You look wonderful. How'd you manage it?"

Becca leaned in and pursed her lips dramatically. "Turns out all my cravings weren't sweets or carbs. I was a sourpuss, if you catch my drift. Pickles, sauerkraut, lemon juice on everything— oh, I guess I did develop a thing for sour cream. But I didn't put it on baked potatoes. I just had a spoonful or two out of the carton every now and then. Minimal damage, I guess you could say."

"You were lucky then. My husband practically had to put in a year's supply of doughnuts and cinnamon rolls. That was my thing—sugar and cinnamon."

Becca pointed to her paper plate. "Well, after everything else I've eaten so far, your meringue is just the light touch I need. This is delicious— especially the sauce. It's so citrus-y."

"Why, thank you. There's a lot of orange and lemon in it, of course," Olla said. "That's a right high compliment, comin' from you, Miz Brachle. I used to listen to *The Becca Broccoli Show* every single morning it was on. Set my alarm by it. You can ask my husband, Marty. He used to complain all the time about me wakin' him up that early."

Olla pointed to her ample waist and gave her prominent right thigh a playful pat. "Speakin' of figures, I don't keep mine anymore. I gave it permission to run away and hide long ago."

Becca laughed. "I'll have to remember that one if it ever happens to me. Very diplomatic way of putting it." Then she finished off the small piece of meringue she had bought, running her tongue quickly across her lips. "You know, all of you out here today are making it very difficult when it comes to casting my vote. Every time I think I've made up my mind, something else I eat changes it. I haven't found anything I don't like so far."

Indeed, since her book signing had ended—and earlier than expected since she had sold out completely and had to apologize profusely to the few who were still standing in line—Becca had mingled among the other Chericoans crowding the venue and made stops at the following other tents with their big signs:

MRS. FRIEZE'S CHEEZE BALLZ
GOURMET SANDWICHES TO GO

173

HOLA, AMIGOS!
GET YOUR NO-SUGAR-ADDED DESSERT HERE
JUST WATERMELON
ALL-AMERICAN APPLE PIE
PAULA'S PEACH ICE CREAM
THE SPAGHETTI IS READY
APPETIZING APPETIZERS

She felt just like a little kid at the circus, trying to cram as much food as possible into a compressed amount of time and practically daring her stomach not to cooperate.

"Please tell all your friends to try me," Olla said, as Becca dropped her paper plate and fork into the nearby trash can.

"Will do, and I'll give your dessert strong consideration, believe me. Who knows? You might be the winner."

"I've got my fingers crossed."

"Good luck to you."

Becca had no sooner turned around than she bumped into Periwinkle and Parker Place, still making their rounds of the food tents.

"Too many people have recognized me," Periwinkle said, giving Becca a nudge. "And they all keep asking why I just didn't go ahead and have a Twinkle tent. But I just know they would've voted for my food even if I told them not to. I'm stickin' to my guns on that."

"You've never seen so much finger-pointing and

gasping in your life as we've walked around today tasting this and that," Mr. Place added. " 'Oh, you work down at The Twinkle, don'tcha?' and 'I just love your pies and your crème brûlée,' and that sorta thing. All these wonderful folks have made us feel like rock stars, if you'll pardon the comparison."

Becca laughed and patted Periwinkle's hand. "What a wonderful predicament! To be the only restaurant game in town. But look at it this way—it's when they stop recognizing you that you'll have to start worrying."

"You got yourself a point there," Periwinkle said. "But you know what? My taste buds have already told me there are some really talented cooks sellin' their food out here today. I may have to schmooze some of 'em and get their recipes. That Chicken on the Sofa lady, for instance. I wish I could talk the way she does—you know, sorta elegant and slow the way Martha Stewart does. Be sure and try her dish, Becca. Why, if I put that on The Twinkle menu, I bet it'd outsell our tomato aspics by a country mile, Parker."

"That would be saying something," Becca added.

Mr. Place looked down and patted his stomach a couple of times. "I'm getting near as full as a tick, and we still have some more tents to sample. You about ready to move on, Peri?"

"Full speed ahead. We'll catch up with you later, Becca."

As they walked away, Becca realized she, too, was getting uncomfortably full even before she had finished her sampling. First, she had over-indulged at the Tuminello family's The Spaghetti Is Ready tent. "Won't you try our spaghetti with a little kick? We don't mind telling you our secret is red pepper flakes and a little cayenne. If you like spicy, you'll like us," the jolly, overfed Valerie Tuminello had told her as she walked by.

Then she had eaten one too many Dijon deviled eggs at the Appetizing Appetizers tent, which belonged to the enthusiastic and diminutive Mrs. Penny Murphy. "Mine aren't your average, boring deviled eggs," Mrs. Murphy had insisted. "No, sir. You just try one. Bet you'll have two if you do. Maybe even three or four after that. My family just gobbles 'em up whenever I fix 'em."

Stuffed to the gills or not, Becca intended to find room to give that Chicken on the Sofa a try. Beyond that, she was enjoying all the activity going on around her. The adults were laughing and chatting, eating and drinking, and occasionally bumping into one another while politely excusing themselves. The children were slurping up slices of watermelon and spitting out the seeds right and left, or tugging at their parents' sleeves and begging them to buy a taste of this and that, "pretty please"; a few were even waving tiny American flags that the library had been giving out free all day. Here and there, the most hyperactive of the children could be seen running amok with sparklers, brandishing them high above their heads as if they had captured blazing comets out of the sky.

In short, her fellow Chericoans were doing everything people should be doing during a celebration like the Fourth of July.

Maura Beth had assigned ballot box duty to Marydell Crumpton and her newest front desk clerk, Helen Porter. The voting precinct, so to speak, had been set up on a small table with a red, white, and blue tablecloth halfway between the food tents and the front door of the library. Maura Beth would have had her oldest clerk, Emma Frost, involved as well, but her husband Leonard's Alzheimer's was requiring more and more of her time, and Emma had asked for the Fourth off—despite the Grand Opening. Voting for Best Appetizer, Best Entrée, Best Dessert, and the Queen of the Cookbooks title, itself, had been going on all day, but there was the annoying little matter of Bit Sessions and Gwen Beetles to expunge from the results before proceeding any further.

"Helen, you have my permission to take the box into my office and remove all ballots cast for those two ladies," she was explaining in hushed tones. "It will look fishy if you do it out here in front of everyone. We don't want anyone to think the contest is rigged. Marydell, I want you to stay here at the table and tell everyone that voting will resume in fifteen minutes or so. You don't have to go into detail."

"What if they press me? I was thinking I could tell them some mischievous child had dropped a cricket in there just to play a joke, and we needed to deal with the little fiend," Marydell said, halfway serious about the suggestion.

Helen looked completely baffled. "Which one is the fiend?"

"The cricket, of course," Marydell answered, shifting her eyes back and forth. "But it really doesn't matter one bit, Helen, since we've made both of them up out of whole cloth. Honestly."

"You sure do things differently here in Cherico."

Maura Beth thought it all over and broke out in a smile. "That's not half-bad, Marydell. Yes, let's go with that."

Helen still seemed all at sea, being the new kid on the block. "We go with cricket removal?"

"More or less," Maura Beth said. "Everyone's having such a good time with the food and the library tours, I believe they'll just shrug it off as par for the course. And, yes, you're right, Helen, we definitely do things differently here in our little town. You'll get used to it. I know I had to. Now, I just embrace it all and consider myself a true Chericoan."

And with that, Helen was off to the races.

Shortly after, Periwinkle Place sidled up to the table, chewing her customary wad of gum a mile a minute, and patted Maura Beth on the back. "You should be proud of yourself. Everybody seems to be havin' a real good time inside and out. Hey, I even learned somethin' today when I went into that book processing room or whatever it is, and I got to beep that scanner a few times on those bar codes. That was fun. I was like a little kid with a new toy at Christmas. There's a lot more to libraries than people think, and you've found lotsa ways to show it."

"Couldn't have put it better myself," Maura Beth said, turning her way. "Where's your talented, handsome pastry man?"

"Parker's over there finishing up with the desserts. He says he's decided he's only gonna vote on the sweets since that's his bailiwick. By the way, I've finally eaten more than my fill of everything, so I'm ready to do my duty and vote. Where do I do that?"

Maura Beth decided to give their little white lie a trial run. "Can you come back in about fifteen minutes? A cricket somehow jumped into the ballot box slot when no one was looking, and we're right in the middle of extracting it. As far as I know, it's not registered to vote, so we're not violating its civil rights."

"You are somethin' else, girl. But the crickets have been out in droves this summer. We even

179

found one on the floor of the kitchen down at The Twinkle. We figured it crawled up through the drain. So we had to have the drains flushed. Maybe I shouldn't mention that too loud, but it's kinda like one a' those old-fashioned science fiction movies where gigantic insects take over the world. Well, I guess I can come back a little later to vote. When are the polls gonna close?"

"Four o'clock. That'll give us a good hour to tally the results, and then Councilman Sparks will do his cheesy politician thing and announce the winners in our mini-auditorium at five."

Periwinkle's laugh was prolonged. "Now, please don't tell me you're still at war with him?"

"Not so much anymore. It's just that . . . well, Durden Sparks will be Durden Sparks no matter what. You should have been here this morning when he took full credit for *his* new library. He's always running for office."

"Yes, that didn't set too well with my sister," Marydell added from behind the table. "Mamie's all about being the center of attention, as you all know. But she and I did match Durden's generous donation, so I think we deserved at least a mention of some kind."

"I agree with you, of course. Where is your sister, by the way?" Maura Beth wanted to know. "I haven't seen her since the ribbon cutting."

"She went home fretting—said she had a headache. But I think Durden got to her with all that speechifying. And she used to think the world of him. If you want my opinion, I think she's always had this secret crush on him. But now I think she doesn't like the fact that you've gotten so chummy with him lately. And to be honest with you, I think it still bothers her that I work for you at the front desk. She says it's so plebian for a Crumpton to be doing such work, but as I told you when you hired me, it's such a relief to get out of the house and get away from her bossiness. That just hasn't dawned on her yet, but despite everything, I don't have the heart to tell her the truth. Imagine that—me wanting to spare *her* feelings."

"You'd think she'd have gotten over my hiring you by now, but I don't know what I'd do without you—and Renette and Emma and Helen. Because, really, it wasn't all that long ago that I was doing front desk duty myself in that dark old dungeon on Shadow Alley we used to call a library."

Periwinkle chucked her on the arm playfully. "You wore many hats, girl. Same as I still do down at The Twinkle, and so does my Parker."

As if on cue, Mr. Place sauntered up and joined them, raving about the last of the dessert he was devouring on his paper plate while gesticulating with a plastic fork. "This is something else, ladies. You've got to try it."

"What is it?" Maura Beth asked.

His angular, mahogany-tinged features lit up.

"Pigeon peas cake from that Hola, Amigos! tent. I even asked that delightful young woman if she'd share the recipe with me. But she shook her head pretty emphatically and said it was a family secret. Now, that's something I can fully appreciate. You never want to give away the franchise in this cutthroat business. Next thing you know, somebody's making hay off your pet recipe and swears they invented it."

"Ah, yes. Ana Estrella, Cherico's newest citizen. She'll be doing PR for Spurs 'R' Us. In fact, I think she's already doing it by entering the competition. I certainly think they hired the right person for the job."

"Looks to me like she's doing quite well out there today. I had to stand in line for my slice." Then he screwed up his face as if reconsidering. "But, you know, I'd also have to say the same thing about the lady with the no-sugar-added cherry cake. She had a few takers, too, and she got me to thinking—I really ought to offer at least one no-sugar-added dessert down at The Twinkle. Lotsa diabetes running around these days. We ought to cater to that market, too."

"Just as long as you don't cut back on your tried-and-true treats," Periwinkle added. "We don't want to throw the baby out with the bathwater. As you say, we send Barry out in the delivery van every day with orders for your grasshopper pie and all the other goodies you've become famous for."

"Which is why it would've been wrong for us to put up a food tent. We needed to give some other folks a shot at winning."

Maura Beth pointed to her watch. "Well, it won't be too long before we reveal the winners."

"Speaking of which, I'm ready to vote right now," Mr. Place said. "I know something new under the sun when I taste it."

Maura Beth and Marydell exchanged amused glances, and Maura Beth said, "The ballot box will be back in a few minutes if you can wait around. There's an unexpected glitch we have to take care of first."

Periwinkle leaned in to her husband, chuckling under her breath. "Somethin' about crickets runnin' amok, I hear."

He drew back as he swallowed the last of his cake. "You don't say? Well, I guess they have to celebrate the Fourth, too."

Maura Beth was especially proud of the new library's mini-auditorium. Draped in red, white, and blue bunting throughout and seating up to four hundred people with a stage as well, it was the perfect setting for the announcement of the food tent winners. There was standing room only as Councilman Sparks tested the microphone on the stage just after five o'clock with Maura Beth standing beside him waiting to hand out the awards.

"Uh, one and a two and a three," Councilman Sparks said in imitation of Lawrence Welk's trademark phrase.

Maura Beth was caught off guard but managed a smile. "An unexpected touch of humor this afternoon, I see."

He backed away from the mike and lowered his voice, speaking out of the side of his mouth. "Why not? Isn't this a happy occasion? Haven't you . . . I mean, haven't we gotten what we wanted?"

The slip wasn't lost on Maura Beth. It reminded her once again that she had forced the man's hand behind the scenes where the construction of the new library was concerned; but if he still held a grudge of any kind, he was just going to have to deal with it. There were rows and rows of smiling, chatting Chericoans seated in front of them to provide proof that this much-needed addition to the town's infrastructure was a huge hit. She had stood her ground and risen to the task of dealing with a good ole boy politician who had had it in for her from the very beginning. Still, her instincts were to be gracious and say nothing about the past.

Councilman Sparks returned to the mike, cleared his throat, and continued in his usual, schmoozing style. "Good afternoon, ladies and gentlemen. If you're like me, you've stuffed yourselves on some mighty good food that was offered out there today in those food tents. I know I had some tough choices to make, but then, that's always the case with me when it comes to eating. I guess I'm one of the lucky ones who don't put on weight too easily—one of those metabolisms, you know."

There were a few groans in the audience, perhaps from those who struggled mightily with their caloric intake on a daily basis, and Councilman Sparks realized almost instantly that he had struck a nerve. Best to move on.

"At any rate, the results of our food tent competition have been tallied now, and we have our winners in the Best Appetizer, Best Entrée, Best Dessert, and overall Queen of the Cookbooks categories. There's some big prize money on the line here, I've been told. So, how're we doing out there with the suspense, ladies and gentlemen?"

The level of audience buzzing only increased, and someone even shouted, "Don't give us indigestion, Councilman. Get on with it!"

He laughed as if he'd just heard the funniest joke in the world, even though he had had better days at the podium; but he finally took a sheet of paper out of his jacket pocket and thumped it for effect. The man would have played to an audience if he had been sleepwalking. "Message received loud and clear. I just thought a little build-up would be nice, the way they do on television." He referred quickly to the sheet and began. "So, our big winner in the Best Appetizer category is . . . oh, well, whaddaya know? It's Mrs. Marzetta Frieze for her cheese balls. Did I pronounce it right? Is it Mar-zetta? And is your last name pronounced like *freeze?*"

A startling, high-pitched scream managed to fill the auditorium even as Councilman Sparks was speaking, as Marzetta popped up out of her seat and raced to the stage as if someone had set her on fire. There, Councilman Sparks shook her hand and offered his congratulations, after which Maura Beth handed her an envelope, and said, "Now, Marzetta, don't spend it all in the same place, as they say."

"I thought your MRS. FRIEZE'S CHEEZE BALLZ sign was pretty darn clever. Smart marketing, and I've seen my share of it," Councilman Sparks added. "What do they call it—alliteration?"

Then came the torrent of words that only Maura Beth was prepared to expect. Unfortunately, it would have been very bad form to forbid Marzetta to ramble as she did. There was nothing left but to grin and bear it.

"Yes, you pronounced my name perfect, sir. Marzetta it is, and when I was little, I used to think my mama and daddy were playin' the worst trick in the world on me with that name, but then I kinda liked it as I got older 'cause there wudd'n anyone else with a name as close to crazy as mine. But, anyway, I just knew if I took a few chances that I would win—I mean, what's investing in a box of toothpicks these days? And my mama—may she rest in peace—would be so proud I took the bull by the horns 'cause that was her recipe I fixed, and I guess all of you know I wasn't shy about giving out samples, but I figured why not get everybody hooked and coming back for more. But, anyway, I live out in the country and don't come into town all that much except to shop for groceries at The Cherico Market 'cause you can't live on cheese balls and cheese balls alone, you know, and I do thank each and every one of you for voting for me today and also for coming out in the first place because it was really hot out there. But the air conditioning here inside this new library sure feels mighty good, doesn't it?" As if to convince everyone of this vital truth, she actually stopped to fan her face with her hand, and said, "I didn't see anybody doin' this."

Having fortunately been given the merest hint of an opening, Maura Beth lost no time in running with it, and said, "No, I think everyone was very comfortable in the library today. So, let's give Marzetta another big hand, shall we, folks? And then to relieve everyone's suspense, let's move on to the Best Entrée category, shall we, Councilman Sparks?"

He took her cue and referred once again to the list of winners, as Marzetta returned to her seat, brandishing her envelope above her head. "And in the Best Entrée category, our winner is . . . Mrs. Aleitha Larken for her . . . uh, Chicken on the Sofa. Am I reading that right?"

"That's right," Maura Beth whispered. "I tried it, and it was absolutely delicious. She would have gotten my vote."

Again there was vigorous applause as the elegant Aleitha sashayed to the stage to receive her prize envelope. Then someone in the audience shouted, "We want a speech!"

"I'd be happy to express my emotions," she began, as poised a speaker as Marzetta had been all over the map. "First, I want to thank all of you who voted for my little family tradition. Now that my children are grown and out of the house, it's a thrill to bring back all those memories with this recipe, and I shall use this prize money to travel to see them for the holidays this fall. They are scattered to the winds. But again—thank you for honoring my divine Chicken Divan—alias my Chicken on the Sofa." She paused to wink at her audience. "It's the sour cream that does the trick, if any of you are interested. You taste a little something different, but then, you don't quite know what it is."

"Are you sharing your recipe?" someone in the first row asked.

"I'll be most happy to. It's easy as pie. We'll exchange e-mail addresses if you'd like. Catch up with me after the ceremony."

And with that, Aleitha made a delicate, wand-like gesture as if she were imitating Glinda the Good Witch from *The Wizard of Oz*, nodded gracefully to light applause, and headed back to her seat.

"Lovely, Mrs. Larken. Just lovely and graceful. And next," Councilman Sparks said, "we have the Best Dessert category. Now there was a lot of competition for this one because who doesn't have a sweet tooth, especially on holidays like this? I know I do." He paused to milk the moment further. "I know we had meringue and chocolate pie and brownies and ice cream and several different cakes and other pies to choose from." There was one last pause and then, "The winner is . . . oh, it's Mrs. Maribelle Pleasance for her no-sugar-added cherry cake."

Maribelle rose excitedly, clutching a hand to her chest in dramatic fashion as the applause exploded around her. "You're kiddin' me?"

Ana Estrella jumped up nearly simultaneously, hugging her newly found friend. "You deserved it, Maribelle. Your cake was beyond delicious. You march right up there and get your prize."

Maribelle appeared to be in shock as she made her way to the stage, shaking her head in disbelief, and she kept staring at the prize envelope Maura Beth handed her as if it were a star that had fallen from the heavens into her hands. When she finally spoke, her voice was trembling, coming in spurts.

"I just never thought I'd win, folks . . . but I thank y'all from the bottom of my heart. . . . Now, I know everybody's talkin' about these healthy recipes all the time . . . I mean, how good for you they are and all . . . but just between you and me and the fence post, some of 'em are a bit much to swallow, if you know what I mean. All my friends who have to watch their sugar intake swear by this one, though . . . in fact, my best friend, Fern, says, 'You don't feel like you're bein' punished for your sugar sins.'"

The audience laughed, and someone even said, "You got that right, sister."

"Well, anyways, I'm glad y'all liked my recipe. And I'll be happy to share it with any of you who'd like to try it for yourselves . . . I mean, all y'all have to do is just come up to me after this is over, and we'll share our contact information. Now I know I sound like I oughta be livin' in another century with the way I talk, but I'm up on all these e-mailin' and Goog-er-lin' computer things and such as that, believe it or not. Thank y'all again so much."

On the way to her seat, Maribelle was inter- cepted by a rather thin woman wearing a straw hat and a pair of white slacks who got everyone's immediate attention by whistling with her fingers. How could such a loud, sharp sound come out of such a small woman? It caused more than a few wide-eyed faces across the crowd.

"I'm Nan McCrary, and I just wanted to say to everybody real quick-like that I have to watch my diabetes real close, and the only thing I had out there today at the tents was unsweet tea to drink and a little slice of this good woman's cake. It was real sweet a' you, Maribelle, to think about those of us who aren't as worried about calories as much as we are about sugar. It's hidden everywhere in just about everything. So that's why I voted for you, and I'm so glad you won."

There was another smattering of applause, and then it was time for the big moment. The coronation of the Queen of the Cookbooks and the $5,000 prize money that went with it. Once again, Councilman Sparks announced the category but held back longer than was necessary. It was safe to say that nobody had any idea who might actually claim it.

"And the winner is . . ." he said finally. "Oh, wow . . . it's Ana Estrella for her pigeon peas cake. Come on up here, Ana, and let us crown you Queen!"

Now it was Maribelle's turn to embrace *her* friend. "I can't hardly believe it. We both won something."

If anything, Ana was even more incredulous than Maribelle had been once she'd reached the stage and accepted the congratulations of Councilman Sparks and Maura Beth. Her prize envelope and a trophy followed; then a tiara, which Councilman Sparks pulled out of his coat pocket and carefully placed on her head.

"I now crown you—Ana Estrella, our very first Queen of the Cookbooks of Greater Cherico!"

Ana gasped with genuine delight as she reached up to touch the tiara gingerly. "These aren't real diamonds, are they?"

"Costume jewelry," Maura Beth whispered, leaning in. "But still sparkly. I had one that was just like that growing up that I wore at every Mardi Gras parade until I was twelve."

Then Ana's public relations skills kicked in effortlessly. "What a surprise, ladies and gentlemen. I am truly overwhelmed. But I did tell myself that if I managed to win, I was not going to keep the prize money for myself." She turned Maura Beth's way. "Instead, Mrs. McShay, I would like to donate it to the library with the stipulation that you use it to purchase bilingual and English as a Second Language materials. Perhaps you can start a section dedicated to that."

Maura Beth was smiling but also seemed slightly taken aback. "Are you absolutely sure you want to do that, Ana?"

"Yes, I'm sure. With Spurs 'R' Us coming to town and the plans the company has for expansion down the road, I can tell you as their public relations specialist that there will eventually be people moving to Cherico who might be able to take advantage of ESL materials. I'm just thinking ahead."

"It's a good thought. Up until now, we haven't had the budget for ESL books and audios, but we certainly have the shelving for an expansion like that. Perhaps we can call it the Ana Estrella Collection."

Ana handed the envelope back with a gracious smile. "What a wonderful gesture on your part. Then it's all settled. Except . . . I will keep the tiara. Or do I have to turn it in next year when a new winner is crowned?"

Maura Beth and Councilman Sparks exchanged wide-eyed looks. "Actually, the councilman and I hadn't thought about it. But I think we can afford to give a new one to the winner every year, don't you?"

"City Hall approves."

"There's your answer."

"I'm almost in a 'tiaras for everyone in the audience' mood," Councilman Sparks added, grinning at the crowd.

"Well, isn't this all just too cozy for words!" an angry female voice suddenly shouted from the back row.

Everyone turned practically in unison in time to see Bit Sessions popping up and wagging a finger at the proceedings on the stage. "This whole thing was rigged from start to finish. You gave the top prize to that woman because she's in cahoots with Spurs 'R' Us, and this is just a big pat on the back for them. Plus, you kicked me outta the competition unfairly, Miz McShay, and you know it!"

Councilman Sparks looked baffled and then squinted at the audience. "Who is that, and what on earth is she talking about, Maura Beth?"

The two huddled for a few moments with their backs to the audience, while Ana looked on uncomfortably. Finally, Maura Beth came up for air and began addressing the charges hurled at her. "First of all, Mrs. Sessions, I distinctly remember asking you to pack up and leave the premises, and then—"

"I did pack up my tent, and I was almost ready to drive back to Corinth. But then I decided to sneak back in here and stand up for myself."

"As I was saying before I was so rudely interrupted . . . you and Mrs. Beetles were disrupting the entire venue earlier this afternoon. You had everyone gathered around to watch your childish food fight, and we simply couldn't permit you to continue. And our awards were certainly not rigged. Once you and Mrs. Beetles were disqualified, we had to remove all ballots that were cast for either of you, and that was well-supervised. It was the only fair thing to do. Plus, I don't see Mrs. Beetles here making a spectacle of herself."

"That's her choice, but she always was a wimp

of the worst kind, full of preachy, self-righteous words."

"And it's that kind of name-calling that got you kicked out in the first place, Mrs. Sessions."

"It doesn't matter what you say—I intend to sue you!" Bit continued, raising her voice another decibel. "I cry foul right here in front of everyone. This was supposed to be about the food, not personalities. I should be the Queen of the Cookbooks, not this woman that can't even speak English!"

"I beg your pardon?!" Ana said, more surprised than angry. "I speak the King's English."

"Hmmph! Her tent sign was in Spanish. What was that all about?"

"'Hola, amigos' simply means 'hello, friends.' My family originally came to America from Puerto Rico. And this is the Fourth of July we are celebrating today. That's what this country is all about—*e pluribus unum*."

"Now what language are you speaking?"

"Latin."

"You're an outsider, then."

Several women surrounding Bit stood up together, and one of them shouted, "We came all the way over from Corinth today to vote for our friend. We think her food is the best, and we support her completely!"

"Yes, we will not be moved," Bit added. "We're standing right here until we get justice. If necessary, I will snatch that tiara off that woman's head!"

Maura Beth couldn't decide whether to frown or let her jaw drop. "Mrs. Sessions, you will do no such thing. You are way out of line. And calling Ms. Estrella an outsider is completely ridiculous. She actually lives here in Cherico. You don't, and you're giving the good people of Corinth a bad name with your remarks. I know they would be horrified at your behavior."

"You can say what you want, but we intend to stand our ground and fight for our rights!"

"For heaven's sake, don't be so ridiculous. This is most certainly not the March on Washington. We're just judging food on the Fourth of July. You need to stick a pickle in it."

"And I'd say that's some pretty rude language comin' from a librarian. I still insist this woman that won is an outsider. These immigrants are taking over everything these days."

Maura Beth and Ana gasped together.

To say that the mood of most of the audience had become testy as Bit Sessions continued to argue was an understatement. There were even a few boos here and there, causing Councilman Sparks to pull out his cell phone and text Mr. Peters: *Where r u? Come 2 auditorium asap & escort all ladies standing out of building.*

Not long after, the security guard arrived, walked down to the stage, had a few words with

Councilman Sparks, surveyed the crowd quickly, and did not mince words. "All right, ladies, I have orders to those of you who are standing up right now to show you the door. Maybe even a jail cell. So what's it going to be?"

Everyone except Bit Sessions dropped down immediately in almost comical fashion. They were like a family of meerkats who had just spotted a predator, quickly retreating to the safety of their holes.

"You must be talking about me, sir, but I'll tell you to your face that I'm not giving in," Bit said, her voice still full of defiance. "You can use those strong-arm tactics all you want, but you haven't heard the last of me. And if you use police brutality on me, I'm taking this all the way to the Supreme Court of the United States if I have to. I'm completely serious."

"Yes, well, I'll be sure and notify the media," Mr. Peters said, approaching her with deliberation and no little sense of amusement. "Meanwhile, if you'll just come with me, please."

Councilman Sparks, Maura Beth, and the entire audience watched Bit's dramatic departure with her nose held high, but strangely, the Corinth contingent did little more than shake their heads and did not follow in protest. Amazing the effect anyone resembling a law enforcement officer had on most people!

"Well, my fellow Greater Chericoans," Councilman Sparks said, trying to regain control of the proceedings, "that concludes our awards ceremony. Congratulations again from City Hall and the Charles Durden Sparks, Crumpton, and Duddney Library to the very deserving winners, and particularly our very first Queen of the Cookbooks—Ana Estrella."

Ana did a peremptory wave as the crowd applauded weakly and began to file out. "Is Cherico always like this?" Ana asked, turning to Maura Beth.

"No," came the forceful reply. "This was nothing. Usually things are out of left field. You don't see them coming so you can duck or run and hide. But believe me, they find you wherever you are."

Ana looked distinctly uncomfortable and lowered her voice. "Maura Beth, that remark about immigrants got me to thinking—I don't want to be the cause of any ill will. I'm supposed to be promoting good feeling with my public relations job. I certainly don't want this award to backfire on me. Maybe I should just refuse the Queen of the Cookbooks title altogether. My recommendation would be that you give it instead to Maribelle Pleasance. She's a dear woman, and everyone clearly loved her no-sugar-added cake."

Maura Beth replied with conviction in her voice. "Don't pay any attention to what that Bit Sessions said. That immigrant remark was about as rude as you can get. She's an odd duck if I ever heard one quack. You earned that title by the vote of everyone who came out to sample the food. She's not even from Cherico, and I for one am glad to know that. I'd be ashamed to claim her if she were. This town needs new blood, and people like yourself fill the bill and then some. I'm glad you won, and even more thrilled that you're donating your prize money to an ESL collection. That's very forward-thinking of you."

"Well, when you put it that way, I guess I'd be doing a disservice to the library if I turned in my crown, right?"

"Absolutely. As our very first Queen of the Cookbooks, you'll always hold a special place of honor in Cherico."

8

Dressed for Fireworks

After an exhausting day at the Grand Opening during which she had answered over and over again every stupid question that had ever been asked about computer operation, Renette stood in front of her full-length bedroom mirror in her modest little apartment at six o'clock that evening. Could she believe her eyes? Who was that strange girl staring back at her so intently? What watershed moment was she about to experience in her young life?

Mirrors had always been a source of friction between Renette and her parents, particularly her mother, Lula Marlowe Posey, whose lectures were always predictable and labored: "A mirror is just another work of the Devil, Renette. He gets you to stare into 'em in all your idle moments when you are always at your weakest, and that's when he works on your vanity like the deceiver he is. Your sin is the sin of false pride because youth itself is a roller-coaster ride of temptation that makes you think the thrills are what it's all about. It is an illusion that soon fades."

It had certainly faded quickly for Lula. It was hard to imagine that she had ever been a pretty woman; even more difficult to believe that Renette's sweet nature and countenance had come out of her body. These days, Lula's mouth, never sullied with lipstick, was always set in a grim slash, her hair without style and far too long for a woman her age.

"To make any kinda fuss over your appearance is yet another sinful trap," Lula was always saying.

Everything, it seemed, was a sin in the Posey household. But Renette had never allowed herself to really believe it. She longed to live in a world in which she was free to make her own judgments and decisions; and her parents had let her know in no uncertain terms that they did not approve of her job at the library that she had applied for and won after her high school graduation.

"Too many of the books they have in there are the work of false prophets," Lula had told her the night Renette had hardly eaten a bite at dinner in announcing her library job to her parents.

On another occasion a few months later, Renette had further disappointed Hardy and Lula by revealing that she had rented an apartment and was leaving their protection of nineteen years to live on her own. "I've been saving my money from my library job because I think it's high time I lived by myself. I don't say this out of disrespect to both of you."

"But we'll take care of you until you find you a

husband to support you. That's the way it should be. Now, this place you've rented—is it one of those singles apartment complexes?" Lula had asked, bowing her head as if she had just spoken profanity. "I've heard that what goes on in places like that is a scandal."

Renette had explained that it was not one of "those places" and that she merely wanted to see what it was like "out there."

"I'm just starting out in life, Mama. You do remember what that was like, don't you?"

"Your father and I were married when we graduated from high school. That was our starting out in life, and we've never regretted it for a moment. What was good enough for us is good enough for you. Meanwhile, you'd do better to stay under our wing right here," Lula had answered. "There are people out there—particularly these awful men with no morals and their condiments—waiting to take advantage of someone like you. Have we taught you nothing?"

Renette was unable to repress an impish smile. "What kind of condiments would those be, Mama?"

"It's condoms, Lula, condoms," Hardy Posey had added in that unfailingly stern manner of his, stopping just short of banging his fist on the table. "Now, she may not have gotten the word right, but you'd better listen to your mother, Renette. She means well."

But Renette had taken a stand against the control she had been wanting to buck all her life. "Both of you always see the worst in everything and everybody. People are a whole lot nicer than you think they are. When I interviewed for the library job, Miz Mayhew couldn't have been sweeter to me. She said I was just the sort of person she was looking for, and I know I will learn a lot working for her. There's nothing wrong with wanting to make your own way in the world."

Her father had continued his cautionary tone. "But you have no idea what the world is really like, Renette. We just want to protect you from it. What kind of parents would we be if we didn't?"

"But I want to try to manage things on my own for a while. Don't you understand that?"

"What I understand is, that librarian you work for is bad news," Lula said, ganging up on her daughter. "She trades in all those scandalous books that are not fit for decent people to read. It was shameful what we found on her shelves, and when we went to her and asked her politely to remove some of them, she refused. She was right proud about that as I recall. I think that was downright irresponsible. She took no responsibility for the effects they would have on innocent children just like yourself. Witches and vampires and such as that—just to name a few—displayed just right out in the open, brazen as you please. What is the world coming to?"

"I am not a little child anymore, Mother. And I'm not nearly as innocent as you think."

Lula gasped and drew back in horror. "Are you saying what I think you're saying, young lady?"

Renette was up to the challenge and even managed a smile. "How am I supposed to know what you're saying when you don't know the difference between condoms and condiments?"

A vein in Hardy Posey's dome-like forehead with its receding hairline became more prominent as he raised his voice. "Don't you dare go and sass your mother that-a-way, young lady!"

"I wasn't sassing. I just wanted to say that Miz Mayhew takes everything into consideration when she buys every book for the library. She listens to everyone's opinion, but she doesn't believe in censorship. She doesn't think that's a library's role in the community. She says it's a slippery slope, and she wants to stay away from it under all circumstances."

"That I can certainly believe. I'm sure she justifies everything she does so she can keep her job," her father said, calming down only slightly. "People like that do not accept a greater authority in their lives the way we do."

"What good does she really do in that library, Renette?" Lula asked. "Seems to me she sits around all day thinkin' up speeches to yap at her patrons when they come in with legitimate complaints, and then she buys whatever she wants with the taxpayers' money. She's just a dictator is what she is. So I have to ask you again what she accomplishes with that."

"Among other things, she encourages people to read the classics. I remember not liking one bit having to read a couple of them in high school. But Miz Maura Beth has changed my thinking completely on the subject. For instance, have you ever read *The Scarlet Letter*?"

Lula looked like her daughter was speaking in a foreign language. "Read what kind of letter?"

"Never mind. The point is, I've started reading the classics since I went to work at the library. *The Scarlet Letter* is about a woman who has to wear an *A* on her clothing in public because she has committed adultery. But you end up feeling that she is the one who is being wronged and persecuted. I think it sends a very powerful message about not judging people and allowing them to live their lives the way they want."

"You don't even know what you're saying. Decent people wouldn't write about such things."

"Nathaniel Hawthorne did."

"Who's he?"

"The author."

"Never heard of him. Must be one of those trashy romance novelists. They encourage people to do as they please and become the slaves of lust. Why, they even have half-naked people on the covers."

Renette laughed. "How would you even know about that, Mama? Do you read them?"

"I most certainly do not. I would never even touch such trash. I just happen to see them at the checkout counter at The Cherico Market. I've always thought James Hannigan should be ashamed of himself selling those things where even innocent little children can see 'em plain as day. Really, I think your father and I oughta go down there and ask him to remove 'em just like we asked Miz McShay to remove those books at the library. If people like your father and I don't start standin' up for decency in this country, I'd like to know who will."

"No one forces anyone to buy those novels at the grocery store, and no one forces anyone to check out certain books at the library, either. It's still a free country, you know. That's what seems to have escaped both of you."

Lula quickly covered her ears with her hands. "I will not hear any more of this, Renette. You're naïve about the ways of the world, and someday you'll find out that I was telling you the truth. I hate to see you going against all your father and I and the church have taught you. If you keep this up, you are bound to bring shame upon this family. Don't expect us to be here for you if you turn your back on your training. That's fair warning."

As Renette continued to stand before the mirror

and reminisce about the numerous tilts with her parents, her mother's words seemed like a slap in the face on this Fourth of July evening. Here she was, made up to the hilt as she had never even attempted before, and it was all for a country singer she had only met once and might not ever meet again. She had gone through Maura Beth to try to wangle an invitation to something—any-thing—that might allow her to see and talk to him again. A meeting at City Hall with Councilman Sparks and Waddell Mack? Was that in the offing? If so, could she somehow be included in that? Was Waddell Mack coming to the Grand Opening, and could she be the one to show him the ins and outs of the new library as her special guest? Or would the security guards surrounding him because of the concert prevent her from any sort of access at all this time around?

As it happened, the latter turned out to be the working reality for her, and she was left with only the overwrought fantasies that had been playing in her head for months now, keeping her awake at nights. So when the words came out of her mouth before the mirror where she was preening and posing around six o'clock, she was not particularly shocked to hear them.

"You are one wicked little girl, Renette Elaina Posey, and it's high time you showed up and made your mark at something other than helping people check books out of the library." Then she winked at herself several times, again admiring her newly made-up face. "Now get out there, have a little gumption, be brave, and stop putting your life on hold," she said out loud.

Most of the members of The Cherry Cola Book Club were sitting out on the deck of the new library in the random collection of chairs they themselves had rounded up and installed for the Grand Opening in a frenetic display of energy. As a reward for their loyalty, Maura Beth had reserved the best seats for them so they could view the fireworks display that would be taking place in a little under fifteen minutes. The bleachers that had been set up for Waddell Mack's concert were also packed with many of the same people who had patronized the food tents and attended the awards ceremony in the library's mini-auditorium. But first the sun had to give up completely on the long day and allow the required backdrop of darkness. No need to dilute the pyrotechnics to come with too much light.

"I can't believe what you just told all of us," Connie McShay was saying to Maura Beth, who was seated next to her near the deck railing. "I halfway expect those two to fall into the lake at some point. Good thing we all know how to swim in case we need to rescue them. I know I don't much look the part now since I've allowed myself to become so pleasingly plump over the years, but

I was a right good lifeguard during summer vacations when I was in high school. I could blow a whistle and yell at people to stop splashing each other and horsing around with the best of them."

What Maura Beth had just shared with the group was the shocking revelation that Councilman Sparks had put "Chunky" Badham and "Gopher" Joe Martin in charge of the fireworks display on his very own yacht in the middle of Lake Cherico. Their reputation as his consummate lackeys definitely preceded them, and the deck was rife with speculation about whether they could actually pull it off without looking like an episode of *The Three Stooges*.

"Give Durden credit, though. I nearly fell out when he told me that he was going to be out there at the wheel, keeping an eye on them," Maura Beth said, barely able to make out the yacht in the rapidly fading light.

Connie couldn't hold back her laughter. "I certainly wouldn't have expected him to be so hands-on where explosives were concerned."

"Hey, his last name isn't Sparks for nothing," Jeremy added, sitting on the other side of Maura Beth.

"He's been a good sport in general today," Maura Beth said. "I think it's finally dawned on him that our new library is truly something he can show off and be proud of. Their names on these buildings is what gets these politicians' juices flowing every time, and in spite of himself, our councilman has an accomplishment for the ages under his belt."

"You're so modest not to have insisted that your name be on the building, too," Connie said.

"You sound like my mother now. But don't worry, I'm on the plaque inside. That's more than enough for me," Maura Beth said. "Besides, The Charles Durden Sparks, Crumpton, Duddney, and McShay Public Library wouldn't have fit across the front. We would have had to continue all those letters on the side."

"You've always seen the humor in every situation, Maura Beth," Connie added. "That first time we met down at The Twinkle and you told me Councilman Sparks was going to shut down your old library unless you did something drastic, I sensed you were going to bear down and find a way out. What laughs and good times we've had since you created The Cherry Cola Book Club and saved the day. Cherico turned a corner when you came up with that idea."

"You make me sound like a superhero or something. I'm anything but. I just do my job."

"No, I'm just giving credit where it's due."

"We all owe you a huge debt of thanks," Becca Brachle said, a couple of chairs away. "My signing was a huge success, but I'm certain the setting had a lot to do with my sales. I don't think we would have gotten nearly that many people coming out to the old library on Shadow Alley."

"It was a combination of things, Becca," Voncille Linwood pointed out, sitting next to her. "Don't be too modest. You have so many fans who swear by your recipes. Locke and I would've found a way to come by if you were signing in a pup tent smack dab in the middle of the woods."

"Ha!" Becca said. "What an image for my scrapbook—insect repellant for a book signing."

Without warning, the first fireworks exploded in the sky, interrupting all conversation on the deck, as a chorus of oohs, aahs, and gasps broke out along the shore of the lake. There was an array of multicolored aerial repeaters to keep the audience below mesmerized for a good long time; a series of bottle rockets and skyrockets followed, producing a display of stars, strobes, and parachutes. Then came at least a dozen Roman candles that exploded, whistled, and crackled high in the sky. After nearly thirty minutes had passed, the finale consisted of a dozen, multiple-shot parachutes that created various colored-star effects burning brightly as they slowly fell back to earth. On this occasion at least, the three good ole boy politicians from City Hall out there in the middle of the lake had performed their public service duties without a glitch, and better yet—no one had fallen overboard.

Scattered applause broke out everywhere when it was apparent nothing more would be forthcoming, even though there was the occasional "Is that it?" and "We want more!" to add a note of slight disappointment to the addictive festivities.

Maura Beth sighed, turned to Jeremy, and expressed perfectly what everyone else was probably thinking: "That brought out the little kid in me. It was over too soon. I could have sat here and watched another hour of that. What is it about fireworks on these special occasions?"

Jeremy thought for a while, then pointed heavenward. "Maybe just as simple as we all like looking up at the night sky and seeing pretty things in it. Who hasn't seen a shooting star fly by with a long tail and thought it was the most amazing thing to witness, no matter how many times it happens?"

"You're right. And no matter how old we get." Maura Beth checked her watch and pointed in the direction of the stage and bleachers to the left of the deck. "Waddell's on in about ten minutes. Looks like we've got standing room only everywhere. Everything couldn't be going better."

Jeremy stood up to stretch his legs and arms with the rest of the group on the deck. "I take it you aren't worried anymore about what people thought of the mix-and-match furniture in the library? I didn't hear any complaints, did you?"

"Well, no."

"And what about that woman from Corinth

who's threatening to sue you? Are you much worried about her?"

Maura Beth laughed. "The loud-mouth soup-slinger? Ha! With two dozen or more witnesses to testify she went a little crazy with her ladle? I doubt she'll even find a lawyer to take that one on."

"And the woman with the lethal sausage?"

"Hot-diggity-dog. I think she folded her tent for good and hightailed it back to Corinth where she belongs. Except that I really wouldn't wish her on the library over there."

Renette had ogled the fireworks from the top row of the bleachers like everyone else; but during the lulls between the various explosions, her attention had drifted gradually to the young man sitting next to her. It was the musk of his cologne that had first aroused her interest. They had not spoken throughout the entire display, but that had not stopped her from sizing him up out of the corner of her eye. He had the same sort of sexy, scruffy beard that had made her go gaga over Waddell Mack; his features were sharp and chiseled, and he had one of those buzz cuts favored by boot camp soldiers. It made him look strong and dangerous, and she liked the way that made her feel. She also liked the jeans and cowboy boots he was wearing, and it occurred to her that if she couldn't have any actual contact with Waddell

Mack himself, this specimen of the male species would do nicely. But could she actually gather up the courage to speak to him? He hadn't spoken to her at all. Did that mean he wasn't interested? Was she out of his league? No matter. He was sitting next to the new Renette—the one who would finally venture into the land of physical romance. The one who had never even kissed a boy, not even in an innocent game of spin the bottle at someone's birthday party growing up. The one who had been a prisoner of her upbringing for far too long.

"Those fireworks just blew me away," she heard herself saying to the young man, as if someone else had taken control of her body. "I've always liked them since I was a little girl. By the way, I'm Renette . . . Renette Posey." She extended her hand, and he shook it. She felt the power of his grip and experienced a spurt of adrenaline beneath her sternum, spreading throughout her body. Whatever she was getting into, she definitely liked the way it felt.

"I'm Shark," he told her, showing off his beautiful set of very white teeth, which did, in fact, feature a pair of long incisors. "Well, that's not my real name. You prob'ly guessed that. I'm really Josh—Josh Allen Baker, but the buddies I run with all call me Shark."

"Because you like to swim?"

"Because I like to play pool at Billy Ray's

Billiards over in Corinth. I'm not one to brag—oh, hell, yes, I am, and the truth is, Shark here never loses." He laughed wickedly. "I make chum of my chums."

Renette could not believe how liberated she suddenly felt. Instead of talking about boys—or men—with her just-out-of-high-school girlfriends during their weekend sleepovers, she was actually engaging one for the first time since the church socials she had grown up with where nothing more than drinking punch and eating cookies was allowed. No dancing, no physical contact—just polite, forced grins during the singing of hymns.

"You're a big Waddell Mack fan, judging by the way you were chantin' a while back," Shark continued. " 'We want Waddell! We want Waddell!' Maybe you're his number one fan?"

"I'm not sure about that, but maybe I could be in the top ten. Or at least the top twenty."

"Yeah, well, I like ole Waddell, myself. I've liked his easygoin' sound ever since he hit it big a coupla years back. I'm not braggin' about it, but I'm a distant cousin of his, you know."

"Are you really?" Renette could feel her heart beating faster now. Once again, if she couldn't hook up with Waddell Mack . . .

"Sure am. My mama sat me down once and explained to me how we're related a while back, but I lost track of all the 'once removed' and 'twice removed' stuff and just finally gave up on it all. The only thing I can tell you for sure is that we share some of the same genes and DNA. Beyond that, I take no responsibility."

"You're both very good-looking. I guess those are the genes you share. That makes you two pretty lucky fellas in my book."

"Why, thank you, ma'am. We resemble that. A fella always likes to hear that from a pretty young lady."

Renette pressed on with the small talk, feeling driven by some unknown force. "Were you here earlier for the food tents and the Queen of the Cookbooks competition? Seemed like the entire population of Cherico was out today. And lots of people from out of town, even."

"Yeah, I was here for a while, but my visit got cut short a little. I had just tried me some spaghetti and then some cheese balls that tasted mighty good, but then there was this huge ruckus up ahead between these two women. I mean, they were shoutin' at each other and everything, so I joined the crowd to watch, and before I knew it, one of 'em had slung some a' this greenish lookin' soup at the other one. Only she missed, and I was in the wrong place at the wrong time. The stuff was all over my shirt, ham and all. Lucky for me I always carry some extra clothes in my van, so I ended up being able to change so I looked halfway decent again. But I sorta called it an afternoon with the food tents."

Renette gasped, putting her hand over her mouth. "I know about that. Not about you being there and having soup spilled all over you, I mean. But someone rushed into the library to tell me that the fight was going on, and I had to run and tell Miz Maura Beth so they could break it up. She's our library director and my boss in case you were wondering."

Shark was shaking his head. "Yeah, I guess that was the lady who came out to give 'em what for. There was a guy who came out, too."

"That would have been Mr. Jeremy, Miz Maura Beth's husband. They're such a nice couple." Renette paused, deciding to change the subject. "Do you get to hang out with your cousin Waddell a lot? I mean, are you maybe gonna see him after the concert? I saw him here in Cherico last year when he ate down at The Twinkle with the rest of his band. Uh, that's the best restaurant in town that Miz Periwinkle runs. You should try it sometime."

"Yeah, I know about it. But as for my seeing him after the concert—nah. All those security people close in pretty fast to keep the groupies away. Hey, you're not one a' those girls that tries to snip off locks of his hair and tear at his shirt and stuff like that, are you? I woudd'n wanna have to spank ya for bein' outta line, ya know."

Renette blushed and touched her cheek lightly, as if to verify that she was not dreaming such a titillating conversation with such a handsome young man. "No, I'd never do anything like that. I just discovered Waddell recently. It was last December, matter of fact. I suppose you know he's responsible for bringing the Spurs 'R' Us plant to Cherico, don't you? He brightened up everybody's Christmas last year with that news."

"Sure do." He pointed down to his feet. "I got a pair of Spurs 'R' Us on me right now. Top-a'-the-line snakeskin. I own me about six more pair back home—all of 'em different. I kinda like to spend my money on my boots and cowboy hats. It's just my thing."

Renette glanced at his boots and then, without being obvious about it, allowed her eyes to follow the line of his leg up to his belt buckle. He was packed in tightly, and she let something inside of her snap, as she imagined him out of those jeans. Then, a further thought that she knew would have horrified her parents: Was he undressing her the same way? A part of her was telling her it was wrong to hope for such a thing; but this new part of her—this outlaw who had broken out of the jail cell of her upbringing—yearned for the opposite.

She came to as Councilman Sparks, fresh off his yacht with all its pyrotechnic triumphs, stepped onstage, bowed crisply to the five-man band that was awaiting him, and made the announcement. "And now, ladies and gentlemen, without further ado—what you've been wanting to hear all day as the finale for our Grand Opening Fourth of July celebration—the country music hits of Nashville's hottest recording star—Waddell Mack!"

The crowd exploded as impressively as the colorful and noisy fireworks display they'd just witnessed for the last hour or so.

After several minutes of applause and cheering, Councilman Sparks continued. "Now, as some of you probably know, Waddell Mack is the name of this great band. But we'd like to introduce each member to you individually before they all start to sing and play for us. Let's begin with Lonnie "Fingers" Gholson, who plays rhythm guitar for the group."

Tall, lanky Fingers waved and took a quick bow; then Councilman Sparks introduced the others in turn who did the same: next came Johnny Davis, the hulking bass player, then Sam Torrey, the wiry drummer, Trent Lightman, the never-without-a-smile fiddle player, and finally, the charismatic, curly-haired, heartthrob Waddell Mack, himself, who played lead guitar and sang the original songs he'd written.

Fortunately for the enterprising young man and his pocketbook, the country music nation had embraced his sound in record time, elevating him to the pinnacle of success, and it was with that considerable fortune that he had acquired forty percent ownership of Spurs 'R' Us and had the clout to bring their new manufacturing plant to the little town of Cherico.

"Let's give them all one last Greater Cherico welcome, and then we'll ask them to let 'er rip!" Councilman Sparks concluded, much to the audience's raucous delight. "I'm sure they'll make this Fourth of July one we'll never forget!"

With that, Waddell stepped up, removed his hat, and said in his most charismatic voice: "Ladies and gentlemen, before me and my band here give y'all what you came for, I'd like to ask all a' y'all to rise, take those hats off, and place y'all's hands over your hearts while we sing 'The Star-Spangled Banner' for ya. Wouldn't be a concert on the Fourth if we didn't do that, now would it?"

For the record, his breathy, slowed-down rendition of the national anthem crackled in the night air with a unique energy that reached out and involved everyone. Even those who couldn't sing a note were at least trying to join in. His stylings were definitely bringing a diverse group of people together on Independence Day, and it didn't get any better than that.

9

Jailbait

Waddell Mack had begun singing his opening number, his current big hit that was number one on the country charts, "Don't Sell Me Short When I'm Longin' for You," causing Renette and many others surrounding her to sway back and forth in unison to the easygoing beat. It was definitely cultish. Every fan in the bleachers knew the lyrics as well as he did, and the song rose like an anthem into the humid night air:

"You don't know I'm thinkin' of you
   most every day,
But I'm just half-crazy and I guess that's
   my way . . .
I wake up each mornin' with my heart
   broke in two,
But don't sell me short when I'm longin'
   for you . . ."

Renette and Shark stole quick, pregnant glances at each other during the brief pause between verses— glances that had more to do with what might come next between them than the song they were singing together. Then the second verse began.

221

"I saw you last night with that guy at the
   bar,
I just never thought you would take it that
   far . . .
You told me it's over and I guess that it's
   true,
But don't sell me short when I'm longin'
   for you."

Then came the bridge.

"They say every guy has his gal . . .
But I want much more than a pal . . ."

And then the final verse.

"So this is fair warnin' that I'm not givin'
   up,
Half-full or half-empty, I'm still raisin'
   my cup,
I'm not gonna settle for just stayin' this
   blue,
So don't sell me short when I'm longin'
   for you."

When the enthusiastic applause and cheers had
finally died down for the opening number, Renette
was ready to take her flirtation with this man who
went by the dangerous name of Shark to the next
level. She didn't have to say anything to him—

somehow he knew it. Then he dug into his black leather jacket pocket and flashed something shiny and metallic at her for just a split second.

"I got a flask," he whispered to her, quickly pocketing it afterward.

"Of what?" she whispered back, leaning in to him.

"Whiskey, of course."

The sound of the word vibrated somewhere deep inside of Renette. It conjured up images of things that she had been forbidden to consider all her life. Only sinners drank alcohol of any kind. Only the weak sought it out and let it run their lives. Many a church sermon she had heard had railed against it, warning her that it ruined people right and left. But whiskey was maybe the worst of the lot, her preacher, the always frowning Elder Warren of the Church of the Eternal Promise, had insisted to his congregation more than once.

"Never doubt that it is far worse than the demon rum!" he had shouted, while pointing to the church ceiling and jabbing at the air as if trying to spear those demons himself with his finger. "Because the day you walk into that liquor store is the day your life'll begin falling apart. You will tumble down that hill, and your bones will not be the only thing that get broken. Your spirit will be broken, too, and there will be no doctor in any hospital that can make you well again. Not if you stray from the straight and narrow that is planned for you."

"Say, how'd you like to check out that van of mine?" Shark whispered, bringing Renette back to the current reality she was facing on the back row of the bleachers. "It's really state of the art. I got an HDTV hooked up in there and everything else for all the comforts of home."

She was not naïve enough to misinterpret him. Shark's invitation was making her think about all the things teenagers might do in the back of a van—things they weren't supposed to do but did anyway. Not that she had experienced any of them, although she'd seen a few teen movies with that type of scene in them containing dialogue played strictly for laughs. Nothing horrible ever happened in those plots—which was probably why they were so popular. Oddly, she felt intrigued and emboldened by her imaginings. And then she heard herself whispering to Shark, "So, where is your van?"

"Parked in the library lot."

"Yeah, my car's there, too. But the concert's not over yet. I want to hear all of Waddell's music. I love his CDs, but this is the real thing that doesn't come along too often."

"Sure makes a difference, don't it? But what I meant was, we might go back and take a look at my van after the concert's over."

"Yeah, I know what you meant. Let me think about it for a while."

Well, there it was. Without giving much thought

to it, Renette found herself refusing to give him an outright no. Then he put his arm around her shoulder and she did not flinch. It was something she wanted him to do, but she knew the request had not come out of her mouth. Was he reading her mind? Were they on some kind of special wavelength? This didn't feel so dangerous. It was exciting.

"You'll know when the right man comes along," her mother had told her over and over in her lectures. "It is out of your hands. There is a plan for you, and if you deny the plan, you will never find peace in life."

So—picking up on her mother's solemn pronouncements—was Shark part of a grand plan? Was she merely rationalizing to believe that he just might be the one? Or—casting her mother's lecturing aside—was she finally letting life catch up with her after all these years of being afraid to venture forth?

The band began their second number, "The Muddy Waters of My Heart," and Renette concentrated on the music and lyrics for a while, careful not to pull away from her Shark in the process.

"You say you think I'll hurt you,
'Cause I've done it once before . . .
But I just wanna tell you,
That I finally know the score . . .
I know we've had our fallouts,

And our quarrels from the start . . .
But please just help me clear
The muddy waters of my heart . . ."

"I really like his voice, don't you? It's so sexy,"
Renette said, allowing herself to relish Shark's
shoulder embrace even further as the first verse
ended. In some sense she could not begin to
identify, she felt that she somehow belonged to
him, even though they had just met.

"Well, I wouldn't exactly call it sexy, you
understand. That's for you girls to say, but I
woudd'n be here if I didn't think he had it goin'
on. I betcha he gets plenty a' action all the time."

Then Waddell tore into the second verse.

"So here we are together,
As we've done it in the past . . .
I know you've thought our lovin'
Was just never gonna last . . .
But here I am to tell you,
That we're never gonna part . . .
If you'll just help me clear
The muddy waters of my heart . . ."

The band did an instrumental bridge and then
Waddell repeated the second verse while Renette's
mind returned to the man whose arm rested on her
shoulder so naturally, so protectively. She could
almost feel the protectiveness seeping through

into her warm flesh. Nothing about what she was feeling seemed muddy to her at the moment. Waddell Mack's lyrics seemed to be encouraging her to clear up her emotions once and for all. Was this the way true romance started? Was it as simple as straightforward physical contact of an innocent nature? Taking it all slowly, one step at a time, didn't seem out of line in the least.

"All of his songs seem so real to me," Renette said after the second number had ended, and she had actually shouted, "Waddell rules!" several times along with her applause.

"Yeah," Shark told her. "Wonder which one they'll do next. They kinda like to keep you in suspense at these things. Guess it's part of the act, huh?"

"Doesn't matter to me. I like all the songs."

"Don't compare to the way I like you, though. Sometimes things can happen real fast between people. That's what makes it so much fun, ya know. You just walk the path and see where it leads ya, darlin'."

Renette's mind was racing now. His arm continued to feel so good around her. She found herself wanting even more of an embrace from him. At the same time, his cologne made her want to kiss him. It would be her first kiss ever from a man, something she had been dreaming about for as long as she had had fantasies about the opposite sex. She had not touched a drop of the whiskey in that flask he had whipped out for a brief second a while back; but was this what it was like to be drunk on love?

Brief flashes of her mother's grim face and wagging finger only emboldened her. This was her life, not her mother's or father's. What had worked for them might not necessarily work for her.

The moment Renette stepped into Shark's decked-out panel van, the uneasiness began to eat at the bravado she'd cultivated so carefully in the bleachers. The stale-smelling, brown shag carpet that stretched from behind the captain's chair to the rear doors set the tone. Then there was the brown sofa big enough to seat two people if they chose to watch the HDTV on the opposite side of the van. Or do something else besides watch television. A black mini-fridge next to the sofa completed the somewhat claustrophobic picture.

"Make yourself at home, darlin,'" Shark told her, pointing to the sofa. "I mean, if you'd like to slip into or outta somethin' and get more comfortable, please be my guest." Then he winked at her twice. "This is my home away from home, if ya know what I mean."

Renette's uneasiness continued to mount as she sat down, and said, "I'm fine for right now."

"Maybe you'd like a little drink to relax ya? I got a little bag a' ice cubes in the fridge."

"A drink of that whiskey?"

He smirked. "What else? I take mine straight, but like I said, I can get some rocks for ya if you want. Or a mixer."

"Rocks? A mixer?"

"Yeah, ice, soda. I got 'em both. Which do you want?"

Renette hesitated. "Uh, rocks . . . I guess."

She watched nervously as he poured their drinks into red plastic cups, taking a deep breath when he handed hers over.

"Wanna make a toast to start things off right?" he asked her. "Maybe you got you a favorite?"

"You make it. I'm not good at things like that. I get my words all jumbled up, and it doesn't make sense."

He thought for a moment and then said, "Well, let's just keep it simple. To Shark and Renette on the Fourth of July. Down the hatch."

She hoisted her cup with her heart in her throat and then slowly brought it to her lips. Her first big swallow of whiskey burned all the way down to the pit of her stomach. For a moment she thought she was being poisoned. She coughed violently several times; then she found herself sucking in as much air as there was in the van in order to catch her breath.

"You okay, darlin'?" he asked. "Did you swallow the wrong way? I don't buy cheap booze, ya know. That's Maker's Mark."

"I . . . I wouldn't know the difference."

He took a generous swig from his cup and frowned. "Don't tell me that was your first sip a' bourbon?"

She finally recovered enough to answer him. "Uh . . . yeah, actually it was. You aren't disappointed in me, are you?"

"Disappointed?"

She was looking down at the carpet now, avoiding eye contact. "Well, the truth is . . . I'm not a drinker."

"You shoudda said so. I woudda poured you a Coke or club soda or whatever. Shark aims to please the ladies. I have to admit I don't meet many teetotalers these days, but to each his own."

"I was . . . afraid you wouldn't like me if . . ."

"If what?"

Instead of answering his question, however, she put her drink down on the carpet and stared straight into his eyes. "Never mind the part about the drinking. I didn't come here to do that, anyway. Is this where we kiss?" Then she closed her eyes and puckered her lips, holding her pose as if she had been turned to stone.

Now it was Shark's turn to feel uncomfortable. "Whoa, now!" he managed. "What's goin' on here? How old are you? Please don't tell me you're underage. That's the last thing I need."

She opened her eyes and was surprised to see that he had backed away from her. "I'm nineteen."

"Yeah, well, I was thinkin' you wuz twenty-somethin'. But you're not tellin' Shark a lie, are ya? You're not jailbait, are ya?"

"What's jailbait?"

He made a soft whistling noise. "Now I'm convinced you are, askin' me a question like that."

"No, really, I'm nineteen. My driver's license is over there in my purse if you'd like to check it out. It's just that I don't like the taste of that whiskey. It's pretty strong, and the vapors went up my nose. But I would like for you to kiss me. Is there anything wrong with that?"

"Boy," he said, swilling more of his drink. "I don't know what to say. Up in the bleachers all friendly-like the way you were, I coudda swore you were lookin' for a good time. Now . . . well, I'm not sure you even know what a good time is. Not the way I mean it."

"Sure I know what a good time is."

"Do ya?"

"You don't want to kiss me then? Please . . . kiss me."

He said nothing for a while. Then he put his drink down atop the mini-fridge, moved to the sofa, and snuggled up to her quickly, embracing her tentatively. "Okay, then. Since you asked me so nicely and all, I'll kiss you."

Before Renette knew it, his lips were on hers. They felt hot, but she could also smell and taste more of the strong whiskey that had been such a shock to her system. She decided it was an altogether unpleasant sensation and nothing like she had expected and wanted her first kiss to be. It was then that she came to her senses in the nick of time, realizing that the wicked little girl she had fancied in the full-length mirror was just an illusion. She wanted the kiss to end, but the two of them suddenly seemed attached at the lips. She realized for the first time just how muscular he was and that it was not going to be easy to back off and get out of her predicament. He didn't just look strong, he was strong. More to the point, the entire experience was becoming increasingly unpleasant, if not alarming.

Finally, and with some effort, she was able to pry herself loose, holding him at arm's length while she caught her breath. "I'm . . . I'm sorry. I shouldn't be here with you like this."

Irritation crept into his face. "Is that right?"

"This . . . this is all wrong."

He took a moment but kept his voice calm and steady. "Well, I think I prob'ly agree with you, darlin'. But you just asked me to kiss you, and I did. I do wanna go on record that I never had any complaints about my kisses from anyone before. I reckon you'd be the first."

"Please don't be mad. I've . . . I've just never been kissed before—I mean, not that way—and I've never tasted liquor before. Any kind of liquor.

My parents never allowed any of that stuff in the house when I was growing up."

His mood changed quickly from annoyance to forced laughter. "Man, I can guess what's comin' next."

"I don't know what you mean."

He leaned into her, blowing more of his whiskey breath into her nostrils. "You're a virgin, aren'tcha?"

"Oh," she said, almost in a whisper. "That."

"Then you are?"

"Well . . . yes."

"Oh, brother."

Her voice began to tremble, and she could feel her heart racing faster. Only it wasn't from excitement any longer. It was from a new and different visitor—fear. Sudden fear. "Please . . . don't be mad at me."

Everything went silent between the two of them for what seemed like an eternity, even though it was probably less than a minute in reality.

Then, to Renette's great relief, Shark's attitude changed completely, his tone becoming almost fatherly. "Listen, Renette, I'm not mad at you, and I'm not disappointed. The truth is, I'm no saint, but I got my standards when it comes to how I treat women. You got lucky tonight 'cause some guys woudda pressed on and took advantage of you if you got this far with 'em. I mean, in a New York second, they would've. But now, let me tell it like it is, and I want you to listen real close to what I say. This idd'n your fault. I made a snap judgment about you tonight out on those bleachers, and that's all on me, but it almost got both of us in trouble. I don't know what's goin' on in that little head a' yours right now, but just take my word for it, this ain't the way to go about things as nice and trustin' a girl as you really are. This bid'ness we were about to conduct here in my van—and I think you understand what coudda happened so easily—it's not for you. You're not ready for it—no way, no how. And believe me, I really do know what I'm talkin' about. Shark's been around the block a time or two."

Renette felt a wave of embarrassment sinking down to the tips of her toes. "I . . . I don't know what's gotten into me. It's this crush I have on Waddell Mack. I haven't been able to think about anything or anyone else. I came to the concert with my head spinning about him, even though I knew I wouldn't be coming anywhere near him. And then you came along and I just let everything happen without even thinking. I was trying to be somebody I'm not, and I guess you figured that out. I guess I figured it out, too. Do you think I'm crazy? Do you think I'll be punished for what I've done?"

This time he patted her shoulder without a hint of sexual innuendo. "Punished? What? Where did you git that from? You haven't done anything. No way, darlin.' You just got carried away with your crush is all. It happens. You gotta right to make a mistake in judgment. Looks like I did, too. But now, I think you oughta go home and get you a good night's sleep. You just take my advice and you wait around until the right guy comes along for a real romance—and you'll know it when he does. You won't have to freeze up like you did and ask somebody to kiss you. You make up your mind to be in control of everything all the time, now. You be the one to call the shots, okay? Will you promise Shark you'll do that?"

Her embarrassment faded as she smiled. "I promise, and what you're saying makes a lot of sense. Right now, I feel exhausted. It sure takes a lot of energy playing games, doesn't it?"

"You got that right. I do too much of it myself." He exhaled. "One a' these days, maybe I'll even settle down and make my parents happy. They worry about me all the time, ya know."

"Same as my parents do me. But if they knew about all this, they'd disown me. But then, they don't like anything about my life. They even think there's something wrong with my working at the library for Miz Maura Beth. To their way of thinking, she's the bad guy. Or gal, I guess."

"You're kiddin' me?"

She shook her head emphatically.

"What's wrong with you workin' at the library? Seems like that'd be the nicest, quietest place in the world to work."

She laughed good-naturedly. "My parents are convinced it's a den of iniquity. Or worse."

He stood up and straightened his shiny belt buckle. "Now that's right funny. A library as a den of iniquity. Shark'll have to remember that one and tell all his buddies next time we play a round a' pool and I clean out their wallets. Now there's your real den of iniquity—the pool hall I go to with all the beer flowin' and the smoke swirlin' so you cain't tell who's who and what's really goin' down." He paused to gaze at her affectionately. "Well, darlin', this has been real nice and all, but I think it's high time Cinderella went on home."

Renette stood up and gave him an impulsive hug. "Thanks. You're right. I did get lucky tonight. Thanks for being a gentleman about it all."

"No problem, sweetheart. You good to drive?"

"I think so," she told him, even if she still had a slight buzz from the swallow of straight whiskey that was still hanging around.

Then he cemented the feel-good exchange they were having as he checked his watch. "I don't think your car'll turn into a pumpkin just yet. Got you a good hour or so before midnight."

She was almost out the door when she turned at the last second, and asked, "Just for the record, are you really Waddell Mack's cousin? Were you telling me the truth?"

His grin was toothy and handsome, and he took a moment. "Like I said—distant . . . real distant."

By the time Renette got home, she felt completely wrung out. Maybe some of the things her parents had been telling her all this time were right after all. She had indeed led a very protected life, and this incident with Shark had brought it home dramatically to her. Suppose he had been a different type of guy? And then, what if that awful whiskey had taken over for the both of them? More than anything else, she felt she needed to talk things out with someone who would listen and understand. Or at least use someone as a sounding board so she could move on.

Two people came to mind: her mother and her mentor, Maura Beth. She went back and forth about it, and finally she reached the point of no return. She had to dispose of it all emotionally because keeping it to herself was not something she could handle. But first, she simply had to take off all that makeup. She had come to the conclusion that it was messy, complicated, and way too overrated. All those ads in the fashion magazines made it look like all a girl had to do was put it on, pose for the camera, and her world would fall into place as if by magic. Maybe someone needed to sue the cosmetics companies for false advertising.

For instance, the talking-a-mile-a-minute saleslady with the beehive hairdo who had sold it all to her and shown her how to apply it was just too slick for words. "Sweetie pie, this is just the right shade for you, but you know, you need something to bring out your cheekbones a little more. You have such beautiful, high cheekbones. And you also need to bring out your eyes. Such, beautiful blue eyes they are, too. Just try this shadow, try this blush, try this eyebrow pencil, try this lip gloss, try this foundation . . ."

Ha! Did these department store people work on commission or what?

Once she was in her soft, roomy pajamas that smelled of fabric softener, she sat down on the edge of her bed and made her decision. It was as if all that makeup had penetrated her pores, entered her bloodstream, and traveled to her brain cells, making them unable to function. There was some risk involved, but she ultimately erred on the side of talking to her family about what had happened after the concert. Maybe, just maybe, her mother and father would understand and approve of the way their daughter had been honest enough to share her experience in the van. After all, nothing bad had happened. She had actually done nothing wrong; and fortunately, neither had her cruising Shark.

She could picture her mother saying something soothing to her like, "The angels were looking out after you, Renette. Your father and I have always told you there were angels out there. You just need to know where to look for them."

Yes, that would be her mother's response. Surely that would be her calm, collected response, and that would be the end of it.

10

The Rabble-Rouser

How on earth had things come to this in a matter of a few days? How had the joy and sense of accomplishment Maura Beth had felt at the opening of her new, state-of-the-art library overlooking the waters of Lake Cherico vanished in the face of these baseless charges against her?

She kept trying to deny the upsetting reality of it all, but here she was in City Hall Chambers, Jeremy on one side of her, Renette on the other, defending herself against a request by Hardy and Lula Posey, Elder Warren, and the Church of the Eternal Promise that she be removed immediately as the director of the Charles Durden Sparks, Crumpton, and Duddney Public Library. At the other end of the long, highly polished meeting room table sat Councilman Sparks, flanked by Chunky Badham and Gopher Joe Martin; and halfway between those two contingents were Maura Beth's accusers—Renette's thin-lipped parents and their embalmed-looking pastor. As she silently observed Elder Warren closely, she was unable to detect even the tiniest tic on his pale, frowning countenance with its glazed, dead eyes; and it even came to her that he had a

240

great deal in common with a flawless work of taxidermy. Then she came to as Councilman Sparks made his opening remarks.

"As you well know, Miz McShay, since City Hall has jurisdiction over the library in Cherico, it is our duty to take these accusations against you seriously. We must give Mr. and Mrs. Posey and Elder Warren their say in this, but you will have the opportunity to rebut them afterward, of course."

Determined at all costs to keep her cool, Maura Beth said, "I understand perfectly, Councilman Sparks."

She and Jeremy had spent a great deal of time the evening before exploring her responses to every possible angle the Poseys might pursue in this hearing, which was not open to the public, and she felt reasonably confident that she would prevail in this challenge to her qualifications as a librarian.

"I've changed the balance of power in Cherico," Maura Beth had reminded Jeremy during their rehearsals. "Those first few years when I was struggling to make ends meet for the old library, I wouldn't have won this battle. I would have been down for the count and maybe even blaming myself for getting the short end of the stick. But this is a new day, and we've got a new library now."

Jeremy had not been quite as optimistic,

remaining cautious. "I hope you're right, Maurie. I just have a hard time trusting Councilman Sparks with all you've been through."

Back in the meeting room, Councilman Sparks was officially opening the proceedings, turning his attention to the Poseys and Elder Warren. "Which of you wants to speak first?"

"I will," Hardy Posey answered, raising his hand. He glared at his daughter and then cleared his throat. "As we told you when we came to your office before, Councilman Sparks, our daughter, Renette, hasn't been the same since she came to work for Miz McShay at the library right after she graduated from high school. She was just a sweet, innocent girl back then." He paused to point dramatically at Maura Beth. "There Miz McShay sits next to our daughter."

"Yes, Mr. Posey," Councilman Sparks said without emotion. "Everybody knows who everybody else is at the table. We can dispense with more introductions. Please proceed."

"Our Renette was happy to live at home with us before she got that job. We had high hopes for her happiness, and we just knew she would find the right young man and get married and give us grandchildren—which is the plan intended for everyone. Then, she started tellin' us about all these books that Miz McShay would buy and put on the shelves. Stories and such we don't think are proper to have for people to check out. They could influence young people the wrong way, you know? That was when we first started to worry about Renette. Especially when she told us she was movin' out and gettin' a place of her own and—"

Councilman Sparks interrupted. "Excuse me, Mr. Posey, but what were some of these stories that you thought were improper for the library to have? Should I be worried about it?"

"Why, anyone would think they weren't fit for a library, sir," Hardy continued, his round, fleshy face reddening. "Those *Harry Potter* novels that glorify sorcery, for starters. And then there were some actual books on witchcraft and Wiccan stuff. How to practice it, mind you. We got no bid'ness havin' that material in our library. Some of the fiction is about teenagers who become vampires or want to become vampires—which we know is ungodly. Now, who in his right mind wants to be promotin' that? And there's more fiction that is not about churchgoin' people like ourselves. How are we supposed to keep our children on the straight and narrow when they have temptations like that to read? You do see my point, don'tcha, Councilman?"

"I do see what you're saying, yes," Councilman Sparks told him, his tone once again calm and deliberate. "Please go on."

"Well, as if Miz McShay fillin' our shelves with all that wudd'n enough, Renette told us about what happened to her at that Queen of the Cookbooks to-do out at the lake the evening the new library opened up. She came to us all emotional the day after it happened, and that's when we knew we finally had to do somethin' then and there about Miz McShay. That Queen of the Cookbooks contest was her idea, we've heard, and she ran it like a dictator. We saw her actually kick people outta the contest just because they had a few words with each other. They didd'n do nobody harm, and it was kinda funny watchin' them carry on the way they did. And then, look what it led to with our Renette."

"What exactly did it lead to, Mr. Posey? Please elaborate for us again because I thought all the contest led to was people eating good food and listening to some country music and having a good time."

"Drunk behavior and nearly some fornication is what it led to, no thanks to Miz McShay, and not only that—"

"That is not what happened, Daddy. That is not what I told you, and you know it. You've twisted this thing to make it sound horrible and a whole lot worse than it was. I sure wish I hadn't said anything at all about it to you and Mama," Renette interrupted, nearly in tears, while Maura Beth comforted her with a couple of gentle pats on the shoulder.

"Miss Renette, I promise you that you'll get

your turn," Councilman Sparks told her. "We'll give you plenty of time, but we must get both sides of the story here to make a fair decision."

Renette exhaled vigorously, her hands knotted in fists, and then offered a barely audible, "I'm sorry to butt in like that."

"No, you don't have anything to be sorry about. I understand that this is difficult for you."

"Well, as I was sayin' before my daughter's outburst," Hardy continued, "there was some people that had flasks of liquor in the stands, and one of 'em invited my daughter back to his van after that concert was over by that singer whose songs don't have any morals to 'em. They're all about drinkin' and people who cheat on each other and that sorta thing from what I can make out. But that Waddell Mack, he sure makes lotsa money off 'em. That's how it is these days in this world." He paused to stare at the faces of the three councilmen, searching for a sympathetic reaction, but found not so much as a nod in his general direction.

"Anyhow, this man in the stands offered my daughter whiskey and tried to get her drunk, and I ask you straight out—would any a' that've happened if Miz McShay hadn't come to Cherico and changed things the way she has? She's been a bad influence on our daughter, and there's no way of tellin' how many others have come into that library and found those materials and lost their way. This never happened when Miz Annie Scott was there. My wife and I think Miz McShay needs to be reigned in, and things need to go back to the way they were before. We tried to get Miz McShay to take those books off the shelves. We asked her nicely, but she just wouldn't do it. She told us no way would she ever do it. So let's forget this Queen of the Cookbooks bid'ness for a moment. That's the least of it. I'd just like to know who made Miz McShay the Queen of Cherico who answers to nobody? Can you answer me that?"

Councilman Sparks continued maintaining his composure. "I don't intend to answer that question at all, Mr. Posey. I'll let Miz McShay handle that when the time comes. Meanwhile, do you, your wife, or Elder Warren have anything else to add to your side of the matter? Please don't leave out anything. We want you to have your day here in court, so to speak."

Elder Warren stirred in his seat and raised his eyebrows, as if coming to life after a long nap. "I'd like to say something. After all, I am Renette's pastor."

"Go right ahead."

Elder Warren suddenly became even more animated, reverting to his preaching style. "Well, it seems to me that Miz McShay fancies herself some sort of gatekeeper of all knowledge in the world. Imagine the false pride in that, and we all know that 'pride goeth before a fall.' Seems she thinks she's alone in this task and the rest of the community must abide by what she does. Mr. and Miz Posey have every right to be concerned about their daughter's behavior, and they should know when it started to change.

"At the Church of the Eternal Promise, we preach that no one is above Our Father's plan and purpose. But Miz McShay seems to believe that she is indeed above that and can dictate what Chericoans can read, for starters. I don't believe what happened to Miss Renette would ever've taken place without Miz McShay and her ideas, either. Miz Annie Scott, may she rest in peace, was what a librarian should be. She attended our church regularly, by the way. She never had opinions about politics or these trendy subjects or anything else. She kept quiet and in the background, and everybody loved her until the day she died. Miz McShay—she's a rabble-rouser, and that's not what we need here in Cherico. That's not what anyone needs in this life."

Councilman Sparks waited for a few moments, unsure that Elder Warren had finished his sermon. Then he pointed to Lula Posey, who had struck an indignant-looking pose. "Did you have anything to add, ma'am?"

"All I know is, my daughter honored her parents and the word of the church before she went to work at the library. After that, she seemed to worship the ground Miz McShay walked on. The woman could do no wrong. But thou shalt not worship false idols, we all know. And look what it almost led to. Who knows what might happen in the future if this woman continues on as our librarian? We need to think about this long and hard before we let her keep runnin' things. We are just thinkin' of the well-being of everybody in Cherico."

Councilman Sparks remained silent, surveying everyone in the room and then taking a deep breath. "I'm sure that is a laudable goal we can all agree with. So, is that it, Miz Posey?"

"I could say more about all this, but I won't."

"Thank you. Then that concludes the charges against Maura Beth McShay. Now we will entertain her rebuttal."

But Renette raised her hand and spoke up immediately. "If Miz McShay wouldn't mind, I'd like to say something on my behalf first."

"Of course I don't mind," Maura Beth said with a smile. "I think it's important that we hear from you, Renette. All you have to do is tell the truth, and I'm sure everything will be all right."

It took a few moments for Renette to gather herself, and she was careful to avoid eye contact with her parents and Elder Warren when she began speaking so that she wouldn't fold. They were shooting daggers at her all the while.

"I begged my parents not to pursue this,

Councilman Sparks, but they were determined to make a fuss where none was really necessary. I thought they would actually be proud of the way I handled what happened after Waddell Mack's concert. Guess I was foolish to think so and should've kept my mouth shut. Or told Miz Maura Beth about it to get it off my chest. That's what I should've done. Anyway—yes, I got carried away sitting in the stands next to this fast-talking young man who swept me off my feet. But it had nothing to do with Miz McShay. It was just me being a naïve teenager is what it was. I had this wild crush on Waddell Mack and his music. How many teenagers have crushes on singers of all kinds these days? I think they always have. That's nothing unusual, seems to me. But when I went back to this fellow's van and he offered me a drink, I soon realized I was in the wrong place at the wrong time after I took the first sip. No one got even close to being drunk, and I left before anything happened. The young man I was with became a complete gentleman in the end, which I appreciated. I thought my parents would also appreciate hearing that. They'd always told me that I was naïve and didn't know squat about the ways of the world. I even told them they were right about that when I went to them and confessed everything. Instead, their heads just exploded, and now they're trying to take it all out on Miz McShay, and I just think that's wrong.

This whole thing is so wrong, and I feel better because I've stood up for myself . . . and Miz Maura Beth."

"Thank you, Renette," Maura Beth said, blowing her a little kiss. "That was very eloquent."

"I didn't expect my daughter to say different today, but what about all those books, Miz McShay?" Lula Posey put in. "All those stories you allow on the shelves that could lead people astray. Seems like you just make up your own rules. Other people have opinions, you know."

Maura Beth gave Councilman Sparks an inquisitive glance. "Is it time for me to speak now?"

Councilman Sparks gave her the go-ahead with a nod of his head.

"Thank you. I'll start by saying that when I first came to Cherico, the old library, such as it was, had a collection that would have been outdated during World War II. Some of the pub dates I weeded out were downright embarrassing. For instance, I found a book on entertaining at home from 1946 that had an entire chapter on—and I quote—that newfangled notion the savory party dip. Can you imagine my horror? Talk about your volumes collecting dust. And that was just the tip of the iceberg. Even though I had almost no budget to work with—but thank goodness I do now—I made it my business to refresh and update the collection with topical subjects that the students were researching for their school assignments and others were asking for. We go out of our way to supplement the high school library, of course.

"These books, which the Poseys have objected to, were not something I wished to impose upon the citizens of Cherico. Their content does not necessarily reflect my opinions either way. They reflected what my patrons were asking for all the time—what patrons all across the country are asking for. It seems to me that we ought to try to please and accommodate the taxpayers where we can—within reason, of course. When I put any book into the collection, I always try to balance what people are asking for with community standards. There are some subjects, whether works of fiction or nonfiction, that are best left to the private purchase of our patrons. We recognize that the library cannot buy everything under the sun, of course." Maura Beth paused briefly to catch the proud expression on Jeremy's face, and that was more than enough to refuel her.

"So when Mr. Posey asks who appointed me the Queen of Cherico, I answer respectfully that rather than being the gatekeeper of all knowledge, as Elder Warren put it, I prefer to say that I am the gatekeeper of the taxpayers' money that funds the library. I try to be the best steward of that money that I can be. From time to time, librarians get challenges to the materials they select for their patrons, and of course the patrons have every right to file complaints; but I would guess far fewer get challenged on their ability to hold down their jobs as a result. In my estimation I have done nothing wrong here, and no harm has come to my employee, Renette Posey. I'm truly sorry that she is having problems with her parents, and I hope she can work them out. I would never knowingly come between parents and their child. But I also hope Renette will continue to work for me as a front desk clerk and assistant, as she has always done an outstanding job. I have nothing more to add."

Jeremy leaned over and gave his wife a kiss on the cheek. "Well done, Maurie, well done."

"And I intend to continue working for you, Miz McShay," Renette added, sitting straight up in her chair. "I also want to say to you again that I would never have brought up what happened the evening of the concert to my parents if I'd known it would lead to this."

"I know that, sweetie. I certainly don't blame any of this on you. Your parents had made it clear before that they didn't approve of the job I was doing. This just brought it all to a head."

"Never mind all that back-patting between the two of you," Hardy said, staring his daughter down. "We already know you're thick as thieves. What is your decision on this, Councilman Sparks? You told us when we requested the hearing that you'd give us your answer right away. We've been considering this for a long time now. So, what's it gonna be? Does Miz McShay go or stay?"

Councilman Sparks did not hesitate, drawing himself up. "She stays, Mr. Posey. I agree with Miz McShay and Miss Renette, herself, that these problems you and your wife are having with your daughter have nothing at all to do with the library, and I trust Maura Beth implicitly to run the library that bears my name in a totally professional manner. It's as simple as that."

"You two are obviously in this together. We shoudda known that from the start. So you've forced our hand," Hardy said, gesturing toward Elder Warren. "Tell him what we intend to do now."

"We agreed that if you didn't see things our way, Councilman," Elder Warren began, rising from his chair somewhat histrionically while puffing himself up, "the Church of the Eternal Promise will picket the library, and that's what we're gonna do. We'll have our entire congregation out here every day with our signs demanding that Miz McShay be fired and replaced with some-one like Miz Annie Scott, who minded her own business when it came to the old library. Why, you never even knew she was there most of the time."

"Boy, does that say a mouthful," Maura Beth pointed out. "The invisible librarian just collecting a paycheck. If I live to be a hundred, I don't think that horrible old stereotype will ever die."

Elder Warren pointed a finger accusingly. "You can say whatever you want about yourself, missy, but there's no need to insult the memory of a righteous woman like Miz Annie Scott."

"If I might, Elder Warren," Councilman Sparks said, "there's also no need to keep standing up before us like you are. This isn't the Nuremburg Trials. Please have a seat, sir."

Elder Warren complied, but the resentment and reluctance clearly showed in his bony face.

"I'd like to point out to you," Councilman Sparks continued, "that times have changed, and what worked for Miz Annie Scott in her day will not work now. I've had that pointed out to me in the last year or so by Miz McShay. Frankly, I'll freely admit that I was behind the times and out of step regarding our library. I didn't think it mattered, and I resisted change as much as I could for as long as I could. I can't honestly say that any longer. I'm right proud of that Charles Durden Sparks, Crumpton, and Duddney Public Library out there on the lake with its grand deck overlooking the water. It's your right to picket it if you want to until the cows come home, but judging from the reaction of the citizens of Cherico on opening day, it won't do you much good. I don't think they're gonna agree with you about letting Miz McShay go. My advice is to accept things as they are. Otherwise, I think you'd just be wasting your time and energy. It's the worst time of the year to be picketing, by the way. Even football teams wait a few more weeks to start their practices. Meanwhile, you'll need plenty of water and mosquito repellant."

"I guess we'll see about that, won't we?" Hardy Posey said. "Come on, Lula, let's go back to the church with Elder Warren and plan our strategy. We need to get the congregation behind this all the way and then get busy making our picket signs. We've got lots to do."

"I wish you wouldn't do this," Renette said. "You're not gonna change anything by it. I think something Councilman Sparks just said applies to the three of you. You're all behind the times and out of step."

Lula rose from her chair, shaking her head. "I would never've thought I'd live to see the day when my daughter would talk to me that-a-way, so smart-aleck and all. But you've chosen your path apart from us, Renette. Now you're stuck with it and all the consequences, too."

"There are no consequences that I'm aware of. I'll be fine, Mama. Don't you worry about me."

"You may be sorry you said that, Renette."

"I don't think so, Mama."

Lula Posey's tone became more and more stern as her face darkened even further. "Honor thy father and thy mother, Renette. Have you forgotten that particular commandment?"

"No, I haven't. I just don't think the way you've both been acting lately is worth honoring."

"That does it. Let's get outta here, Hardy."

After the Poseys and Elder Warren had left the room in a huff, it was Councilman Sparks who stood up and struck just the right note. "You know, Maura Beth, I think I can say for sure now that you and I are finally on the same page, same paragraph, same sentence, after all these years."

Unable to resist the opening he had given her, Maura Beth laughed warmly and said, "It's about time."

The dream Maura Beth had that night featured images both familiar to her and making their debut in her head. The first-time scenes were a partial replay of the City Hall hearing that had gone her way. Only, in this version, everyone in the room was pointing a finger at her and calling her a "rabble-rouser"—even her Jeremy and sweet, loyal Renette. She felt betrayed that they had joined this loud chorus of her adversaries. The dream world could be so cruel at times.

"No, I'm not!" she shouted to them all. "I'm just doing my job. Don't you know the difference?"

"Rabble-rouser! Rabble-rouser! Rabble-rouser!" they all repeated together, the decibel level increasing all the while until Maura Beth had to cover her ears to keep from going over the edge.

In a flash, Elder Warren's grim face hogged her visuals in a huge close-up, and she had to listen to him going on and on about how Miz Annie Scott was turning over in her grave at what was going on in Cherico now. "She doesn't like what's happened to her library one bit. She told me so the last time I talked to her, and I talk to her all the time, you know. Her and God."

"She did not say that!" Maura Beth shouted back. "I just put flowers on her grave the other day and she thanked me for them!"

The cries of "Rabble-Rouser!" continued until Maura Beth was forced to flee the meeting room. She could stand it no longer. She found herself running down the hall, out of the building, and down the steps, but she had no idea where she was going. She only knew she had to escape everyone's constant badgering before she went out of her mind.

Then there was a dissolve to the familiar— that recurring dream during which she always wandered about in a fog or a mist, feeling lost and abandoned. Until that light-filled clearing showed up ahead. But this time, instead of waking up, Maura Beth pressed on. Something told her that this time her dream journey would reach its conclusion and perhaps stop tantalizing her with its frequent appearances during her sleep.

Finally, she reached the clearing, and it was then

that she heard the cry of a baby. Not the sort of crying a baby makes when it is hungry or thirsty or needs changing, but the sort that is more like expressing wonder at being alive after that first breath in the brave but dry new world is taken.

It was then that Maura Beth woke up and understood. She looked over at her wonderful, incredibly understanding Jeremy, sound asleep and facing away from her as he always did. How many times had they made love to each other since taking their vows? Way too many times to count.

So that was it. After all these months, that was what the dream was all about. What a wondrous thing the universe was! Wasn't it all a hoot and a half?

11

Three

Maura Beth had been sketchy with all The Cherry Cola Book Club members about the reason for calling an emergency meeting in the new library's mini-auditorium just two days after her hearing in City Hall Chambers.

"But this is way too short notice for me to coordinate the menu," Becca had pointed out over the phone. "If I don't check with everybody in advance, we'll have three desserts and no appetizers or something like that. Although I did want to run something past you. At my signing, Locke and Voncille Linwood suggested that we use only recipes from my cookbook next time we met. I said I'd ask you about it. So what do you think of the idea?"

"I think we can hold that good thought for another time. But this is not going to be that kind of meeting. No food, no review, no inspirational stories. Just trust me," she had told her, "we have some urgent business to tend to, so if there's any way you and Justin can clear your calendar, please do. Bring little Markie if you want. It's just way too complicated to go into right now."

As it happened, there was no one among her

loyal core of followers who was unable to attend. All to the good, since she needed as much participation as possible to thwart what was coming at her fast and furious out of left field. If nothing else, Cherico was always full of surprises and then equally surprising solutions.

"Starting tomorrow," she began the afternoon of the meeting, standing onstage behind the podium and surveying the attentive faces of all the best friends she had in Cherico, "our magnificent new library with all the bells and whistles will be picketed by the entire congregation of the Church of the Eternal Promise." She paused, knowing that the name alone would stir things up.

"Please run that by me again, girlfriend. The church of the . . . what?" Periwinkle Place said, nudging Mr. Place, who was sitting next to her in disbelief. "Who the hell are they?"

"They'd get you for that kind of language, Peri," Maura Beth told her, snickering for good measure. "But seriously, they're some quirky little church out in the country somewhere that actually challenged my job qualifications recently. They asked Councilman Sparks to fire me because they didn't approve of my book selection policy and a few other things I don't need to go into at this time."

Jeremy cleared his throat, stood up, and turned around from his vantage point in the front row. "To cut to the chase, folks, they wanted censorship big-time. They claimed that Maurie's ruining our young people and leading them into temptation, if you will, but to his credit, Councilman Sparks was having none of that nonsense. He dismissed their accusations and sent them on their way."

"Well, that's refreshing," Connie McShay said, exchanging surprised looks with Douglas. "But my goodness, why didn't you tell us about any of this before now, Maura Beth?"

She shrugged as she brought her hands together. "I wanted to wait and see if these church people were serious about picketing us. Today, Councilman Sparks informed me that they have done everything they're supposed to do legally to begin picketing. He says they told him they won't give up until I'm fired. So, it looks like anyone who wants to use the library will have to dodge these picketers for the time being. I hate the thought of it, but there it is."

Periwinkle assumed her feistiest demeanor. "Just who the hell do they think they are?"

Maura Beth couldn't resist one more time. "And there you go again with that language."

"This is serious, girl. The very idea of anyone questioning your credentials. It's like somebody saying I don't know how to cook, or Parker doesn't know squat about desserts."

Mr. Place sounded nearly as feisty as his wife. "Damn straight, and I used that language on purpose."

"I like your analogy," Maura Beth continued, giving Periwinkle and Parker a thumbs-up as everyone chuckled. "But I think we all need to go on the offensive here, and I don't mean we're going to picket in return. We just need to get all our friends and family members to tell everyone they know to keep on using the library—now more than ever. Don't let those church people stop anyone from coming out to use the computers, or to bring the little ones for one of Miriam's story hours, or to just check out a book and read a little of it out on the deck overlooking the lake. Everyone's raving about all of it. Now that we've got such a state-of-the-art resource, we can't lose our momentum by letting these picketers discourage people from using it. You spread the word. If you hear someone you know saying, 'Well, I would go out there, but I don't want to get involved with those crazy people,' you tell them we've reached a point in our society where we can't let the crazies win."

"Atta, girl!" Periwinkle shouted, pumping her fist. "Don't you back down. You tell 'em!"

"I appreciate the enthusiasm, Peri," Maura Beth said, "but we also need to keep our cool in this business. No matter what those people say to any of us, and no matter what they've written on their signs—and who knows what all they may come up with—we need to walk right past them and go into the library as if they aren't even there. No shouting matches, certainly no tussles. Just cool, calm, and collected will get the job done."

"Maura Beth's right," Douglas added. "And if they should try to block anyone from entering the library, they'll go to jail. I'm sure we can get Sheriff Dreyfus to see to that. They have their rights, but the patrons will still have theirs. Connie and I will be more than happy to tell all our friends out here what's going on. As Maura Beth said, I think the best approach for all of us will be to pretend they don't even exist, and I'll bet your circulation figures not only won't take a dip, they'll soar."

Maura Beth gestured toward Douglas and with great warmth in her voice said, "Thank you for that. I certainly hope so. It's definitely true that our phones have been ringing off the hook since the Grand Opening—patrons complimenting us on everything from the spacious design and all the light to the wonderful new staff. And, of course, they all love the location right here on the water. They've all said they intend to start using the library much more often than they did before when it was on Shadow Alley in that dark old ex-tractor warehouse. So, that's why I've called this meeting, and now all I ask is that The Cherry Cola Book Club does its thing as only it can. We've been tested before, as you all know."

Renette raised her hand, and said, "I'm sorry to have to tell y'all that my parents are behind this picket line thing. Well, with the support of their church. They were the ones who held Miz McShay's feet to the fire at that hearing. I was there, too, and it was pretty bad with a lot of finger-pointing and hysteria on their part. I wish I could change their minds, but they don't believe in anyone's ideas but their own, and they want to impose them on everyone else. Just please know that I support Miz McShay and the library and will do whatever I can to help her weather this storm."

"That was a very courageous thing to say, Renette," Maura Beth told her. "I can't tell you how much I appreciate it, and I'm also quite sure no one here blames you for any of this."

The group gave Renette instant validation with overlapping comments like, "Of course we don't," and "Don't you worry about that for even a second," and "We're all in this together."

"I have a further suggestion," Connie said. "I don't think it's enough that we just tell all our friends about this and we show up out here once or twice a week. I think each of us should make an effort to come out to the library and use it every single day and encourage our friends to do the same thing. Why, Douglas and I can come over three or four times a day since we live right next door. Those picketers will get sick of our faces before it's all over and done with. We all just need to find time to do it to send a message. None of us would have to stay long. We could obviously check out a book or use the computers, but we could also just read a newspaper or a magazine or browse or walk out on the deck and take in that magnificent view of Lake Cherico. Anything to outnumber these self-righteous people on the picket line. Hopefully, they'll soon see they're swimming upstream."

Maura Beth applauded lightly. "That's excellent. Let's all make a resolution not to miss a day without a library visit. As we've discovered more than once with our Cherry Cola Book Club, there's strength in numbers."

Everyone had been sitting and buzzing in suspense ever since Maura Beth had concluded the emergency meeting with the cryptic statement, "And now, if my dear, sweet Jeremy will come up here onstage, we have another important announcement to make to all of you."

Unlike an Oscar winner practically climbing over the seats to claim that coveted golden statue onstage, Jeremy seemed to be taking forever, taking baby steps, in fact, and it was Periwinkle who took him to task first.

"Will you please get the lead out, Jeremy McShay? You're shufflin' along like an old man."

"Yep, that's just what I am—an old man."

Periwinkle suddenly gasped, covering her

mouth with her hand, but Maura Beth caught her in time. "Shush, Peri! Let us tell everybody."

Jeremy then sped up and was soon by Maura Beth's side with a smirk on his face. "Ladies and gentlemen," he said, "yes, you heard it right. I will soon be somebody's old man. Eventually, I mean. Maurie and I are thrilled to announce to all of you, our dearest friends here in Cherico, that we are officially pregnant. How about that? Our family is expanding from two to three."

The auditorium exploded with cheers, applause, and congratulations, and not a single person stayed seated, all of them rushing the stage to get closer.

"How long have you known?" Becca asked, reaching Maura Beth first and giving her a hug and a peck on the cheek, while Justin vigorously shook Jeremy's hand with his big, ex-quarterback paw.

"We just found out. I went up to Memphis to confirm it yesterday. I knew I was late, so I wanted to check things out, and then there was this dream I had . . . actually, I kept having it . . . oh, never mind, I probably sound as crazy as those church people that'll be out there tomorrow on the picket line."

Becca was amused. "But yours is the good kind of crazy. Isn't that right, Stout Fella?"

"I'm here to tell you that your life'll never be the same from now on," her Justin said with his best grin. "Not much sleep ahead, and lots of cryin'—from the baby, I mean, not you. But it'll all be worth it in the end, believe me. I hate leavin' our little Markie for even a second. I'd take him to work with me if Becca would let me. Matter a' fact, I'm downright jealous of the babysitter as we speak."

"We can't wait to get to where you two are now," Maura Beth said. "Three instead of two. What a wonderful number."

Then Ana Estrella stepped up and took Maura Beth's hand in hers. "I'm so excited for you both, and I'd like to do my part for the library as Queen of the Cookbooks. I've checked out that enormous kitchen you have in the staff lounge, and I was thinking that if I offered baking lessons, the same people who voted for my pigeon peas cake might want to come out and learn how to make it. All we have to do is move a few more chairs in there, and we have lots more patrons for the library, right?"

Maura Beth gave her a hug and said, "I think that's an absolutely brilliant idea. And if I can manage to get away from my desk for a while, I'll be right there taking notes with the rest of them. I've been trying all sorts of recipes since Jeremy and I got married, and I'd love to try this one, too."

"Then it's settled. I'll be using my title for another good cause."

"First ESL books, and now this. You wear your crown well."

Ana was giggling to herself. "Most tiara-wearing queens like to talk about world peace on the runway, but I'll just settle for more practical things like reading and baking. You can always count on those."

The rest of The Cherry Cola Book Club took turns with their schmoozing and good wishes, and for a while everyone forgot all about the distressing revelation that had brought them together. But despite the warm, fuzzy feeling Maura Beth was enjoying, she was not about to adjourn the meeting without a reminder.

"Be sure and come out tomorrow and do your part to counter those protests. Remember, we let them do all the shouting. We just walk in and take advantage of the greatest little library in the state of Mississippi."

12
Signs of the Times

Connie and Douglas McShay were standing in the parking lot of the Charles Durden Sparks, Crumpton, and Duddney Public Library in the humid morning air of July, completely aghast at what they were witnessing. They had set the alarm to rise bright and early to make sure they were ready to face all the protestors from the Church of the Eternal Promise, walking past them into the library with their heads held high; but they were completely unprepared for the over-the-top signs the group was carrying. Had these people stayed up all night concocting these witless slogans?

MIZ MAYHEW CONDONES WITCH-CRAFT . . . MAY LIGHTNING STRIKE THIS LIBRARY . . . DENY FALSE PROPHETS . . . TURN IN YOUR LIBRARY CARD NOW . . . MIZ MAYHEW IS A DICTATOR . . . THIS LIBRARY DOES NOT PROTECT THE INNOCENT . . . TELL CITY HALL TO FIRE MIZ MAYHEW . . . and comprised the collection.

The contingent had already begun circling—in silence for the time being—but perhaps it was only a matter of time before they started chanting something equally outrageous. No sentiment, it appeared, was off-limits.

"You can't make this stuff up," Connie said out of the side of her mouth. "I'm trying very hard to fathom the world these people live in, but I keep coming up with nothing." She checked her watch. "Maura Beth should be here soon to open up. I'm glad we'll be here for her."

Douglas could only shake his head, looking down at the asphalt. "And I trust the rest of the club will start showing up. We need to have a steady stream of people to counteract this disgraceful display."

A few minutes later Maura Beth drove up, and the McShays greeted her as she got out of her little Prius and took it all in. "We didn't want you to face this alone," Connie told her.

"No way should you face this nonsense by yourself. We'll be here for you no matter what," Douglas agreed.

Maura Beth did not speak right away, and the three of them watched the blank-faced protestors trudging around, practically mesmerized by the spectacle. "Well, I've been the villain before— according to our dear Councilman Sparks not all that long ago—so I guess I can be the villain again," Maura Beth said finally.

"You are no such thing," Connie said. "You're the best thing that ever happened to Cherico, and you know it. By the way, where's Jeremy?"

"He's coming. I asked him to run by The Cherico Market to pick up some milk and a loaf of bread and a few other things we need as long as he was out and about. I'm terrible at keeping track of staples."

"You see? That's what you and Jeremy should be worrying about—last-minute grocery shopping and mundane things like that," Douglas said. "Not this insane side show."

Maura Beth nodded and took a deep breath. "Well, what do you say? Shall we run this blockade?"

It was at precisely that moment that the Brachles and the Places pulled up in their cars and quickly headed over.

"So, what's the game plan here?" Justin asked, rubbing his hands together and sounding like he was about to call a play at the line of scrimmage. The mindset of ex-quarterbacks died hard. "I call personal foul on this bunch."

Douglas shook hands with his friend and chuckled. "I think we were about to execute the old end around."

Becca stood frozen in place, shaking her head. "Those signs are unbelievable. Are they serious?"

"Crazy serious," Periwinkle added with a frown. "There's protests, and then there's protests. But this here is like a comedy skit. Only, it's not very funny."

"Yeah, they want our Maura Beth's head on a plate," Mr. Place said. "We gotta do something about this, folks. Connie, you were right, we need to come out here as often as we can to make a statement."

"Let's do just that right now for starters," Maura Beth told the group. "We're The Cherry Cola Book Club, and we know how to get things done the right way. So, y'all ready?"

Then the group efficiently linked arms and walked in lock-step silence around the picket line straight into the library. In response, the believers of the Church of the Eternal Promise raised their signs higher, as if to invoke heavenly intervention against the heathens daring to oppose them.

"The forecast predicts an unusually hot, muggy day," Maura Beth said, once she and the McShays were inside the deliciously air-conditioned lobby. "I know I should be a little less petty about all this, but I can't help it if our friends out there enjoy triple digits, can I?"

By the time another hour had passed, the protestors had begun chanting mindlessly.

"Maura Beth must go! Maura Beth must go! Maura Beth must go!" was their mean-spirited mantra of choice. Perhaps it was the flood of patrons who were beginning to show up—many who were members of The Cherry Cola Book Club, of course—who had inspired the noise. It had to be unsettling to the Church of the Eternal Promise that their presence was most definitely not keeping people away. Indeed, the exact opposite was true.

When Councilman Sparks, himself, showed up and headed into the library, Elder Warren could no longer restrain himself, getting out of the picket line and bringing his sign down to his side long enough to accost him.

"I guess you're goin' in to huddle with Miz Mayhew, aren't you? We knew you and her were in cahoots, Councilman. Like I said the other day, that whole hearing in City Hall Chambers—why, it was rigged from the start. This proves it. You're all swoll up with pride with your chest puffed out in your fancy suit and tie because your name is on that library. Everybody in Cherico knows you didn't give a hoot about the library until then. You even wanted to close the old library down. But it's the love of the material things in life that sends us to Hell, you know. You'll have to account for this when the time comes to meet your Maker. I just hope you're ready to face what'll be comin' to you."

Councilman Sparks addressed his accuser with his best reelection smile. "Well, Elder Warren, I may end up going to that Hell of yours, as you predict, but it won't be because I'm proud as I can be of this library. I've done a whole lot worse than that in my lifetime—including making all sorts of trouble for Miz McShay, when all she wanted was to do her job. But I'm sure I'll be forgiven for that. In fact, I already know Miz McShay has forgiven me for that and a whole lot more. So, oops! I guess I don't get to go to your Hell after all."

"You're a blasphemer!"

"Hell, yes, I guess I am."

Elder Warren was fuming now, left completely speechless by the exchange. All he could think to do was to hoist his sign to the sky again and rejoin his comrades on the line.

"By the way," Councilman Sparks added just before triggering the sliding glass doors, "you folks need to be sure and stay good and hydrated out here on the picket line. There's no rain predicted today, and I know you don't wanna burn up before you get to Heaven."

Perhaps the most stunning blow to the picketers came when at least a dozen cars pulled up one after another into the parking lot around noon, honking their horns in random, staccato fashion to announce their arrival. Five or six people bounded out of each car, and they all gathered together in one spot where they were addressed by James Hannigan of The Cherico Market.

"Ladies and gentlemen, here we all are, ready to go in and enjoy our new library. I know all of us have had nothing but memorable experiences with Maura Beth McShay, and we can never thank her enough for providing us with this outstanding facility. Cherico's been long overdue for a library we can be proud of. I, for one, will never forget how she led me to the shelf where all the books on grief were. My mother had just died in her sleep, and I was having a real hard time with it, as anyone would. There were things I learned in those books that helped me through those dark times, and I will forever be grateful to Maura Beth for guiding me to that much-needed information. A priest or minister could not have done a better job. Meanwhile, as I've done in the past for so many other good causes, it was my pleasure to make announcements over my PA system in the grocery store to all of you, my best customers— this time about what's going on with these church people—and I'm overwhelmed by the number of you who chose to follow me out here today. Hey, I'm happy to shut down The Cherico Market for an hour or so to help out. As Maura Beth's always telling us in our Cherry Cola Book Club meetings, there's strength in numbers."

He paused briefly to turn and glance at the

picketers behind him. "Seems like it's a sign of the times to go overboard protesting everything under the sun. To my way of thinking, some of it's legit, and you gotta stand up for what you believe in if it's halfway reasonable. That's what this country is all about. But this business going on over there in front of our library, well, I think these people need to get a life instead of running their mouths like that about our librarian."

The group cheered, and there was even a bit of applause before Mr. Hannigan continued. "Anyway, let's don't waste any more time yakking at each other and get busy inside our library. I know I've got me an issue of *Progressive Grocer* I've been meaning to read in the periodicals area, and I just love how you can look up and see a fishing boat or somebody skiing out on the lake when your eyes get a little tired from the reading. Bet some a' you have some best-sellers you can't wait to check out, too. So, just follow my lead, and we'll file in silently one by one and pay no mind to those signs and those insulting slogans."

It was almost comical the way everyone made a straight line and began the short journey to the sliding glass doors. No group of kindergarteners coming in from recess could have done it better. There must have been close to fifty people in all, and the procession was enough to halt the picketers in their tracks and stop their chanting, if only until everyone was safely inside.

At the front desk, Renette and Marydell Crumpton had taken note of the oncoming flood and given Maura Beth a heads-up over the intercom. She soon emerged from her spacious corner office overlooking the lake—what an incredible contrast it was to that dark, claustrophobic closet she had toiled in before; then she rushed into the lobby to give James Hannigan the biggest hug she could muster as the group behind him began to disperse.

"You sweet, lovable man," she told him, the affection radiating from her eyes. "You've done your part and then some, haven't you?"

He drew back and waved her off. "Nah, it was nothing I haven't done before for ya. Those people out there are way off base, and everyone in Cherico with half a brain knows it."

"I feel so vindicated," she said. "Not that I needed to be. I like to think I've always been on the side of the angels. But Councilman Sparks was here earlier, and we went into my office and had the best chat we've ever had. It was like we had always been the best of friends, which was anything but the case. He told me how genuinely sorry he was for ever making life hard for me here in Cherico and that he was glad I had forced him to realize what a great resource the new library will always be to the town. I truly feel I've fulfilled my mission as a librarian."

"You are preaching to the choir," he told her

with a fatherly wink. "But I do wish there was some way we could get through to those people out there. And they call themselves a church. That's not truly spiritual, what they're doing out there."

"Oh, let them have their laughable moment. Councilman Sparks assured me once again this morning that I would continue to have my job come hell or high water. I don't know about the hell part, but I have it on good authority that Lake Cherico never overflows."

Maura Beth had been trying to track Jeremy down all morning. When he had not shown up at the library a good half hour after she had opened it up, she had texted him. Picking up milk and a loaf of bread couldn't possibly take that long. He had replied that he had a surprise in the works for her and to give him a little more time to get things together. Then an hour or more passed. Connie and Douglas had browsed, checked out books, and then left; Councilman Sparks had come and gone; Voncille and Locke Linwood had put in an appearance, heading straight to the genealogy room; and James Hannigan had brought practically every Cherico Market customer of his out to the library; and still no Jeremy.

His cell kept going to voice mail. She was beginning to worry that something out of the ordinary had happened. Had he been in another terrible accident of some kind? Oh, please, anything but that. He had flirted with death once during their courtship days in that freak encounter between his car and that frightened deer darting out in front on the Natchez Trace Parkway. So she nervously texted him again.

Nuff surprise talk. Where r u?

To her profound relief, he answered.

On way with surprise.

If it was more patrons for the library, it wouldn't be much of a surprise. That was what everyone was supposed to be doing—dragging every relative, friend, and acquaintance who still had a pulse to the library to make a point to the picketers; and so far, the strategy had been a huge success. The building was overflowing with people taking advantage of everything the library had to offer them in the millennium; it was alive with patrons reading and learning and browsing and being a part of something that was the repository of their culture—past, present, and even suggesting the direction the future might take.

Fifteen minutes later and not bothering to knock or have himself announced, Jeremy stuck his head in his wife's office doorframe, looking slightly sheepish. "Sorry it took me so long."

"Where have you been? Did you drive all the way to Corinth and back to get those groceries?"

"Nope, just hold on."

Then he pushed the door open, stepped aside, and in walked his sister, Elise, wearing her long blond hair parted down the middle as usual and a tie-dyed smock that echoed the hippie styles of late sixties San Francisco. The same sister who taught Women's and Feminist Studies at the University of Evansville and had offended most of the McShay family with her unrelenting militant politics. The very same whom Maura Beth had had to plead with in a letter to attend her only brother's wedding in Cherico last year. And the same who had insisted on a do-over when she had inadvertently caught the bridal bouquet Maura Beth had thrown because, as she had pointed out loudly to everyone at the reception right then and there, "I don't approve of the institution of marriage, and this symbolizes it precisely." Or something to that effect.

"Annndd heeerrrre's Leesie!" Jeremy said in imitation of the classic *The Johnny Carson Show* intro and the hand gestures of one of those corny game-show spokesmodels.

"Hello, Maura Beth, it's so good to see you again," Elise said, moving across the room quickly with open arms to embrace her sister-in-law.

"You were right, Jeremy, this is a surprise,"

Maura Beth said after the hug, pulling away slightly with a smile. "And it's good to see you, too. What brings you down to Cherico? Don't tell me you came all the way from Evansville to see my new library? That would be the highest of compliments to pay me, but it's way beyond the call of duty. Please, have a seat and let's have a nice chat."

Once they were all settled around the room, Elise took the lead, shaking her head emphatically. "First, I have to tell you how disturbing that scene is out in front of your library. Jeremy brought me up to date in the parking lot. Talk about your Neanderthals. I didn't know people like that still existed. The knowledge-is-a-dangerous-thing crowd, I mean. The spirit of book burning is alive and well."

"Yes, it's unfortunate. I've had to pinch myself sometimes to make myself believe it's really happening," Maura Beth told her. "But I can assure you, they will not get anywhere with their shenanigans. My job is secure."

"Thank goodness for that. We can't let censorship win, or we're dead as a society. Don't get me started." Elise paused, leaning forward in her chair with an earnest expression on her face. "Maura Beth, I hope you don't mind my barging in like this, and please don't blame Jer for all the sneaking around he had to do this morning. I didn't give him much advance warning, I'm afraid."

"Was he sneaking around? I did think he was up to something, but he kept me in the loop. Sort of." She gave her husband a coy glance.

"I surprised Jer, too, just like I did when I showed up out of the blue for your wedding. Yesterday, I decided to drive down from Evansville to share some news with the two of you, and I wanted Jer to show me the way to your new library when I finally got here. He's been waiting all morning for me to arrive so we could do that. Seems I'm always late for things."

Maura Beth settled back in her armchair, resting her hands comfortably in her lap. "Well, now that you're finally here, what's your news?"

"First order of business is, I've taken a sabbatical from the university. A year off to accomplish something very important to me."

"That's nice. Are you going to travel abroad or write a paper or book or something academic like that? Everyone needs a real vacation now and then. I think our honeymoon was the first one I've had in years."

Elise exchanged glances with her brother, and any objective observer could have seen that something of note was passing between them. "No, nothing like that." There was a deep breath and then the payoff. "I'm pregnant."

Maura Beth sprang to life, her interest sparked. "Oh, my sincerest congratulations! Well, that makes two of us. I assume you got our text about our little one on the way? We couldn't reach you over the phone last night. I guess you'd already left on your trip down. Looks like you and I will be producing first cousins for the McShay family. Won't that be exciting?"

"Yes, I certainly trust it will be. Actually, I did get your text on the way down, but I decided to wait and congratulate you both in person. So, here I am wishing you and Jer all the best."

"There's more," Jeremy added, sounding cryptic and impish at the same time.

"I imagine so," Maura Beth continued. "I didn't even know you were seeing someone. Did you meet him at the university? Who's the lucky guy?"

"I don't know who he is." Elise's reply brought the conversation to a dead halt for a good thirty seconds.

Caught completely off guard, all Maura Beth could manage was a polite but forced, "Oh?"

"It's really very simple. I decided I wanted to have a child before I got too far into my thirties, but I definitely do not want to have a husband at any age. You both know how I feel about marriage."

Images of Elise holding that bridal bouquet at arm's length as if it were day-old roadkill bubbled up from deep within Maura Beth's scrapbook of wedding memories. "Yes, I remember that quite well."

"I know I'm keeping you in needless suspense with all this, but the fact is that I went to a sperm bank. It was all very impersonal, but it got the job done. There, I said it."

"I told you there was more," Jeremy said, wagging his brows at Maura Beth. "Leave it to my sister not to do things by the book."

"You sound a bit disapproving in that tone of voice, Jer, or is it just my overactive imagination?"

"No, not at all, Leesie. Sorry if I gave you that impression. We're both grownups now. If this is what you really want, it's perfectly fine with me. Just a hunch, but I'm assuming you haven't told Mom and Dad yet about this? If you had, I know I would have heard from them long and loud by now."

"No, I haven't. I was thinking maybe around Christmastime when we all get together. Of course, I'd be showing quite a bit by then, so I probably won't have to tell them a thing. They'll get the message when I walk through the door. Do you think they'll have a fit when I tell them about the sperm bank? They're so traditional about everything the way you are."

Jeremy thought for a while, shifting his eyes back and forth with the hint of a grin forming. "It might be better to give them some advance warning. But they've always wanted grandchildren from us, if that's what you meant by traditional. Now it looks like they'll be getting one each from both of us really close together. Maurie'll be due about the same time you will, right?"

"I'm about five weeks along, so I'd say yes."

Maura Beth put her hands atop her desk, assuming her most serious, director-of-the-library pose. "So. What a brave new world, huh? You plan to bring up this child all by yourself?"

"Of course. I make very good money at the university. I have tenure, you know. I don't see why a woman should be forced to choose between having a career and having children. She should be able to do both. Why does everyone bring that up for women but not for men?"

"I didn't mean to imply that a woman couldn't."

"It seemed like you were."

"Believe me, Elise, I'm not the enemy."

Jeremy intervened before his sister reverted completely to her customary argumentative alter ego that had alienated so much of her family. "Leesie, you and I have had our political differences—we probably still do—but you need to understand that neither Maurie nor I will be judging you. I'll just cut to the chase right now and prove it to you by asking what we can do to help you out. I'm assuming that's why you came all this way to tell us. I mean, you could just as easily have done it over the phone. I know you too well."

Elise seemed to relax a bit, sounding placated. "That's very perceptive of you, brother dear. Because I've decided I want to stay down here in Cherico throughout the pregnancy. I know it

285

might shock you to hear it, but I think I'd like to be around at least some family while I'm going through this. I'm not a total lone wolf. Mom and Dad are out, of course. I just couldn't tough it out up there with them in Brentwood with all their friends nosing around. So, believe it or not, I'd very much like my baby to be born right here."

"Wow! I'd be lying if I said that doesn't surprise me just a little bit," Jeremy said. "So you'd like to spend most of your sabbatical down here instead of up in Evansville where all your friends are? Cherico's just a very small town, you know. The medical facilities might be a lot better up there when the time comes. Have you thought about that?"

Elise made a dismissive gesture with a broad sweep of her hand. "Yes, I've thought about it a great deal, of course. I didn't just decide to do this on the spur of the moment, Jer. I've concluded that delivering a baby is just about the same everywhere. I mean, it's not like I'll have to use a midwife who'll have to chew off the umbilical cord with her teeth."

"I'll try very hard to get that image out of my head," Maura Beth said, clutching a hand to her belly reflexively.

"I was hoping you and Jeremy could help me find a place to rent for the next year," Elise continued. "It doesn't have to be much, but I've already sublet my apartment up in Evansville."

Jeremy's puzzled tone seemed genuine enough. "Come on, now. We don't have to look very far, Leesie. Honestly, Aunt Connie and Uncle Doug live right next door to the library. They've got two guest rooms upstairs in the lodge within walking distance of here. That's my first suggestion, and since you're family, they might not even want to charge you."

"I'd absolutely insist on paying them something. That is, if they'd consider taking me in."

Jeremy couldn't repress a chuckle. "For heaven's sake, Leesie, you make yourself sound like some forlorn character out of Charles Dickens. Sorry for the literary reference, but you're not an orphan all alone in the world. This tactic is unworthy of a tenured professor."

Elise's reaction was a cross between a wince and a smile. "It's just that I know I've annoyed the family more than once with my sociological views. I'm wondering if Aunt Connie and Uncle Doug will hold that against me. I did carry on quite a bit at your wedding right in front of them in their house. Sometimes I just can't seem to help myself."

Then Maura Beth spoke up. "You're exaggerating, Elise. I think most people thought it was kinda funny—the bit about you and the bouquet, I mean. But I really can't see your aunt and uncle rejecting you. They generously donated the land this library is standing on so the town of Cherico wouldn't incur extra costs, and it got the ball rolling much sooner on construction. I certainly didn't ask them to do that. They came up with the idea on their own. Maybe it's been a while since you've had any substantial contact with them, but I think you might be surprised at their reaction if you approached them. I agree with Jeremy. They're your first option."

"Leesie, we have a guest room at our house on Painter Street we'd be happy to offer you, but we'll be converting it to a nursery for the baby soon," Jeremy added. "Otherwise—"

Elise and Maura Beth both laughed simultaneously, and it was Elise who enlightened her bewildered-looking brother. "Two pregnant women in the same house? Do you have any idea of the raging river of hormones you'd be dealing with? Actually, it'll be more like a waterfall, or so I've read. I just had this hilarious image of you flailing your arms and screaming while being swept over in a barrel."

Maura Beth wrinkled her nose a couple of times, clearly a sign of her unbridled affection for her husband. "I'm afraid she's right, Jeremy. Having one pregnant woman on your hands is probably all you want to take on—even if you had superhuman powers. But, anyway, Elise, Connie and Douglas have already been here once today to show their support, and they said they would be coming back after lunch. So, you're welcome to wait here and chat a little more, or you and Jeremy can walk on over and break the news to them."

Elise was gazing out Maura Beth's wraparound office window at all the recreational activity on the lake. In the distance, an athletic young man was doing showoff tricks on his skis, sending a wake in the direction of a small yacht with several people casting their lines. Closer to shore, there were a couple of dinghies bobbing about with lazy, cane pole fishermen aboard. Could there be anything more relaxing on a hot summer day? "If you two don't mind, I think I'll stay right here and wait for Aunt Connie and Uncle Doug to show up. This scenery is so restful and just to die for. It's almost like a form of meditation."

"Isn't it?" Maura Beth said. "It remains to be seen how much work I actually get done as time goes on. And, no, I don't mind one bit if you hang around. I may have to answer the phone or pop up now and then, but meanwhile, you and I can discuss pregnancy and all that goes with it. I'm so glad we have this in common. We can go through it together."

Elise's sigh almost seemed to be one of relief; then she launched into one of the intellectual monologues everyone had come to expect of her. "Yes, we can. You know, I wasn't sure how you and my brother would take this. Jer has probably told you that we haven't been all that close over the years, and then you wrote that sweet letter to me practically begging me to come to your wedding. But just so you both know, I appreciate the understanding. These days, we seem to have become a society of judging people who do things a little differently and don't fit whatever normal is—oh, how I hate that word, especially the way it's used to bash people over the head. As I always tell my students, that's not what this country is supposed to be about. The proof that we've gone off the rails a bit is that kooky bunch parading around out there with those ludicrous signs. They have every right to picket, of course, but I don't think they're going to win any arguments with those semiliterate opinions."

"I think we can all agree on that, Leesie," Jeremy said. Then he rose, moved to his sister, put his hands gently on her shoulders, and began a gentle massage. "Welcome to Cherico."

"Yes, I think you'll like it here, despite the antics of those people outside. They don't represent the vast majority of our citizens," Maura Beth added. "But here's a little tip—I wouldn't mention your sperm bank visit to them on your way out. Not that I think you should be intimidated by them. But you'd probably end up on their signs like I have. Actually, I consider it a badge of honor since they basically don't have any idea what they're talking about. Their foolishness only strengthens my resolve as a library professional."

Elise rolled her eyes and made a clucking noise with her tongue. "Believe me, I wouldn't give them the time of day."

"That's been our approach all along," Maura Beth continued. "You can tell that what they desperately want is confrontation and some long, drawn-out shouting match that lowers us to their level. But we just aren't going there. All of my Cherry Cola Book Club members have been showing up with regularity and giving them the silent treatment, and I know it's driving them crazy."

"Not a syllable from me," Elise said, putting a finger to her lips. "I'm used to talking to students who want to learn something about the real world, not a bunch of posturing and posing."

"Substance over style," Maura Beth added. "That's what I've been about since I got this job. If I hadn't been, I wouldn't have lasted a day. Instead, I've toughed it out for seven years and won the day."

Elise was smiling now. "I'm very glad you're my sister-in-law, Maura Beth. And to think— we'll be expectant mothers together."

"Well, nothing usually brings most families together like baby news," Maura Beth said.

Then she found herself wondering why she had inserted the words *usually* and *most* in her statement. There were circumstances under which pregnancies were not welcomed at all. Would it turn out that way for Elise?

13

Pigeon Peas, Please!

It took exactly three days of enduring the record temperatures and humidity of midsummer on the picket line for the members of the Church of the Eternal Promise to give up the ghost. That, and the incessant stream of Chericoans frequenting the library as the ultimate reminder that the "believers" just might be on the wrong side of this particular issue.

The Cherry Cola Book Club members, in particular, had even cobbled together a schedule for their visits to the library around the clock. Connie and Douglas McShay had volunteered to make at least one morning and one afternoon appearance for as long as the protests continued; Periwinkle and Parker Place would show up midmorning before their luncheon preparation at The Twinkle; Audra Neely had agreed to delay the opening of her antique shop on Commerce Street to drop in and read various newspapers and magazines at her leisure; Locke and Voncille Linwood would continue to make visits to the significant genealogical section where she conducted her ongoing research for her "Who's Who in Cherico?" meetings; Justin and Becca Brachle would each take turns at home minding Markie while the other visited with Maura Beth to keep up her spirits; and even Mamie Crumpton agreed to do her part, putting aside her disenchantment with her sister, Marydell, long enough to do a daily browsing of the stacks to find something to read at one of the windows overlooking the deck. Wasn't that a kick in the pants?

To the dismay of the protestors, they were finding out that Maura Beth McShay was untouchable and off-limits, a veritable community icon; and the new library was such an overwhelming, state-of-the-art contrast to the old, inadequate facility, that Chericoans from all walks of life simply couldn't stay away. The shortsighted—no, more like profoundly myopic—members of the Church of the Eternal Promise definitely hadn't counted on that.

Still, Elder Warren had made a final appearance at Maura Beth's office door unannounced, and she had resisted the powerful urge to call security and have him ushered out quickly. Instead, and probably because watching the sun glinting off the lake all morning had produced its usual calming effect on her, she had generously allowed him to remain and say his piece. What could it possibly hurt to be the bigger person here?

"You may have won this round, Miz McShay," he told her, not willing to cross her threshold, "but the truth is on our side. You'll see. You can't just shove us under the rug."

"We haven't done that at all. You've had free reign—no one has blocked your path. You've had your say out in the open, but it appears that no one was paying much attention."

Elder Warren thrust out his chin defiantly and pointed his finger accusingly. "Yeah, I've heard it's 'cause that snotty book club a' yours put the word out on the street. Mr. and Miz Posey told me all about it 'cause their daughter Renette's got herself all brainwashed by you. I could tell she was all mixed up at the hearing the other day. It's got to where some say you and your club practically run this town now. You've even got Councilman Sparks crawlin' around on his knees. Don't know how you managed to beat him down so bad like that, but the word is that he hasn't been the same man since you came to Cherico."

Maura Beth's laugh was prolonged and somewhat incredulous. "You have quite an overwrought imagination there, Elder Warren—especially your ridiculous depiction of Councilman Sparks. It's true that he and I have had our differences in the past, but now we're on the same team. We've extended the olive branch to each other for good. And your information is bogus about my Cherry Cola Book Club, too. I can assure you it's a voluntary organization devoted strictly to the appreciation of good literature, enjoying potluck dishes, friendship, and the promotion of community spirit. We welcome everyone with intelligence. Even a hint of it."

Elder Warren narrowed his eyes, which added an extra layer of anger to his hard-boiled features. "You can say all the rude, smart-alecky words you want to, missy, but like I've said many times and like our church believes, the way of godliness is on our side."

"And yet you have such an ungodly way of demonstrating it."

"We are only exercising our rights as Americans. You just don't happen to agree with us."

"I will certainly agree with you on exercising your right to protest, but I also highly doubt your effectiveness."

"You haven't heard or seen the last of us."

"I'm sure, but I believe this conversation has gone on long enough. All I have left to say to you, Elder Warren, is good-bye, sir. I'm sure you can find your way out." And with that, Maura Beth mentally put the entire episode to bed as she watched him leave, turning to look over his shoulder and glare at her every now and then.

But the protests had not ended without constructive results, bringing a record number of people out of the woodwork to support their library. Little wonder, then, that most of them were aware of the Queen of the Cookbooks' first baking lesson in the library's state-of-the-art kitchen one week after opening day. Maura Beth had allowed Ana Estrella to post notices all around the lobby and at the circulation desk, and twenty-six patrons had signed up for the program so far. It was going to be a bit of a tight squeeze with all those chairs moved into the kitchen for the program—and thankfully the library's real furniture had finally arrived to replace the odds and ends the club members had provided at the last minute; but what did that really matter when the goal of record library usage was being realized and then some?

COME AND LEARN HOW TO MAKE PIGEON PEAS CAKE IN A FREE DEMONSTRATION, the flyers had proclaimed. Since Ana's dessert had propelled her to the overall title on the Fourth of July, it was easy to conclude that lots of Chericoans wanted to make it for themselves whenever they developed a craving. That had to be the ultimate tribute to her culinary skills.

"*Bizcocho de gandules,*" Ana Estrella was saying to all the patrons sitting in their chairs placed throughout the library's kitchen. They had gathered at the appointed hour to learn how to make her prize-winning recipe and were giving her their full attention.

She in turn was standing behind the gleaming marble island countertop that Maura Beth had insisted architect Rogers Jernigan include in the staff lounge blueprints. What a battle that had

296

been with him as well as Councilman Sparks for a first-class design; but she had not given an inch and won out! Because of that, Ana had plenty of room for mixing bowls and measuring cups and all the other utensils she needed to do her show-and-tell without feeling cramped and compromised.

"That's pigeon peas cake in Spanish, of course. But first, I want to thank those of you who voted for me and made it possible for me to win the Queen of the Cookbooks title. You have no idea what that means to me, being a newcomer to Cherico. I feel very welcome here already, and sharing this recipe with you is my way of giving back. As a part of Spurs 'R' Us, I want to be a good citizen. Now, as I go along, please don't hesitate to ask any questions you like."

"I have one off the bat," Becca Brachle said, raising her hand in the middle of the cadre of Cherry Cola Book Club members present. "Why pigeon peas in a cake? Don't get me wrong. I think it's delicious, and yes, I was one of the many who voted for you because I thought it was such a revelation when I tried a piece on the Fourth of July. Nothing much surprises me anymore when it comes to food, but this did, and I had to come up with all sorts of unusual dish ideas when I did my cooking show on the radio all those years. You run through recipes so fast, it's a bit dizzying, and then you start worrying that you'll run dry. But enough about that. Please tell us all about those peas."

"Yes, the very thought of making a cake from peas has me obsessed," Voncille Linwood added.

Ana adjusted the apron she was wearing and smiled. "I'd be delighted to tell you all about it, of course. Back in Puerto Rico where my family is from originally, pigeon peas are a staple. Mixing them with rice for a savory dish is how they are usually used. But then because they are so plentiful, someone came up with the idea of using them in a cake. Who knows where these strange inspirations come from—maybe there was nothing else in someone's pantry at the time—but you'll find that most cultures use what they have lots of and what's cheap in a variety of very creative ways. It's also a good way of stretching your budget in tough economic times. These days, I think we can all agree that that's a big plus."

Mr. Parker Place's hand shot up. "That's definitely true. Black folks didn't have a lot of money way back when, but they found ways to turn greens they could grow out in the yard and chicken parts and sweet potatoes into an art form. We stewed the greens, fried up the chicken, made pies out of the sweet potatoes, and ended up calling all of it soul food somewhere down the line. None of it's particularly fancy or even what you'd call gourmet, but it sure hits the spot when your stomach's growling. Necessity being the mother of invention and all that."

"Different cultures can learn a lot from each other, and I promise I'm going to sample some of yours as soon as I can now that I'm living down here in Mississippi," Ana told him.

"I can give you some tips about where to eat in Memphis where I used to work, if you'd like," he said. "Just get with me after this is over. Whatever kinda food you prefer, I can put you on its trail."

"I'll look forward to that. Now," Ana continued, "please refer to the handouts I had printed up for all of you. First up on the list of ingredients, you'll need one cup of *gandules*, as you can see. You can get them in the fifteen-ounce can that I'm holding up, and I was a little proactive about this and asked Mr. Hannigan to stock them at The Cherico Market for everyone. I knew you'd all be making a beeline to the grocery store sooner rather than later. Let's give him a round of applause for making that happen, shall we?"

James Hannigan seemed slightly embarrassed by the extra attention but stood up briefly and acknowledged it with a wave of his hand. "Hey, that's what we do for one another here in Cherico all the time. Just hope I don't run out, judging by the size of this crowd."

Ana and many of the others laughed good-naturedly. "As long as you folks don't double up on the recipe, I think it'll all work out. And once you open those cans, be sure and drain off the liquid. That's vital, or you'll end up with a very runny batter. You'll also find that fifteen ounces is too much for one cake—just use one cup of the peas and then you can save the rest for a savory recipe. As I said, maybe you can try the peas with some rice for a different side dish. It's a very versatile ingredient. Once you've tried it, I think you'll be hooked."

"I'm looking down the list of the rest of these ingredients and all this mixing and blending we're going to have to do," Marydell Crumpton said. "I didn't know it was going to be this complicated. Mamie and I have always had help to do our cooking, so I think I'm a little intimidated."

"Don't even worry 'bout it," Jellica Jones whispered to her employer, who was sitting next to her. It had taken some doing on Marydell's part, but Jellica had finally given in and allowed herself to be talked into participating in the program. "I can follow any recipe, Miz Marydell. Mama Surleen, she was the best cook ever, and I learned errything I know about cookin' at her side. You and Miz Mamie, you've never had no complaints about my food, so just calm down."

Up at the counter, Ana continued her spiel without missing a beat. "Well, everyone, I have to admit there are quite a few other ingredients to deal with. There's coconut milk and regular milk, butter, sugar, vanilla extract, eggs, flour, cinnamon, nutmeg . . . you know how it is with cakes. They don't make and bake themselves, the tasty little devils. But just follow along step-by-step—it'll all be worth it when it comes out of the oven and fills your house with unbelievable aromas. Your family members will all come running every time, begging you to cut it while it's still warm. I know I always did when I was growing up."

"It sure was irresistible during the Grand Opening," Connie McShay added. "I especially loved how dense and moist it was."

"I admit it's a little extra work with all the preparation and such," Ana said. "Just remember to be patient for the payoff, and you'll have a treat your family will always be requesting."

Meanwhile, Maura Beth—who had found time in her schedule to take in Ana's presentation—sat back in her chair, silently observing with a great deal of pride the interaction between Ana and her cadre of diverse patrons. This was what a library should be about—involving the community in a variety of ways, making it seem as diverting as a movie theater or a county fair with all the crazy rides that took your breath away. To the point that the public would always be wondering what fun, enticing event was going on at the library. To the degree that it would always be a relevant part of the lives of Chericoans.

After seven years of trying as hard as she could

and against some significant odds, Maura Beth McShay had finally achieved her goal of being the director of a state-of-the-art library that was making a difference. Perhaps Councilman Sparks had not always understood her mission. Heck, he'd even gone out of his way not to. Perhaps her own parents had been puzzled by her dedication, as well as her unwillingness to budge on where and how she lived her life. But none of that mattered now. She had reached the light-filled clearing of her recurring dreams, and it was as sparkling and exhilarating as the sunlit waters of Lake Cherico. The only thing better than that was the knowledge that she had a brand-new human being growing inside of her—made from the love that she and Jeremy shared.

Life was very good, indeed.

14

Buns in the Oven

"I could live out here on this deck all the time," Elise was saying to the two couples on either side of her.

Her Aunt Connie and Uncle Doug were sitting to her right sipping clear, potent cocktails, while Maura Beth and Jeremy sat at her left with their Virgin and Bloody Marys, respectively. Elise, meanwhile, had also taken a vow of sobriety because of her condition and was reluctantly nursing bottled water with a slice of lemon. The five of them were enjoying the view of the lake from the McShays' fishing lodge, watching the mercurochrome sun ringing down the curtain on another sizzling midsummer day in Cherico.

"You *do* live here all the time, Leesie," Jeremy said, giving his sister a playful nudge. "Thanks to Aunt Connie and Uncle Doug."

"Lake Cherico has to be the best-kept secret on the planet," Elise answered, soaking up as much of the sunset as she could before it paled and diffused, bleeding out onto the surface of the water. "But I'd say the town of Cherico needs to guard against overdevelopment so the cat doesn't get let out of the bag. I hate to see pretty trees toppled and bulldozers grading the land down to dirt. Why not work around the trees? It takes decades for the saplings they plant after that to make a difference. In fact, it takes a lifetime."

"Don't say things like that in front of Justin Brachle," Douglas added. "Everything out here bears his distinctive subdivided imprint. Except the library, of course. That we owe to our esteemed librarian."

"And the two of you donating the land next door, don't forget," Maura Beth reminded them. "You saved us a great deal of time and money by stepping up to the plate the way you did."

Two weeks earlier, it had all worked out perfectly, even though Elise had had her doubts, and she'd been more than a little uptight when she had approached the Cherico McShays about the way she had become pregnant and then chosen to exit Evansville for a while. Would it be too Bohemian for them? Would they tell her to take her unconventional choices elsewhere? For morale purposes, she had asked both Maura Beth and Jeremy to be there with her around the dinner table that watershed evening when she broached the subject.

"Well, of course, when I worked at the hospital all those years, I was aware of a few single mothers who had taken that route," Connie had said over her grilled catfish and hush puppies following the initial revelation. "It's not particularly helpful to judge patients when you're in the nursing profession. I was always shocked when one of my cohorts, Vivian Rutledge—and I was never very close to her—did just that now and then in the staff lounge. 'How could any woman think of doing something like that?' I remember her saying to me once. To which I responded quite calmly, 'It's not our place to speculate about such things. That's not what any of our patients are looking for from us.'"

Elise had pressed on valiantly. "I appreciate all that, but what do you think about my staying here with you, Aunt Connie? Would it be too much to ask? Please be honest with me. If you think it's a terrible imposition, just say so. I'm in uncharted territory here."

"We certainly have the room," Douglas had said, smiling at his niece. "What do you think, Connie?"

She put down her fork, pursed her lips for one brief moment, and then exhaled. "This is what I think, Elise. You shouldn't keep this from your parents until the last minute the way you say you're going to do. You can't just show up around Christmastime and pull that kind of surprise on them. Paul and Susan have the right to know and have some time to prepare for this. It's not business as usual."

Elise was all frowns and downcast eyes. "But I know I just couldn't go up to Brentwood and stay with them under any circumstances. I've said too many things in anger over the years that I . . . well, that I regret. Yes, I'll admit it. Maybe I'm mellowing just a tad bit."

"We all do, sweetie. Life kind of forces your hand, and you realize you don't know it all. But I think you may have misunderstood me," Connie told her. "I didn't mean to suggest you should go up there and live with them. As Douglas said, we have the room, and we'd be delighted to be a part of this adventure of yours while you're on sabbatical. If this is what you want, then we'll support you. That's what close families do for each other. Just tell your parents about it. You need to give them the opportunity to be a part of this, too. Even if you don't know who the father is, we all know who the mother is. That's what we all need to focus on from here on out. Your welfare and the baby's welfare."

"I think you might be surprised by their reaction," Douglas added. "Trust me, your father's no slouch when it comes to understanding the unconventional. Paul didn't teach psychology at Vanderbilt all those years for nothing. I'd be shocked if my brother couldn't handle this."

Elise was pushing food around her plate with a look of resignation. "What about Mom?"

"Susan will come around," Connie said. "Your mother is sophisticated. Just give her a chance. She'll get used to the idea. What's done is done."

306

"Both of you make it sound so easy. Like all I have to do is walk through the door and snap my fingers and they'll understand."

Connie gave her a skeptical glance and minced no words. "Sweetie, what you've chosen to do won't be easy at all. Bringing up a child is anything but. Your uncle and I just kind of winged it when your cousin Lindy came along, and you'll have to bear down and do the same thing. Minus a husband at this point. But you should have your family around to help out now and then. And that includes your parents. Take my advice—don't shut them out."

Thus, and with the understanding that Elise would definitely tell her parents all about her pregnancy, Connie and Douglas had agreed to let their niece use one of the upstairs guest rooms as her base of operations over the next eight months. She could come and go as she pleased and was always welcome to break bread with them, but Elise had insisted on paying them for her room and board.

The deck at sunset had therefore become a favorite spot for the five of them since Elise had moved down from Evansville. Maura Beth and Jeremy would walk over after the library closed down, and the McShays would have a few canapés and drinks ready; then they would chat, share with one another how the day had gone, and eat a leisurely meal together. Sometimes, Connie would fix dinner; other times they would go into town to The Twinkle to enjoy one of Periwinkle's specials and Mr. Place's ooey gooey desserts, taking turns picking up the tab.

"Years from now," Elise said, returning to her lemon water and the flotilla of activity out on the lake, "I think I'll remember this delightful routine of ours the most. I'll be able to tell my son or daughter how the sun seemed to set just for the five of us, almost like a long-running Broadway play nobody else could ever get tickets to."

"Wow, Leesie," Jeremy said, "I wish I could come up with prose like that for the novel I'm always trying to write. Later on, I'll remind you to say that to me again so I can take notes."

"If I can remember. But, yeah, how's your writing coming along? You told me you started on something during your honeymoon in Key West."

"He did start it. I can vouch for that," Maura Beth added, raising an eyebrow. "But then our honeymoon sorta got in the way. Actually, it's still going on. The honeymoon, I mean. The novel— not so much."

Jeremy blew his wife a kiss and took a sip of his Bloody Mary. "My beautiful, redheaded bride speaks the truth because right now, I've got the Berlin Wall of writer's blocks."

Elise thought for a moment. "What are you trying to write about? I mean, what's the plot? Maybe that's the problem."

"I guess you could say I'm trying to write the classic Southern novel. It's set in Mississippi right after the Civil War. The family I've created is struggling to make a living now that their plantation has gone up in flames. The creature comforts they once enjoyed have vanished, and it changes the equation for them. They no longer rule the roost, and it's a huge reality check for them."

Elise fished the lemon out of her glass and started sucking on it, causing her to make a sour face.

"Hey, no fair. You haven't even read a word of it yet, Leesie. Your mugging is uncalled for."

"Very funny, Jer. I was just giving the baby a little vitamin C. Your plot sounds fine as far as it goes, but maybe . . ."

"Maybe what?"

"Don't you think the aftermath of the Civil War has been done to death and then some? Do you really think anyone will ever top what Margaret Mitchell wrote? I'll bet you anything there are hundreds of thousands of unpublished manuscripts floating around out there on the same subject. Maybe you should be just a little more forward-thinking and try your hand at something more contemporary. After all, we are living in the millennium now."

Jeremy finished off the olive floating in his Bloody Mary and gave his sister an expectant stare. "Well? Any suggestions?"

Her eyes moved to Maura Beth and then she gave a little gasp. "It just came to me—wait for it . . . wait for it . . . here it is . . . my contribution to your literary career—buns in the oven."

Jeremy frowned. "What?"

"Don't you see, Jer? It would be perfect. Both your wife and sister have buns in the oven at the same time. You'd have to fictionalize us, of course, but you wouldn't have to do much research. You could just check in with us as we trudge through the trimesters with our ever-expanding waistlines. I mean, you obviously can't live the reality of being pregnant, but we'd be the next best thing."

Connie spoke up. "I know I'd read it with a great deal of interest. What about you, Douggie?"

"If my nephew wrote it, I'd read it." He shrugged. "Whether the subject is the Civil War or birthin' babies—either way, I'm on board."

Everyone laughed, but Jeremy looked particularly intrigued. "That's not a half-bad idea. I could create two female characters who were related and going through pregnancy together."

"Something on the order of Tweedledum and Tweedledee," Maura Beth said, obviously pleased with herself.

"It's not like I've done a whole lot with *Forlorn Legacy*. That's my working title. I know, I need to come up with something a little less trite. It almost sounds like one of those romance novels with the

310

shirtless man holding the busty lady in his arms. But I've only managed to write thirty-five pages in a little over six months," Jeremy added. "Good thing I have a paying job as a teacher, right? I was excited about it when I started writing it in Key West, but as I said, I'm just totally blocked. So why not *Buns in the Oven*?"

"Then I guess that's settled," Elise said. "Maura Beth and I will expect to appear on the acknowledgments page, of course."

"It's a done deal, Leesie. Or maybe I'll just decide to dedicate the novel to both of you. *To the women in my life.* Or something like that. That is, if it ever gets published. They say it takes even longer to get a book out than a baby."

It was two evenings later that Maura Beth and Elise found some time to discuss their pregnancies without the distraction of an audience. They were both leaning against the deck railing of the McShay fishing lodge while the men and Connie had gone into town to pick up some tomato aspics and desserts for the weekend from The Twinkle.

"Have you thought about names yet?" Maura Beth asked, wondering how such a delightful breeze could be coming in off the lake in this oppressive heat. There weren't many to point to in late July and early August, but this one seemed intent on keeping the two pregnant women just a little cooler as it rearranged their hair ever so slightly.

"No, I haven't," Elise said. "I'll eventually get around to it, though."

"Well, I have. If it's a boy, I'd like to include both Jeremy and my father in the name. Either Jeremy William McShay or William Jeremy McShay. That is, if Jeremy will go along with it. I'm very much opposed to juniors, though. Or thirds or fourths. It's just too pompous. Everyone should have the right to their own name. Jeremy and I haven't even discussed it yet, though, so I don't know how he feels about it. I guess I'll find out soon enough."

"And if it's a girl?"

"I thought I'd play it safe again. Maybe Cara for my mother and Susan for yours. Cara Susan or Susan Cara."

"Well, aren't you the little politician?"

The swirling wind once again caused a few strands of Maura Beth's hair to tickle her forehead, and she sighed softly as she swept them back with the palm of her hand. "What can I say? I like your mother—have from the first time Jeremy introduced us. And there was also a time not too long ago that I liked her more than I liked my own mother."

Then Maura Beth finally addressed the elephant in the room. "You won't have any in-laws, of course. Does that bother you?"

"No, it's a relief, actually. I'd probably just alienate them with my strong opinions, too."

"I think everyone has to deal with in-laws in their own good time. Have you told your parents about being pregnant yet?"

Elise managed a sheepish grin as she looked away. "No, I still haven't gotten that far. I keep putting it off, and I know I promised Aunt Connie and Uncle Doug that I'd take care of it. As confident as I am about this when I'm by myself, I can't help imagining their secret disdain for what I've done. The last time I got into a huge argument with them about politics, I told them they lived in the nineteenth century. There's a part of me that wonders if I've already burned my bridges with them. Things were still a bit strained at your wedding last year."

"Well, there's only one way to find out. But if they're like most parents—and I think they are—they'll still want the best for you as their only daughter. No matter what, the child will carry some of their genes."

"I'm sure you're right. For all my bluster and posturing, I guess I really need them to approve of my decision. I want my child to have grand-parents, as conventional as that sounds." Elise hesitated. "Do you think that makes me a fraud? I wonder if my students would think so. By the time I see them again, I'll have a child to take care of. I can picture some of my militants—and I've brought it out in many of them—wanting me to bring the baby to class as a show-and-tell, expecting me to be completely objective about it all without a hint of emotion. That's how I've presented myself to all of them in the past."

The image sparked Maura Beth's imagination, and she could suddenly see herself sitting in a desk on the front row of one of Elise's classes, peering into a baby carriage and taking detailed notes in case there was a pop quiz. "That's an amusing little concept, but it wouldn't make you a fraud. There's nothing wrong with wanting your child to be loved. We all need as much of that as we can get. Just remember—our children will be first cousins and have all the fun that comes with it. Better than those sibling rivalries, I hear. I can hardly wait for that to happen."

"Eight more months to go," Elise said, sighing. "Do you think we'll turn into awful monsters as our hormones rage? I keep reading these articles about women who practically chased their husbands out of the house at times with a broom. Maybe we'll become the worst ever."

They both laughed, and the slight tension the conversation had generated melted away. "I hope not," Maura Beth said. "Jeremy's been such a prince on a white horse so far. He was so thrilled when I told him the news, even though we had both thought we wanted to wait a little longer to get pregnant. At any rate, I really don't want to test his limits."

"Jer has them, I can assure you. He's told me

where to go more times than I can count during our arguments over everything under the sun. Politics, religion, what women are supposed to be, what men are supposed to be—you name it. Sometimes it felt like we were members of a debate club instead of brother and sister. But let me emphasize this again. Being in love with you has changed him for the better. I recognized it the first time I saw him around you. You've brought out the sweetness in him, and the opinionated lover of literature who thinks technology is changing the world for the worse has taken a backseat a little. That's something you can definitely be proud of, believe me."

Maura Beth impulsively embraced her sister-in-law, feeling no resistance to such closeness. "What a nice thing to say to me." Then she pulled back, smiling. "I think we better get in our hugs while we can. A few more months and we'll be way too big to do this."

The two women laughed and then went silent for a while, continuing to enjoy that rare summer breeze that was making their conversation on the deck more than tolerable in all the humidity.

"Are you scared?" Maura Beth asked finally, having gathered up her courage with a woman she still barely knew but definitely wanted to get to know better. It was "all in the family" now.

"Don't let my militant behavior fool you. I still have my core beliefs, but I'm terrified at what I might be getting myself into. But there's some part of me deep down that keeps urging me on."

"Your biological clock?"

Elise eyed her intently, and for a moment there, it was difficult to tell if the remark had been viewed as offensive or merely straightforward observation. "There was a time I would have denied such a thing existed. Hell, I practically made an assignment of it for my students, footnotes and all. Refute the biological clock, I told them. Do it with a vengeance, I said. No, I wasn't foaming at the mouth or anything close to that, but I'll readily admit I had tunnel vision."

"And now?"

"Now . . . I don't see things in terms of black or white so much. It seems to have come upon me rather suddenly—like one of those violent summer storms you have down here. Go figure. Does that make sense?"

"Perfect sense. And I understand the part about being terrified. I really want to do this right. I guess every parent says that at the beginning, but I don't want to have the misunderstanding between myself and my child that I had for way too long with my mother. We were just two different people with the same name. Thank God, we ironed it all out in time for my wedding, and when we talk to each other now, all the tension is gone."

"Well, let's just agree to lean on each other," Elise continued.

"Like sisters? You do know I'm an only child, right?"

"Yes, I do. I never had a sister, either. You don't know how many times I've wished Jer was a girl, and don't you dare tell him I said that. The macho side of him will take it the wrong way. So it'll be a new experience for the both of us, this little kingdom of ours with a population of two."

Maura Beth's smile conveyed the comfort zone she'd just entered. Perhaps she should press things just a bit more, feeling the way she did. "Four, if you count our babies. I was wondering, though . . . do you ever see yourself letting a man into your life? Not that I think it's necessary, you understand."

Surprisingly, Elise's features softened, and she lowered her voice almost to a whisper. "I'm not going to lose any sleep over it. Let's just say that I will try to keep myself open to all possibilities."

"Sounds like me. And, you know, it's paid off where my library career was concerned."

Then Elise made a gesture as if she were scribbling something in midair. "And just think, Jeremy will be sniffing around throughout the whole eight months taking notes for his novel and asking us to describe all our aches and pains and cravings. Oh, I bet he really presses us about our cravings. Jer can be quite analytical at times. Are you ready for that?"

"I think I can handle it," Maura Beth added. "And who knows? Maybe the three of us will all give birth at the same time."

Recipes:
And the Winners Are . . .

For our recipe section this time around, we thought we would feature the dishes that won Best Appetizer, Best Entrée, Best Dessert, and Overall Best Dish in the Queen of the Cookbooks Competition during the Grand Opening of the new library on the shores of Lake Cherico. Each of these dishes was contributed by loyal Ashton Lee readers around the world, and each fan has been gratefully credited at the end of each recipe. Interestingly, all came forward to Ashton Lee himself to offer these dishes on their own without prodding. These are people worth cloning. Please try all the recipes at your leisure. Some are very easy to fix, but all are quite tasty. Meanwhile, we know you'll be looking forward to the next installment in The Cherry Cola Book Club series, coming soon. Those babies are on the way!

Mrs. Frieze's Cheeze Ballz

Ingredients you will need . . .

2 eight-ounce boxes of Philadelphia
(Original) cream cheese
1 envelope Hidden Valley Ranch Seasoning
2 tablespoons garlic powder
2 tablespoons onion powder
2 cups shredded cheddar cheese
1 can Hormel ham
1 package chopped pecans

Mix first six ingredients together thoroughly and then roll mixture into balls. Roll cheese balls in the chopped pecans until completely covered. Refrigerate for at least 2 hours. Best served with crackers.

—Courtesy Mignon Pittman, Director, Calloway County Library, Murray, Kentucky

Aleitha Larken's Chicken on the Sofa
(Chicken Divan)

Ingredients you will need . . .

2 cups cooked chicken, sliced or large pieces
1 package dehydrated onion soup mix
1 pint sour cream
2 packages frozen broccoli, cooked
1 cup heavy cream, whipped
1 tablespoon Parmesan cheese

Bake chicken breasts or dark meat—whichever is preferred, or use both. Slice chicken into large pieces. To make sauce for cooked chicken, add soup mix to sour cream and beat with rotary beater until well blended. Arrange cooked broccoli in shallow casserole dish in a single layer. Spoon half of sauce over broccoli, then add layer of chicken. Fold whipped cream into remaining sauce and pour over chicken layer. Bake at 350 degrees for 20 minutes or until bubbly. Sprinkle Parmesan cheese and brown under broiler. Recipe serves 4.

—Courtesy Margaret Trigg Kuehnle,
Natchez, Mississippi,
and Margaret Kuehnle Fulton,
Lake Concordia, Louisiana

Maribelle Pleasance's
No-Sugar-Added Cherry Cake

Ingredients you will need . . .

1 can pineapple tidbits in own juice
1 can cherry pie filling (no sugar added)
8 ounces walnuts (or pecan pieces)
1 box yellow cake mix (no sugar added)
1 stick real butter

Preheat oven to 325 degrees. Combine pineapple tidbits and cherry pie filling, and stir together in an ungreased pan. Do not drain pineapple tidbits. Layer nuts on top of fruit. Add cake mix dry. Do not stir in, just level out. Melt stick of butter and then spoon over dry mixture. Bake for about 45 minutes until brown on top.

—Courtesy Marilyn Cadle Holkham,
London, United Kingdom

Ana Estrella's Pigeon Peas Cake

Ingredients you will need . . .

1 cup *gandules* (pigeon peas) (if using canned *gandules*, which come in a 15-ounce can, drain the *gandules* first and use 1 cup for this recipe; save the rest for a savory dish)
¼ cup coconut milk
¼ cup 2% milk
1½ sticks unsalted butter, softened
2 cups granulated sugar
1 teaspoon vanilla extract
2 large eggs
2 cups cake flour
½ teaspoon baking soda
2 teaspoons ground cinnamon
½ teaspoon freshly ground nutmeg
1 tablespoon Maxwell House International Café Hazelnut Flavor powder
3 ounces baking dark chocolate, coarsely chopped

In a small food processor, mix the *gandules* with both milks and process until it is puréed. Set aside.

In a large bowl, beat the butter and sugar with an electric mixer until creamy. Add vanilla and eggs, one at a time, and mix.

In a separate bowl, combine cake flour with baking soda, cinnamon, nutmeg, and International Café Hazelnut powder and sift once. Remove about 2 teaspoons of this flour mixture and set it aside. Gradually add the rest of the flour mixture to the butter mixture, mixing well.

Add *gandules* mixture to the batter, mixing well.

In a small bowl, mix the chocolate chunks with the 2 teaspoons of flour mixture that was set aside and fold into cake batter.

Pour cake batter into a greased and floured Bundt cake pan and bake in a preheated oven at 350 degrees for about 25–30 minutes or until a toothpick inserted into the cake comes out clean, without crumbs.

Once cake is done, remove from oven and let cool inside the pan for 10 minutes; then invert cake onto a cooling rack. Let cake cool completely. Once it has cooled and is ready to be served, sprinkle with confectioner's sugar. Slice and enjoy with a cup of *café con leche*! *Buen provecho*!

—Courtesy Ana Raquel Ruiz,
Atlanta, Georgia, and San Juan, Puerto Rico

Discussion Questions

1. Have you ever run a food tent such as the ones featured during the Grand Opening of the new library? Talk about your experiences.

2. Do you take advantage of your library's story hours for your children? Discuss some memorable events.

3. How important do you think sex education and awareness of substance abuse are for young people these days, and how do you believe the information is best imparted? (Re: Renette Posey's character)

4. Do you approve of constant library monitoring of Internet use on their computer terminals?

5. Do you think libraries should block certain Internet sites?

6. Which of these newly introduced characters in this novel captured your fancy—negatively or positively—the most: Ana Estrella, Bit Sessions, Gwen Beetles, Maribelle Pleasance, Marzetta Frieze, Miriam Goodcastle, Hardy and Lula Posey, Elder Warren, or Shark?

7. Have you ever had a mad crush on someone the way Renette does on Waddell Mack?

8. Jeremy's sister, Elise McShay, makes her first appearance in the series since Jeremy and Maura Beth's wedding in *The Wedding Circle*. What do you think of her latest unconventional decision?

9. Have you changed your mind significantly about Councilman Sparks? In what way?

10. How would you rate Maura Beth's growth as a woman and a librarian? In which area has she most improved?

Center Point Large Print
600 Brooks Road / PO Box 1
Thorndike, ME 04986-0001 USA

(207) 568-3717

US & Canada:
1 800 929-9108
www.centerpointlargeprint.com